Mantis

By

Erica Summers

By

Erica Summers

RUSTY OGRE PUBLISHING

A NOTE FROM RUSTY OGRE PUBLISHING:

Even though this book was proofread thoroughly by professionals, mistakes happen. We want our readers to have the best experience possible. If you spot any spelling, grammatical, or formatting errors, please let us know so we can rectify them immediately. You can reach out to us at: Rustyogrepublishing@gmail.com

Screenshots are lovely, but if unavailable, the entire sentence, page number, and format type will suffice! We *always* appreciate your feedback.

REVIEWS:

If you could take the time to leave an honest review after you've read this book, we would greatly appreciate it. We respect your time and promise it doesn't *have* to be long and eloquent. Even a few words or a star rating will do! As a small publishing house, every review allows us to better ourselves. It also helps others determine if this book is right for them. It dramatically helps our ranking and algorithms on those platforms, even if it isn't five stars.

TRIGGER WARNINGS:
(May contain spoilers!)

Profanity (heavy)
Themes & discussion of suicide
Consensual Sex
Death of a wild animal — *chapters with this*
trigger have an asterisk (*) in the chapter title

Other Works by Erica Summers

Vanity Kills
Bad God's Tower
Writhe
Derailed
Feed the Machine
In the Blood of the Martyr

Coming Soon:

Price Slashers
The Rictus Grin & Other Tales of Insanity
Ensuring Your Place in Hell II

"God's light came into the world, but people loved the darkness more than the light for their actions were evil."

- John 3:19

PART ONE:
APOKALYPSIS

In the Beginning

The humidity felt like a pair of thick, angry hands wrapped around her throat, and rain gleaned off her halter top onto her corpse-white breasts. It rarely rained in Tucson, but there had been a downpour every night for the last two weeks. Like the angels were punishing her.

The glowing nightclub sign above pulsed: *The Throne Room.* The neon words bathed her shaggy mop of jet-black hair in green. Her eyes were steely and hard, caked with two-day-old liner, lids heavy from chasing ever-elusive sleep. She reached into the pocket of her tight pants and retrieved a soggy pack of cigarettes with slight fingers.

Grace found her way into Mantis's cluttered mind at odd times like these. Images of drying blood, tangling in crimson streams from Grace's forearms, body half-immersed in sanguine water.

Mantis ground her molars together and peered at the soaked mess before hurling it into the sopping gutter. Loud bass-driven music pounded through the streets. Vibrations rippled obsidian puddles near the soles of her black, always-untied combat boots as she strode across the street with a purpose: to wash away the nightmarish things she'd seen and *done* and chase them down with a wedge of lime and salt.

I Want Candy

Mantis and her sexy new acquaintance, Candy, burst through the door like a wrecking ball, cracking the drywall with the knob. Candy giggled and feigned an apologetic look.

Mantis didn't care about making another hole in the wall. The place looked like shit. She'd never get the security deposit back for the dump anyway.

She shrugged and thrust herself at Candy, lustfully ripping at what little clothes she had on.

"Don't sweat it, Brandy." She kicked the door closed, and the wonky knob hit wrong, kicking it back open a few inches.

"Bitch, it's *Candy*."

She looked hotter at *The Throne Room* but so did everyone *else* beneath the flashing par-cans after hastily-downed tequila shots.

"Aww, I'm sorry, baby." Mantis kissed her softly on her pouting lips and ran a hand up between Candy's thighs. "I *meant* to say Candy." She pulled Candy's panties aside with her skilled fingers and felt the slickness beneath. "Forgive me? Hmm?"

Candy gasped and responded with a frenzied kiss. She yanked Mantis closer with the sides of her halter. Mantis kicked the door shut behind them a second time and tugged up the tight skirt clinging to Candy's firm ass.

Candy pulled away and pressed her back against the door. She looked at Mantis like a hungry tiger ready to feast. She beckoned with a crooked index finger, skin glistening with sweat and glitter.

Mantis walked, instead, over to a cluttered desk, sat on the corner, and kicked off her untied boots.

"You live alone, I take it?" Candy already knew the answer.

"Mmm-hmm."

"Place could use an air freshener."

"Mmmm-hmm." Mantis peered out the window, beyond the fire escape, to the city below.

Tucson had never seemed so silent before. It was unnerving. *Ominous.* Not a single barking dog. Not a single siren or car horn. Not one neighbor cussing at his wife.

Mantis reached into the clutter strewn across her desk and fished out a crumpled half-pack of cigarettes, placing one between her lips. She retrieved a gold, dented flip-top lighter from her tight, leather pants pocket. Its faint, illegible letters were nearly worn away.

For the one who sets my heart ablaze, it said.

Candy shuffled through the pig sty and removed the cigarette from Mantis's lips, tossing it into the mess on the desk.

"I don't want you tasting like an ashtray while I'm kissing you."

Mantis forced a slight, irritated smile.

Candy forced her body behind Mantis, pressing her lips against the skin of Mantis's neck. She cupped her breasts, slowly caressing her nipples through the fabric of her top.

Mantis craned her neck around and kissed Candy, pressing against her curvaceous body.

Candy unclasped Mantis's halter and hungrily took the left breast in her mouth, sucking

3

gently before drawing the rosy nipple between her teeth.

Mantis groaned with pleasure and forcefully shoved Candy down into the unmade bed. She slid Candy's miniskirt and thong down over the gentle curves of her legs and pressed her hungry mouth to the wet flesh between them. Candy moaned at the touch of the skillful tongue.

Candy clutched the black satin sheets in her hands and rolled her head to the side in ecstasy. In the gap between the bathroom's door and floor, Candy watched the silhouette of two feet shuffle.

Candy gasped. "Who is THAT?!"

Her curvy breasts jiggled as she sat up. Mantis raised her head from between Candy's legs like a gopher and licked her glistening lips.

"Hmm?" Mantis seemed dazed.

The feet moved again.

"What the fuck? Is someone there?"

"No." Mantis closed her eyes, agitated.

Candy flashed Mantis an accusatory glance. "Is some pervert in there *watching us*? I didn't sign up for fucking weird-ass *sex games*—"

Mantis cut her off with a roar. "Nobody's fuckin' *here*, Mandy!"

Candy shoved Mantis out from between her legs. "It's fucking *Candy*!"

"*Goddammit.*" Mantis flopped back on the bed and barked out a frustrated sigh, bare tits bathed in moonlight.

Why were the women I bring home always such a pain in the ass, she wondered.

"Fine." Candy shifted gears and pawed at Mantis.

Mantis rolled her head over. "What? You want *more*?"

Candy reminded her of a needy dog seeking her full attention.

Candy nodded, biting her lip.

"*Beg for it,*" Mantis ordered sternly.

"Pretty-please…" Candy moved in closer. "With *Candy* on top…"

Mantis rolled over in an attempt to salvage the casual encounter.

"Look," she kissed Candy's knee, "I promise it's just *you*," the kisses trailed down Candy's thigh, "and *me*."

Candy closed her eyes, excited by Mantis's tongue as it slid back into her.

"I could've sworn—" Candy could no longer remember what she was attempting to say.

The brass bathroom doorknob turned.

The darkness inside birthed a demonic, three-fingered claw from the crack between the door and frame. The texture of it was like porous volcanic rock, ashen on the outside, illuminating like molten magma through jagged cracks.

A set of ivory eyes peered through the crevasse. Razor-sharp teeth emerged from the blackness, dripping strings of drool. Its bottom jaw ratcheted open like a stiff machine.

Moaning, Candy opened her eyes just in time to catch a terrifying glimpse.

"*Ahhhh!*" She shrieked.

The creature retreated.

Candy pointed to the bathroom door, muttering incoherent babble like a lunatic.

In a huff, Mantis slid out from between her legs, gathered Candy's clothes, and hurled them rudely at her.

"That's enough, sweetheart." Mantis pointed at the door.

"Wait! What? Hey, no, I swear I'm *not* crazy!" Tears welled in her heavily made-up eyes, smearing her mascara.

"Out." She didn't have time for games. She'd salvage the night with a half-bottle of tequila and her vibrator alone. *Less headache.*

Mantis grabbed a dirty, black muscle shirt from the floor and pulled it on. She plucked the cigarette back off the table and lit it with the flip-top lighter, just as she'd done a thousand times before. "You're still here?"

Candy was frozen, unable to take her eyes off the bathroom door and the... *thing*... she saw lurking behind it only moments before. Her voice was filled with fear. "I *swear*, there's something *in* there."

Mantis lumbered over to the bathroom to prove that they were, in fact, alone. But as she reached the bathroom door, she stopped in her tracks.

She *clearly* remembered shutting the door before leaving for the bar. She could sense a dark presence. And that smell...

Sulfur?

Mantis reached into the darkness and flicked the light on.

An unnaturally slender beast loomed over her. Strings of spit dribbled down onto its craggy chest.

She reached into her leather pants and pulled out a black-handled switchblade, the one she never went anywhere without. She held it down by her side and depressed the trigger. The blade fired out of the handle, flashing in the moonlight like a bolt of lightning.

A foot thumped, hard and sloppy, against the wooden floor. *BOOM.*

The other foot slammed down closer to them, rattling the glassware in the tiny nearby sink of the studio apartment.

The savage ashen figure surged fiercely, erupting from the bathroom door. It was followed by an overpowering, elemental smell.

It offered a guttural bellow, powering toward her. Mantis thrust the knife up through the fleshy sac beneath its lower jaw, burying the blade in its head all the way to the handle.

The grim creature stopped in its tracks.

Mantis reared back, whipping the knife out of its rotten skull with a sickening slurp. The beast snatched the switchblade from her and held it in its tri-fingered hand. It sniffed first, then chewed on the metal blade. Dark slime dribbled off of its jagged teeth.

Mantis scanned the room for a new weapon. The creature's teeth clicked against every inch of the glistening blade. Her eyes landed on the wood-handled mop in the corner. Another conquest bought it for her months ago as a backhanded gesture and hint to clean her house. It still had the plastic wrapper on its fabric head.

Mantis bolted forward, snatched the mop, and raced toward the creature, impaling it like charred meat on a bamboo skewer.

It squealed. Jarring. Like a dying hog.

While the night had been uncommonly quiet, the noise in the apartment was ear-piercing. Mantis wasn't sure who shrieked louder: the dying creature or the naked stripper.

Jet-black blood spattered onto Mantis's face like viscous oil, extinguishing her cigarette on contact. She'd driven the mop clean-though, and with another twist of the handle, its shoulders went limp. It fell to the floor, emitting a sound from its dying mouth that shattered the apartment's only window.

It clawed at the handle in its chest, then swiped its razor-sharp talons at Mantis's legs, barely missing her delicate flesh.

Once it was still, Candy raced to Mantis and wrapped her dewy arms around her savior, burying her face in Mantis's neck. "Oh, thank God!" But Mantis didn't believe in *God. Not for some time now.*

"Is it *dead?*"

Mantis grunted something through her cigarette-pursed mouth that sounded like, "*Dunno.*" She pulled away and walked toward the monstrosity. She gripped the pole and twisted it until the gurgling ceased.

"*Yep.*" Mantis managed coolly through the filter of the muck-covered cigarette.

Cleanup

Mantis perched on the edge of her bed, staring at the slain creature in its own dark, pooled blood. Three clear numbers were carved on its palm as if made by a dull blade… *616.*

She picked up her switchblade and examined the blackened goo on its blade. She lowered it to the dead thing's wrists and pushed hard, crunching through tissue and charcoal-gray bone.

Blood oozed from the veins of the severed extremity like black honey. Mantis lobbed the hand onto the cluttered desk. She retrieved a roll of cheap painter's plastic from one of its drawers and unfurled it. She rolled the remainder of the beast in it and wound clear packing tape around the outside, encasing it in a plasticized cocoon.

She struggled to drag the seven-foot-long wiry being toward her closet. She whipped open the door and gagged at the stench seeping from it. She wrestled the carcass to the threshold.

Inside the closet sat two more slumping lumps of plastic, similar in shape. Mantis rolled the fresh corpse against the others and shut the closet door.

***

In a hole-ridden nightshirt and tattered black panties, Mantis packed a torn satchel to the brim. Unable to zip it, she tossed it onto the floor and grabbed a pack of Iron Pillars. She placed one between her lips, lit it, and tossed the gold flip-lighter back down. It clattered against the particleboard nightstand and toppled over a picture frame.

Tendrils of gray smoke dissipated into the night air. She glanced at the tattoo on her arm. In solid cursive letters, it simply said: *Grace.*

Mantis scrunched a handful of messy jaw-length hair and flopped onto her always-unmade bed. She sat the frame back up, fixated on its image through the fog of cigarette smoke. The frame had bold, red letters across the bottom: *Paris.*

In the photo, Mantis and Grace were on a curved Montmartre walkway in front of the *Sacre Coeur.* The lush trees along the walkway to the basilica were a wide array of vibrant fall colors. Grace was frozen in a genuine laugh, and Mantis had an arm lovingly around her. She couldn't remember what the Parisian stranger taking the picture had said to make Grace laugh so hard. Still, she felt grateful to have such a perfect moment forever frozen in time.

She gazed at her lover's warm smile, catching a dim glimmer of her melancholic reflection in the smudged glass.

Grace used to sing her to sleep on nights like this. She'd stroke Mantis's wavy mop of hair. She hadn't gotten a decent night's sleep since Grace died. Though it had been years, the smell of Grace's coffin still haunted her. *The wood. The formaldehyde...* Thoughts of Grace's lifeless body made her feel hollow now.

"*I hate you,*" Mantis whispered to the picture, fighting back a wave of roiling emotion. She slammed her fist into the frame, smashing the glass into sharp shards on the floor.

Mantis leaned over and picked up the largest piece off the chintzy nightstand and held it at her own wrist, feeling the edge press against her pulsing vein…

After a moment, she groaned into the hot air and hurled the shard of glass into the unhygienic abyss. She glanced at the picture, blurry through tear-filled eyes, plucked the photo through the busted frame, and discarded the rest on the floor. Crinkling in her trembling hands, she flipped it and looked at the back.

Paris. '09. Je t'aime.

Mantis lifted the picture to her chest, reclined onto her mismatched pillows, and wiped her face.

PART TWO:
CONQUEST

It was daytime. The bright sky was drained of color. Mantis stood in a smoky wheat field lined with trees, still in her nightshirt and panties. A grotesque lamb with seven cream-colored horns and seven reddened eyes sat on a large rock in the middle of the field. The creature was dirty. Its flesh was sliced, staining patches of its wool a vibrant pink.

An old man stood beside the animal in an ankle-length brown garment over a flowy, white linen tunic. He stepped closer to the bleeding creature, bending grass with every step of his sandals. He presented it an ornate book, a valuable relic adorned with precious metals and glinting gems.

The lamb snorted, blinked its seven strange eyes, and nudged the book with a battered hoof until it opened to the first page.

An eerie beast approached Mantis from behind, standing upright on two furry hind legs. She studied his terrifying expression. He was unlike anything she'd ever seen before. More human than animal, but with distinct features from several recognizable creatures. A lion's mane jutted out from beneath his cloak. Long, fierce horns and the broad snout of a black bull graced his hideous face.

An amalgamation of creatures. A *monstrosity*.

He straightened his hunched posture to get a better look up at her with his three unsettling eyes, the third seated in the middle of his fur-smattered forehead.

He was dressed like a vagrant in tattered rags of mismatched materials. The patchwork creature held out a hawk-like claw and spoke with the lips and mouth of a man.

"*It'sssssss you.*" His low, mesmerizing voice strangely brought a sense of peace to Mantis. He was pleased by her presence. He'd been expecting her.

"I knew you'd come." He gazed up at her in awe. She could sense from his eager demeanor that he had something important to tell her.

"*Come and sssssssssee,*" he repeated.

Mantis reluctantly took his claw and followed him into the foggy wheat field.

Through billows of white smoke, a muscular rider on a pure-white stallion appeared. His gleaming white mask had a painted-on expression so the man beneath could remain anonymous. He wore a gory crown of black demon fingers atop his mask, each crudely stitched to one another. Blood from the severed digits was dried to him like leaked ink. Beneath the bright overhead sun, his white armor shone through the gray haze. Beneath it, he wore a white, belted tunic. On his back, a wooden bow and quiver full of razor-sharp arrows clattered with every clomp. The horseman stared at her for a moment and then rode into the hazy treeline without a word.

The patchwork creature jovially rejoiced. "*Conquessssssssst.*"

"Who *are* you?" She gazed into his snakelike eyes, confused.

Without muttering another word, he raced away, disappearing into the mist.

Long Day

Mantis awoke in a pool of sweat to the earth rumbling violently beneath her. Glassware rattled off kitchen shelves, shattering on the floor. Mismatched plates jiggled out of the cabinets and exploded on impact like fireworks. She'd escaped a vivid dream only to be hurtled into a real-life nightmare. She bolted out of bed, clutching the desk to steady herself.

Outside, a symphony of car alarms blared out of sync. The pavement shook with brutal force, cracking the street violently in two.

Mantis rushed to the bathroom and sat down in the bathtub. A shampoo bottle rumbled off her shower caddy, glanced painfully off her shoulder, and dunked into the toilet. The quake continued. Outside, a woman screamed at the top of her lungs.

A fissure in the ceiling above the tub spread from one wall to another in seconds.

The end of the quake was sudden, halting as abruptly as it started.

The woman's wailing grew. Dozens of alarms and security buzzers sounded off like a casino full of winning slot machines chiming all at once. Mantis crawled out of the tub and looked into the mirror.

CRACK!

The sound rang out, and suddenly, a bathtub from the floor above burst through the ceiling, smashing the tub Mantis had taken shelter in mere moments before. Her heart raced as she looked at the devastation. Staying seated just a few moments longer would've ended her life. Unable to tell if she was utterly cursed or unbelievably blessed, Mantis stared in horror at the demolished bathroom. She had a feeling it was going to be a difficult day.

She had no idea how *right* she really *was*.

***

Mantis couldn't have felt more out of place as her boots whooshed the kickstand of her chopper down onto pristine asphalt. She glowered at the picturesque street, seemingly unscathed by the earthquake, and rested her hands on the high ape-hangers. She turned the key and killed the deafening motor of the flat-black motorcycle.

Fucking suburbia. This part of Tucson was flooded with soul-crushingly dull people. Full of zombified cubicle workers and upper-middle-class *Stepford Wives*.

She flicked a clinging ladybug off the arm of her leather jacket and looked up at a beige cookie-cutter house with its nauseatingly perfect white picket fence.

The vulcanized rubber heels of her combat boots clattered like horse hooves up the sidewalk as she neared the idyllic two-story house.

A scraggly-haired terrier trotted over and rolled on its back submissively at her feet, begging for attention.

"There's no way in hell, you little mutt," Mantis mumbled quietly.

Next door, an elderly woman in a night dress and slippers eyed her suspiciously as she mindlessly checked the contents of her mailbox. "Biscuit, get over here," she shouted disapprovingly.

The dog rolled to its feet and scurried off.

Mantis turned back to the house, dragging her chewed-short fingernails across the stringed bottom of her black crop top. She'd made it herself from a tight, cut-up thrift store tee that said "*Majestic as Fuck*" across the breasts in red lettering.

Mantis looked at the freshly painted front door. Her stomach churned. She'd been dreading this day for *seven years.*

***

Black-Eyed Betty had a rockabilly vibe about her even despite trying to hide it behind a polished veneer. At first sight, she looked poised. Elegant. Every hair of her tight up-do rigidly in place. A vibrant half-sleeve of tattoos peeked out from beneath the rolled sleeves of her pastel-pink blouse.

Years of heartache were etched into the fine lines of her face. It was a hurt from several impossibly hard decades makeup couldn't cover.

Mantis leaned against the fence and watched Betty water a pot of flowers from across the manicured yard. Betty's stare was icy when their eyes finally met. A look of utter disappointment spread across her face.

"Oh, good *Lord*," Betty sighed heavily. "What do *you* want?"

Betty's house was spotless. A flat-screen TV sat atop a glass entertainment stand in the living room. On it, a handsome televangelist in a stark-white suit spoke to his eager flock. Jeremiah Munsey had dominated Christian television, rising in fame yearly due to his mega-church and line of non-fiction books. Nearly everyone in America knew of him, religious or not.

"The time has come, folks! The book of *Revelations* is upon us!" Munsey's fanatics showed their support, hands thrust in the air, hanging on his every word. "There is gonna be a *rapture*... It is gonna be *glorious* when God's flock ascends to the holy kingdom of Heaven!" The audience reacted with passion. "There will soon be a day of *reckoning*! A judgment day." Munsey glanced around at the sea of faces. "Will *you* be ready?"

As the audience cheered, Betty turned the volume down with the remote. "Well, *this* is a surprise." She sounded irritated, leading Mantis through the tidy space into the kitchen toward the squealing kettle on the stove. "Care for some tea?"

"Long Island *iced*, perhaps?" Mantis joked playfully.

Betty didn't laugh. "How about *chamomile.* It's two in the afternoon."

"But it's five o'clock *somewhere.*" Mantis smiled. Her joke fell flat. She cleared her throat. "Yeah, chamomile's fine. Thank you."

Betty retrieved two pure-white teacups from a cabinet and poured boiling water into both. She steeped a tea bag in each and placed them on the island. She slid a brimming bowl of sugar cubes beside Mantis's.

Mantis plopped her dirty satchel down on the immaculate counter.

Betty stared at it anxiously. "When was the last time you *washed* that thing?"

Mantis chuckled and shook her head. "Still a neat freak, I see."

A young boy shuffled into the kitchen and looked up at Betty. She smiled down at him and kissed the top of his head. "Hey, baby."

Betty smoothed his black hair lovingly and then looked up at Mantis. She motioned for Mantis to cover her crass shirt.

Mantis looked down at the vulgar message, mouthed *whoops*, and zipped her jacket enough to cover it.

"Gabe, this is mommy's," Betty tried to think of the right word, "*friend*." But her expression said that term was wildly inaccurate. "*Mantis*."

"Hello, Miss Mantis." Gabriel waved timidly to Mantis and stared with innocent, glacier-blue eyes. "It's nice to meet you."

"We met, actually, but it was a long, long time ago. Your mommy and I go way back like car seats." Mantis was unable to take her eyes off the kid.

"Gabriel, go upstairs and play, baby," Betty said softly. The women listened as Gabriel's feet bound up the carpeted stairs before speaking again.

"God, they really do grow up fast." The words stung in Mantis's throat. She had no idea how strange it would be to see him after all this time apart. "How long's it *been*?"

"Seven years." Betty's tone turned brash. "Get to the *point*. What do you want from me?"

Mantis hated saying the words more than anything. "I... need your help." She grabbed her bag, picking at one of the studs on it with a chipped, black fingernail.

Betty exhaled deeply and pulled a pad and pen from a kitchen drawer near the phone. "I know a great rehab facility in Mesa. They're great. I know a lot of girls who got clean there."

"You think I'm fucking *high?*" Mantis was appalled.

"Watch your *language*! I have a child in *earshot.*" Betty fired back.

"I'm *aware!*" Mantis choked back her fury. "I'm not *high*, Bet. *Hand to God.* I have a *problem.*"

"You have a *lot* of problems."

"I know." Mantis laughed nervously at the slam. "You know, this new attitude, it's *very Christian* of you. I really dig this new *forgiving spirit.*"

"Can you get to the point? I have things to do."

Mantis instinctively pulled a cigarette from a nearly empty pack of Iron Pillars in her satchel. "Yeah, I can see how *bustling* life is here in *Pleasantville.*" She stuck it between her lips and fished around for her lighter. Betty angrily snatched the cigarette from her lips and dropped it into Mantis's cup of tea.

"What the *fuck*?!"

"*Out!*" Betty pointed a manicured, pink fingernail at the door.

"What the hell *happened* to you? You used to be cool." Mantis stood.

"What happened to *me*? What happened to *you*? You're a *train wreck*. You're still dressing like Ozzy Osborne's lovechild, and you frankly smell like *garbage*. When was the last time you *showered?*" Betty crossed her arms.

"Shower's outta commission. Listen, something *big* is going *on* out there. That smell is not me. It's *this* thing." Mantis motioned to the satchel. "It's sulfur. It smells like a friggin' egg fart."

"Nothing is going on out there. It was an *earthquake*. They *happen*." Betty growled quietly.

"I'm not talking about the earthquake." Mantis unzipped her bag and removed the demon's severed hand, flopping the ashen extremity onto the spotless, tiled kitchen island. The pungent sulfuric stench was vile. Betty gagged at the rotting mess. The curled *616* etched into the palm oozed chunky, ebony slime.

"Killed it in my place last night. Killed two more the day before." Mantis shook her head.

"I prepare *food* on this counter!" Betty was horrified.

There was a long pause between them. Finally, Betty spoke. "Let me get this straight: you think they're after you again, right?"

"*Yes!*" Mantis breathed a sigh of relief. Betty was finally on the same page.

"So you came *here*? *Knowing* I have a *child* in the house?"

"*Well*," Mantis realized that her plan, in retrospect, had some serious holes.

23

Just then, an old woman's blood-curdling scream seeped through the screen door.

Lucy

Something sinister lurked above Gabriel in his tidy bedroom. *Something evil.*

"Aren't you going to say hello?" The stunning woman smirked.

Gabe shook his head and fixated his gaze on the beautiful stranger. He placed the action figures in his hands on the carpet near his stuffed bear and stood.

Lucy was a vision, with curves of perfection and irises greener than fresh-cut grass. Her bountiful breasts pressed tightly into a cinched patchwork corset, one fashioned out of human skin. It sported hunks of flesh from every race with irritated, uneven edges sewn together with locks of hair and tendon. The edges were embellished with a row of human teeth, each with the root still attached. Her yellow skirt flowed in the breeze gusting through the boy's open window.

"Mom says I'm not supposed to talk to strangers." Gabriel focused on her, eyes like glowing sapphires.

Lucy felt as if the boy could almost see into her soul. She'd hoped that was not the case.

For *his* sake.

"We wouldn't be strangers if we introduced ourselves, now *would* we?" The woman took a step toward him.

Gabriel shook his head.

"You're no stranger to *me*, Gabriel."

"How did you know my name?"

"I know everyone's name. In fact, I know a *lot* of things. I knew another Gabriel once," she grinned nostalgically, referring to a dark time *eons* ago.

"Who are *you*?"

"*Lucy.*" The woman held out her hand.

Gabriel shook it slowly. She was hot to the touch, painful against his tender, young palm.

"I'm an angel." She smirked."Well, I *was* an angel."

"If you're an angel, where are your *wings*?"

She flexed her jaw muscles. "They were taken from me."

"Why?" His voice was full of innocence.

Lucy smirked. "I've been asking myself the same thing for years."

Believe Me Now?

Mantis and Betty burst out of the front door to see an ashen demon leap onto Mrs. Crandall, Betty's sneering neighbor. The demon growled through its gaping maw. A terrifying, inhuman sound rattled through the air. It sunk its long fangs into the old woman and savagely shook her. The afternoon sun glistened off its tar-like exterior. Glowing, magma-colored blood coursed through the deep crags in its flesh as it devoured her lower extremities like a hungry animal.

A few feet away, Biscuit yapped as if the noise would make it stop eviscerating its owner. The old woman let out another squeal and outstretched a hand toward them, pleading.

Betty didn't move.

The demon whipped its bloody head around and glowered at the women over Mrs. Crandall's disemboweled body. It chewed a long hunk of the woman's intestines while maintaining threatening eye contact with its fogged, ivory eyes. The demon's gaze was all Betty needed to break her momentary paralysis and push back into her home. Mantis followed, locking the door behind herself.

"Believe me NOW?!" Mantis hollered. "I told you, something is *happening*!"

Betty shuffled through her kitchen drawers, searching for something sharp.

"You're a curse, Mantis!" She put her hands behind her head, choking back her anger.

"How did this become *my* fault?!" Mantis poked herself in the chest, offended.

"I haven't seen you in seven years. Life has been *perfect*. Today, you waltz back into my house, and next thing I know—"

"Woah, why blame *me*? *I* wasn't the one that just ate your fuckin' neighbor."

"Look *around you*, Mantis! Everything even *near you* gets sucked into your vortex of *misery*!" Betty was on the verge of tears.

"This was a huge mistake." Mantis grabbed the severed hand in a huff and jammed it back into her bag. "I knew I shouldn't have come." Mantis stormed back out the front door of Betty's home.

Blackened storm clouds rolled out, casting dark patches of shade throughout the neighborhood.

The feeding creature whipped its head, glaring at Mantis with pale eyes, gnashing sinewy musculature out of Crandall's leg.

Mantis dashed toward the creature and hurled her satchel down on the road.

After her chat with Betty, Mantis was aching for a fight. She dug into the pocket of her frayed black jeans and retrieved her switchblade. She flicked the trigger, and the silver sliver shot out.

REEEEEEEEEEEE!

The creature shrieked.

Mantis stopped in her tracks and covered her ears. The nightmarish sound shattered a car window. The creature dropped the leg and leaped straight into the air, landing on Mantis and slamming her hard against the searing asphalt. The switchblade bounced off the ground and skidded beneath her motorcycle.

Mantis screamed as the beast dug into the back of her neck with its talons. She managed to wriggle her feet up and wedge them against the emaciated being's bony ribcage.

The beast was stronger. It drew her close, sinking its rotted nails into her scalp. Hot blood trickled underneath her leather jacket and down her back.

BOOM!

A deafening gunshot rang out.

RAWWWWWWWWOOOO!

The creature roared in pain, knocked backward with the force of the bullet.

BOOM! BOOM! BOOM-BOOM!

Four more shots were fired in quick succession. All crack shots with near-perfect grouping. The beast made an attempt to stand.

BOOM!

Betty fired the final shot into its skull. The bullet blasted through, piercing the front tire of Mantis's motorcycle and deflating the rubber.

The spindly body flopped on the ground and clawed at the smoking holes in its chest.

Mantis smiled at the hand holding the brushed metal .38 special and struggled to right herself. Betty slowly lowered the gun. The beast rattled violently in the throes of death.

"You still scream like a girl." Betty hollered across the yard to Mantis, cracking a little smile.

"Whaaaat? No. That wasn't me. I didn't scream. Must've been the, um, demon thingy." Mantis retrieved her switchblade and motioned down to the stilled lump of tar by her feet. "I totally had him, by the way."

Betty laughed. "Yeah, I saw. You know, you really ought to get a gun one of these days."

Mantis kicked the demon with her combat boot with full force. Its lifeless carcass shook, making Betty emit another genuine chuckle.

***

In Gabriel's room, Lucy lifted the stuffed bear to her face, inhaling its intoxicating scent deeply.

"Mmm. You smell just like your father." Lucy was enthralled, relishing the shivers it sent through her. She placed the bear back onto the carpet, and Gabriel caught a glimpse of the burning number *616* in the meat of her right palm.

Lucy said the magic word:

Father.

She had Gabriel's full attention.

He took a slow, curious step towards her. "You know my dad?"

"All *too* well. He's very," she took a deep breath, "*jealous.*"

"Jealous of *what*?"

"Pfft," Lucy scoffed. "You *name* it. Do you," she grinned, "want to *meet* him?"

Gabriel's eyes widened. He nodded excitedly. Lucy offered her hand to him, and he fixated his gaze on it. The numbers pulsed as if molten lava oozed beneath the gouges. Steam gently escaped the cracks in her otherwise perfect hand.

"Unless you're *scared.*" Lucy's red lips twisted upward into a grin.

***

Mantis picked up her messenger bag and pointed to the flat front tire of her bike. "Your aim could use improvement."

Betty leaned against her fence to get a better look at the damage. "Can you fix it?"

"Yeah, let me just put on my *spare*." Mantis joked, staring at her for a moment. "No. I gotta call a tow truck. Can I use your phone?"

Betty nodded.

Suddenly, the wind picked up, and a chilling breeze ripped through the block, rustling through the trees. Mantis looked around, uneasy, and then followed Betty back in.

"Phone's in the kitchen. Help yourself." Betty walked around to the staircase and hollered up. "Gabriel? Would you bring Mommy the peroxide from the bathroom upstairs?"

Betty stared up the stairs, waiting for an answer.

"*Gabe*?"

But there was no answer.

Only *silence.*

A silence she could feel in the depths of her soul.

Moments later, Betty tore through the doorway of Gabriel's room.

It was silent, save for the pounding of her heart and the icy breeze whipping through the wide-open window with wavering curtains.

On the taupe carpet, a still-smoking outline of an ornate two-foot cross had been burned artfully into the fibers, singed clean-through to the backing.

Mantis reached the doorway just as Betty fell to her knees.

"Did you look in the other rooms?"

Betty nodded. Watery ribbons raced down her cheeks.

Mantis stood like a somber statue for a moment before kneeling on the carpet beside her friend.

Betty noticed her son's favorite stuffed bear lying face-down. There were soot markings on it.

616.

The numbers were smeared into its fur, matching the hand she'd been shown in the kitchen. It was no coincidence.

Thunder cracked loudly outside, drawing their attention out to the sky. It grew dark through the street. Faint demonic growls echoed in the distance. The sound of anarchy and fear rattled through the idyllic suburban neighborhood.

"I have to get him back," Betty whispered.

"We will. I promise."

Mantis held out her hand. Betty took it.

Rock music thumped through the amps on either side of a black, reflective stage, shining like polished onyx. An exotic dancer slid upside-down down the chrome pole in the center by clenched thighs until she could brush the floor with her long hair.

A middle-aged male patron tossed a dollar at her. It twirled like a pinwheel. The dancer crawled across the stage and squeezed her huge, naked breasts together to pick up the dollar. The entranced man lifted a highball glass to his lips and sipped his liquor, never blinking once.

Dylan Goldstein watched the dancers from his DJ booth in the corner with oversized headphones hanging around his neck. He was lanky with a lush head of short, thick black hair. His shy smile gave him a certain boyish charm.

A server in a metallic bikini slammed a drink onto Dylan's cramped DJ station, slopping the pink liquid close enough to his equipment to cause alarm.

"Here's your *Sex on the Beach*," she huffed rudely, scuttling off to serve the patrons.

"Yeah, thanks a *pant-load*." Dylan muttered after she walked away, dabbing at the mess with a stack of cocktail napkins.

As the song ended, the dancer on stage collected her singles. Dylan wrenched the microphone around and held his lips close. He spoke with an exciting announcer tone that didn't fit his scrawny physique. "Alright, alright. That was Trina! *Trina-bina* we will… *see ya*."

As the dancer retreated behind a velvet curtain at the rear of the stage, Dylan started another tune. "This next performer will take your breath away. Open those wallets, folks. Get out those Benjamins. And get ready for a nice, tall glass of southern *Sweet Tea!*"

The track made his heart race every time he heard the opening notes.

It was *her* song.

Just then, a gorgeous, busty blonde strutted through the gap in the curtains confidently. She marched to the edge of the stage in her acrylic stripper platforms and smiled at Dylan. His heart skipped a beat. He beamed back with adoration. *His heart ached for her.*

The few men peppered throughout the barren club whistled and shouted. Weekday evenings were always hit-and-miss.

Sweet Tea slid her body against the pole with precision, strutting her Daisy-Duke-clad ass across the stage with swagger. Dylan sipped on his mixed drink and watched intently. Sweet Tea removed her tied top slowly to reveal a bra bursting with a massive set of breasts. She winked at two men who seated themselves in the front row.

She was *mesmerizing.*

Dylan wanted to work any night she was on the schedule just to see her perfect, curvaceous body in motion.

***

Betty parked her white SUV in front of the club. The neon pink sign looming high above read: *The Classy Lassie.*

Photos of the dancers inside, all clad in metallic bikinis, lined the seedy-looking entrance and darkened windows. A large sign that said: *We Bare All!* sat in the window closest to the front door.

"Mantis, why here? We need to find Gabriel! We are losing valuable time!" Betty growled, following Mantis out of the car and up to the club.

"We *will*." Mantis said calmly.

She had a plan.

"My seven-year-old is *not* going to be in a *strip club*," Betty argued.

"Betty, please. Just shut up and trust me." Mantis held open the door for her. "We're here for reinforcements."

"*Reinforcements?*" Betty reluctantly went inside.

Mantis pulled a messy wad of cash out of her front pants pocket and paid the stocky bouncer at the door the cover charges.

He pointed behind himself. "Sex shop's to the left. Strip club is to the right." He looked at Betty, staring a little too long. "Manager's in the back if you want a *job*, sweet thing."

Mantis yanked Betty by the sleeve of her blouse into the strip club, glaring at the bouncer.

Mantis looked around and spotted the DJ booth. She strode over to Dylan, boots clomping with every mannish step.

She yanked one of the puffy headphones from Dylan's ear and hollered, sending a shock wave of terror and surprise through him.

"Lookin' for Sweet Tea," Mantis yelled.

"She's working the crowd. Who are *you*?" Dylan yelled back.

"A friend." Mantis stared at the pair of brunette dancers on stage grinding the pole with bored expressions. "Thanks, kid." And she was off, weaving her way through the crowd.

Just then, out of the corner of his eye, Dylan spotted something strange. Something tall rustled past the crack in the dressing room door near his booth.

It didn't look human.

***

Mantis approached a patron in front of the stage and looked at his glass of booze. He glared up at her, filthy from a long day of laborious work, and set a small stack of singles on the edge of the stage, folded like a teepee.

She pointed at his glass. "I'll make you a bet. If I can guess what drink that is, you'll let me have it. *Deal*?"

The dirty worker laughed. "What do *I* get if you get it *wrong*?"

"I'll give you a dollar." Mantis leaned in, her hard features accentuated by the colorful par-cans above the stage.

"*Deal*." The man folded his arms and tipped his chair backward on two feet.

"Jack and Coke."

"Nope." He fired back quickly. "*Rum and diet*."

"Ew. What a *pussy*." Mantis rudely grabbed the drink and slurped the contents, avoiding the straw.

"Hey, *bitch*! You got it *wrong*!"

Mantis slammed down the empty glass and slapped the man playfully on the shoulder. She grabbed one of the neatly folded dollar bills from his pile and slammed it on the bar beside him. She walked off, and the exasperated man placed his dollar back on the stage again, cursing beneath his breath.

At the other end of the bar, Mantis sat on a torn bar stool and eyeballed the dancer on stage. She yanked her combat boot off and tipped it upside down, spilling loose change and rumpled singles all over the bar. A businessman behind her watched intently.

Mantis grabbed a small wad of cash, set it to the side, and scooped the change back into her boot with a broad sweep of her arm. She shoved it back on her foot with a jingle and unfurled the damp currency.

"Classy," Betty said, sipping a Shirley Temple. "You've heard of a *purse*, right?" She wiped the seat next to Mantis with a cocktail napkin and sat.

Mantis laughed, tucking a dollar halfway into the neck of her vulgar t-shirt. The exotic dancer on stage lowered herself to her knees and sensually crawled toward her. The dancer dragged her long hair across Mantis's face and removed the bill slowly with her teeth, brushing her nose against the skin of Mantis's neck.

Betty grimaced. "Are we here to get my son back, or are we here so you can get your rocks off?"

"Can't we do *both*?" Mantis smiled.

The dancer nibbled on Mantis's earlobe.

"That's *great*. My boy is out there somewhere, and you're cracking jokes."

Mantis gently pulled the dancer closer and whispered something into the woman's ear. The dancer retreated onto the stage and jiggled for the other patrons.

Mantis rolled her eyes. *"Happy now?"*

Sweet Tea emerged from a room marked PRIVATE, followed by an aroused customer, hiding his hard-on with a mesh trucker hat. She flashed him her signature, bubbly smile and stroked his chest as he walked away.

Dylan was still entranced by the strange sighting. He swore he'd seen something moving beyond the dressing room door. He nearly came out of his skin when Sweet Tea touched him. She wrapped her arms around his chest and pressed her bikini-clad breasts against his back. The feel of it made his pulse pound.

He craned his neck around and smiled at her, and she laid her head on his shoulder. In her thick, southern drawl, she said, "One of these days, we'll leave this place and never look back." She relaxed into him and sighed. Her voice was music to his ears.

The thing in the dressing room shifted again.

Dylan saw eyes emerge from the darkness. He fixated on the *thing* lurking in the shadows.

"Some… woman's here asking about you." He never took his eyes off of it.

"What woman?" She looked around.

Dylan pointed to the women at the edge of the stage.

Sweet Tea squealed and raced away from the booth, bouncing wildly.

She threw herself at Mantis, smashing her breasts into the side of her face. *"Oh my God,* I thought I'd never see y'all again!" She dabbed the tears emerging from her glittery, made-up eyes.

When Betty recognized her, she nearly choked on the last sip of her virgin drink.

***

Dylan stepped closer to the dressing room, zeroing in on the two hideous orbs locked on him.

Suddenly, the snarling demon within weaseled its ashen head through the dressing room door, drooling through two magma-red, glowing lips.

Dylan stumbled, tripping backward over the nest of extension cords behind him, ripping some from the wall socket, killing the booming music instantly. Patrons scanned the room in utter confusion.

The back of his head slammed against the linoleum. On the floor, Dylan dabbed his fingertips against the bloodied curls on the back of his head.

The creature hissed as it crept out of the dressing room.

Mantis arose from her seat with purpose, her smile fading instantly. She pulled out her switchblade and pressed the trigger, shooting the sharp metal blade out of the handle.

The beast emitted a deafening scream, sending the dancers and patrons into a frenzied mob. It lunged at Dylan.

Dylan screamed and kicked his legs frantically. The ashen beast swiped its long talons at the DJ's face. He kicked harder, keeping it as far away as possible. A full-force kick landed and rocketed it backward into a wall, smearing black goo and ash everywhere it made contact.

Mantis wasted no time. She booted the beast, knocking it onto the floor. She stabbed her knife at it, but the creature rolled away in the nick of time, sending her blade point-first into checkered linoleum. It rose again, hunching its back, locking its pale eyes on Dylan. It opened its terrifying mouth wide and launched toward him, barreling through Dylan's equipment, smashing sound boards and turntables beneath its weight to get at him.

It leaped over Dylan, ratcheting its unhinged jaw impossibly wide like a giant python. Skull bones cracked as the top half of its head snapped backward, nearly shearing itself in half at the throat.

Dylan screamed again as the beast smashed against him, trying to drive its ivory fangs into his face.

Mantis grabbed a power cord from the floor and wound it around her fists. She draped it in the creature's wide-open maw, slammed her boot against the beast's back, and yanked back with force. The harsh movement cracked the beast's skull in half. The top of its head toppled backward until its scalp rested against its spine. Dylan saw Mantis through the thin membrane of the beast's shredded cheek and hyperventilated. The creature slumped to the ground, lifeless.

Mantis offered Dylan a hand and tugged him toward her.

Just then, another ashen demon tore into the foyer behind Sweet Tea, hobbling unevenly on three-toed feet. It grabbed a red-headed dancer as she raced by, snatching her with brute force and gnawing a chunk out of her neck. Blood coursed from her shredded jugular down her jiggling, bare breasts.

Sweet Tea grabbed a beer bottle, smashed it against the bar, and stomped toward the gnashing creature with the fistful of brown glass, clacking her acrylic stripper heels the whole way. She stabbed it in the fleshy abdomen. It released its hold on the wounded dancer.

She jabbed it again, grinding shards of broken glass right where its heart should be. Glowing, red slime dribbled from its wound. The light pulsing through its craggy exterior dimmed and slumped lifelessly to the floor.

Sweet Tea knelt on the spattered linoleum to help her co-worker, but it was useless. The redhead choked up a mouthful of blood and gasped one final time before growing limp in the crimson puddle beneath her.

"Betty!" Mantis screamed from across the emptying club. She made her way to the stage and pointed at the ceiling. "Above you!"

Betty ducked, glancing up at the water-stained tiles above her.

A third creature clung to the ceiling like a charcoal bat. It swung open a set of veined wings with a *whoosh* and swiped a knobby fist at her, missing Betty's face by inches.

Mantis slid her knife across the glassy stage to Betty. Betty slammed her palm onto the top of it and grabbed the weapon. She triggered the blade, swung around, and slashed the throat of the hanging creature before it had a moment to react.

Tangerine-colored blood splattered onto Betty's pink shirt and khaki skirt. The beast dropped to the floor with a massive *thud* and let out a chilling hiss as life left it.

Betty flashed Mantis an appreciative glance, and Mantis hollered, "Still got it. Just like old times!"

"What in the absolute FUCK just happened?!" Dylan was undeniably more shaken than the women.

"Shit. Y'all always *did* know how to make one hell of an entrance!" Sweet Tea wiped her blood-spattered hands on the ass of her tight daisy-dukes. She looked down at the dead dancer on the floor and spoke. "*Damn*, Lindsay just started, too. That *blows*."

The curtain on the stage moved. Mantis tensed.

"What's wrong?" Betty followed the woman's gaze up to the slim-covered hand, pulling back the curtain at the rear of the stage.

Sweet Tea confidently held a hand up. "Allow me."

"All yours," Mantis chuckled.

Sweet Tea hopped onto the stage skillfully and danced without any music. She hummed the melody of one of her favorite songs. The partially-obscured creature watched with ghastly eyes.

"*Careful,* Tea," Betty shouted.

Mantis reached over the counter of the bar and grabbed a bottle of tequila. She dumped two random, abandoned glasses on the floor and poured the gold liquid into them. She took one for herself and offered the other to Dylan. He took it with a trembling hand but was too shaken to drink from it.

"Are you just going to let her…" Dylan trailed off, watching the creature creep closer to Sweet Tea.

"She's got this." Mantis tossed the liquor back and slammed the glass down on the bar.

Sweet Tea pressed the curves of her body against the chrome stripper pole.

The creature slowly unhinged its jaw and let out a low, horrendous rattle from the back of its throat.

She smiled, beckoning it to come close with a bent finger. When it did, she gripped the pole up high and spun herself onto it skillfully, drawing her legs in close. The beast crept forward again, and when the moment was right, she exploded her legs straight at it, shooting it toward the back wall. It flailed wild, shearing the giant velvet curtain from its grommets, tangling itself in the loosed fabric.

Sweet Tea danced to the writhing, cloaked creature and drove the heel of her stripper shoe brutally into its skull.

Several times.

Finally, it emitted a gurgle. Mantis clapped loudly from her bar stool.

Dylan made his way out into the middle of the room, surveying the massive damage to the overturned strip club with his hands on his head. The damage done in such a short period was unbelievable.

He looked around at the girls. "Does anyone want to tell me what the *fuck* just happened?"

"Tea? Who is this guy?" Mantis pointed with her switchblade.

"This is Dylan." Sweet Tea motioned between them as she carefully lowered herself onto the ground. "Dylan, this is Mantis and Betty."

Betty growled, nudging one of the dead creatures with the sole of her pink peep-toe heel.

"What kind of a name is *Mantis*?" Dylan winced.

"You *bangin'* this lame-wad, Tea?" Mantis cocked a brow.

"No. We're just friends," Sweet Tea said as she converged with the others at the bar.

The words carved a deep gash into Dylan's angst-ridden heart. He wanted to die hearing them aloud.

Just friends…

"Run along, kid." Mantis waved a hand lazily at Dylan. "The adults need to talk."

"Kid? I'm *24*." Dylan said, scrunching his forehead. "I'm not a child, alright? I'm a *man*."

"Oh, you're a *man*? Funny, you don't *scream* like a *man*." Mantis dug under his skin with her patronizing remarks.

"Dylan, *please*." Sweet Tea held up her hand to quiet him politely.

Mantis spoke to him like a dog. "*Good boy*, Dylan. *Stay*. Stayyyyyy. Now, *sit…*"

"Leave Dylan alone." Sweet Tea grumbled. "Why are you and Betty *here*."

"Someone took my son." Betty fought back a wave of panic and tears. She felt like she'd been waiting *days* to spew the words out.

Sweet Tea gasped. "What?! *Gabe*? No!"

"Yeah, right from his bedroom. We'll find him, but with these things running around again, I thought… why not put the ol' crew back together? We need all hands on deck." Mantis slid her hands mindlessly across the bar's surface. "You in?"

"Absolutely," Sweet Tea said without hesitation.

"Count me in, too," Dylan chimed in.

Mantis immediately made a repulsed face. "Woah, woah, woah, *chucklehead*, you're not invited."

"You *just* said you need all the help you can get." Dylan argued. "All hands on deck, right?" Dylan held both hands up and stared at them, eyes large, to make his point.

Betty's tone was motherly. "Sweetie, it's going to be *dangerous*."

He eyed the destruction around them. "My equipment is destroyed, so I'm basically unemployed now. Plus, I've been dying to leave this God-forsaken town for a while." He stared into Sweet Tea's hazel eyes. "I'll *beg* if I have to."

"That won't be necessary." Sweet Tea put an arm around him. "Dylan's coming with. I insist. *Package deal.*"

"Absolutely not. I just had to save his ass back there!" Mantis pointed to the demolished DJ booth.

"I held my *own*." Dylan locked eyes with Mantis.

Mantis thought for a moment, stood, and banged an index finger into his blood-smeared sternum. "Make me regret it, and I will leave you at the *first* gas station you take a *piss* at. *Understood?*"

Dylan nodded. Mantis turned away.

He cleared his throat. "So, who's the rest of the *crew*?"

"*Excuse* me?" Mantis whipped around, confused.

"You said you were putting the old crew back together. So," Dylan shrugged, "who are we getting next?"

Mantis looked appalled. "This *is* the whole crew, genius."

A look of fear flashed across Dylan's eyes, and he swallowed hard.

"What are we waiting 'round this dump for? The clock's a-tickin'. Let's find Gabe," Sweet Tea said, heading toward the front door.

As soon as Sweet Tea turned around, Mantis snatched Dylan by the collar of his T-shirt. "You're a *liability*. If you get in the *way*, I'll kill you *myself*."

Dylan pretended he wasn't scared shitless and nodded.

Mantis hollered from the rear as they exited, "Tea, make sure you keep your little boyfriend in check."

"He's not my *boyfriend*," she hollered back and then cast her gaze on Betty. "So, where do we start looking for Gabe?"

"Unfortunately, I've got an idea of where he might be." Betty shivered at the very thought of it.

The Hitchhiker

As Betty's wagon sped down a lonesome stretch of Arizona highway, Sweet Tea leaned across the back seat and laid her head on Dylan's shoulder. She closed her eyes, snuggling against him in preparation for the long drive ahead.

Dylan wanted desperately to touch her. To *kiss* her.

To stroke her honey-blonde hair.

…But the timing had never been right. He feared being rejected. Feared ruining their friendship.

But he'd always wanted to be *more*.

In the front, Mantis and Betty sat in silence. Betty's whiskey-colored eyes fixated on the road and the roadside devastation from the day's catastrophic earthquake. The terrain of the desert was cracked, with jagged chunks of earth split apart between the massive, toppled-over cacti. The ground looked like rust-colored paint, flaking in deep hunks.

Betty strangled the wheel, thinking about Gabriel, nauseous every time his abduction drifted into her thoughts. Whenever she remembered his angelic face and those sapphire eyes, her pink pump pressed harder on the accelerator.

Through the window, Mantis saw someone hitchhiking in the darkness. She bolted upright in her seat as the wagon whizzed past the woman on the roadside. She craned her neck to stare in the side mirror, recognizing the woman's face immediately.

It was Grace.

Only it *couldn't be.*

Grace was *long gone*. Nothing more than a rotting pine box full of maggoty bones.

"What?" Betty asked quietly, glancing at Mantis's worried eyes in the reflection of the rearview.

The woman was gone.

"Nothing. I didn't say anything." Mantis slunk back in her seat, thinking about what Betty had said earlier.

Maybe she *was* a curse.

El Paso-bound, the Volvo sped into the ominous sunset that lit the desert terrain up like a postcard.

PART THREE:
WAR

It was sunset. Mantis saw the fading, red light in the sky through a hole in a jagged, slate cave. Through the opening, she could see the grotesque lamb with seven horns, blinking its seven pink eyes. The old man from her last dream stood in the field beside it. He held out the open, ornate book. The lamb shuffled painfully and managed to nudge open a new section of the book with a ragged hoof.

On it, a single word was in inked cursive:

WAR.

The jarring patchwork creature, with the flesh of many different breeds of animal, grabbed Mantis by the hand with his birdlike claw.

"Come and *sssssssee*."

He led her eagerly through the hole in the steep rock wall into the field outside. The dry wheat drummed quietly against her jeans and leather jacket.

A dense layer of red smoke drifted through the land.

The ugly beast yanked her to the clearing of dirt surrounding the lamb. Confusion spread across her face as the patchwork creature released her hand.

From the billows of crimson-tinged smoke appeared a muscular man riding a blood-red horse. He wore a matching crimson mask with a painted-on expression of hatred. He had another tar-colored crown of demon talons atop his head that sliced through the smoke like a razor.

His shining armor reflected the raging fire blazing in the treeline behind him.

In his hand, he held a steel sword.

The red man rode his horse to her.

The patchwork creature rejoiced beside her jovially. "*Warrrrrrrrr.*" It growled in ecstasy and then scuttled off, disappearing into the smoke beyond the horseman.

The arid ground beneath her feet quaked. A design of an ornate cross etched itself into the soil from beneath the surface.

The cross had harsh edges with illegible words on all four ends. She only caught a glimpse of it before rust-red dirt puffed through the widening holes. Slivers of white light cut through the outline, shining upward in blinding beams.

She gasped at the revelation. Mantis realized she had seen the image before…

It was the same cross burned into the carpet in Gabriel's room.

Betty parallel-parked the wagon in a tight spot in front of a string of drab downtown buildings. The abrupt braking shook Mantis awake. She wiped her drool from the door's upholstery, still electrified by the wild dream.

"*Gross,*" Betty whispered, watching Mantis rub the spit into the fabric. Mantis looked at Betty apologetically and used the hem of her vulgar shirt instead.

Betty killed the engine and exited the wagon, starting down the block.

Mantis walked briskly and caught up with Betty. Her boots clomped against the sidewalk with every wide step. Sweet Tea followed close behind, blowing bubbles with her gum, strutting in her blue leather jacket, short jean shorts, and silver bikini top. Dylan brought up the rear, stretching hard from the grueling drive.

El Paso's downtown area was alive with party-goers and hammered Texans drunkenly stumbling toward their ordered ride-shares. Music resonated from a nightclub halfway down the block, vibrating the sidewalk with deep bass.

Betty turned the corner into an alley. A crimson neon sign advertised a basement entrance.

"Wait, are you fucking *kidding* me, Betty?!" Mantis shouted, realizing where they were. "Aww, *hell* no!" Mantis turned on her heel and started back toward the car.

Betty yanked her by the coat. "Stop! You said you were here to help me. You think I'm *excited* to see him again?"

"Are you *serious* right now? You brought us all the way to El Paso for *that prick*?! I'm gonna take his fucking head off!"

Mantis squirmed violently. It was everything Betty could do to restrain her.

"Mantis!" Betty's voice echoed through the alley. "He might have my *son*!"

A tear rolled from Betty's eyes. It was Mantis's weakness. She *hated* to see Betty cry. The woman had shed enough tears for ten people. The woman's life had been unbelievably hard. It was a miracle that she'd survived, much less *thrived*.

Mantis wiped the tear from Betty's face. "Fine," she whispered, "but if this shit goes *south*, I'm gonna gut that motherfucker like a fish." Mantis reigned in her fury, "You hear me?"

Betty nodded and turned back toward the sign. A slew of hookers paced like hungry sharks at the end of the alley.

Seeing them brought Betty back to the days when she'd been a shark herself... hungry for all the benefits the unsavory lifestyle had afforded her. She wanted to run far and fast, but the thought of Gabriel was all she needed to carry on.

Two strung-out prostitutes approached Dylan, touching his shoulders and licking their lips like hungry dogs.

The first pawed at him, glaring at Sweet Tea like a piece of garbage, barely able to keep her glassy eyes open. "*Mmmmmmmmm*, baby. Have you come to get yo' self *covered* in Honey?" Her breathy words wafted a distinct mixture of smoke and malt liquor his way.

"No?" Dylan's nervous reply came out more like a polite question.

The woman rubbed her hand down his abdomen, and Sweet Tea's smile faded. The hooker nibbled his earlobe, and he jerked backward.

"Easy there," Dylan said, fending the woman off with an awkward karate-style movement.

A grinning man emerged from the smoke. Betty recognized him right away, grinding her teeth in anger at the sight of him.

The slick pimp walked toward her and ran a finger across the golden chains that lay over his tuft of exposed chest hair. He rubbed his palm against his chiseled jaw, grazing the uniformed stubble.

"Well, well, well. Look's like the gang's all here." He jested, glancing between Betty, Sweet Tea, and Mantis. He patted his hands against the sides of his pants in rapid succession, like the tapping of a snake's tail, distracting the focus of the prey away from its deadly jaws.

Johnny Four-Fingers. That was the street name bestowed upon him after the loss of his left pinky finger. It's how all the thugs and whores knew him. His moniker held power and clout. Johnny practically *owned* the city's dirty underbelly, and he was a God to most of the degenerates in it.

Betty knew Johnny *before* the power. Before the *drugs*. Before the harem of strung-out, money-hungry women.

And certainly before the *nickname*.

She no longer wanted to feel his talented tongue entwining with hers or feel his gruff hands brush against the tender parts of her body. She no longer desired to feel his skin pressed against hers during sex, causing the orgasmic waves of pleasure rattling through every inch of her body.

Instead, she wanted to feel the bounce of a semi-truck as it drove over his chest like a speed bump… and then reversed for good measure.

"*Where is he*?!" Betty growled.

The two hookers pawing at Dylan like catnip whipped their heads and glared at Betty.

Johnny grinned. His nicotine-stained teeth reflected ruby-red in the neons. "Baby, calm down. You're so *tense*." Johnny reached for her. She swatted him away furiously. "You need to *relax*."

"Touch her again, and I will *end* you," Mantis barked.

Johnny grinned, tempted to test the waters to see how serious the threats were. "Last time I saw *you—*"

"Where is my *son*?" Betty interrupted, her tone loud. Johnny eyed Betty like a juicy T-bone steak. His gaze made her feel filthy.

The second prostitute reached into her thigh-high boot, tugged a pink-handled knife out of it, and pointed the blade at Betty, stepping to Johnny's side. "You need me to cut this bitch, daddy?"

"No, Rosie, I'll be *juuuust* fine." He slapped the hooker hard on the ass, letting his gnarled excuse for fingers linger there.

"Hey," Mantis motioned to Rosie's weapon, "sweet snake-print knife. You know how to use that thing?"

"Betta' believe it." Rosie jabbed the blade, but Mantis looked aroused instead of threatened.

"You look *good*, Black-Eyed Betty. Last time, well, you looked a little *rough*." Johnny chuckled and wiped a tendril of jet-black hair from Betty's eyes, and she flinched. She was furious at the very *mention* of the nickname. It was a cheap callback to her former life, one she tried to forget.

"Last time we were together, you were *indisposed*. Had that sexy little thong knotted around your heels. Face pressed against the ground, lapping up the gutter runoff like a dog with that *lucrative* little tongue of yours."

"*Shut up*." Betty wiped her face where once-perfect winged eyeliner now streaked her cheeks.

Mantis stepped forward, balling her fists, ready to clock the guy.

"Hell, you probably don't even *remember* that night. You were ridin' the white horse, high as a fuckin' kite." Johnny grinned. Her pain always *was* his pleasure.

"Should've done more than cut off your finger that night. I should've *slit your throat,* too.*" Fury roiled behind Betty's eyes.

Johnny neared her with a shit-eating grin on his face. "Did you *enjoy it* when they took turns using your naked body like a fucking *rag doll—*"

Johnny was interrupted by a full-force punch from Mantis's hand.

Betty lunged, throwing herself in the middle of the two as Mantis scrambled to get another shot in.

"Mantis, stop!" Betty growled. Her terrified eyes flitted back and forth between both of her former acquaintances.

Johnny held his chin and chuckled, checking his lips for blood. Rosie bolted toward Betty, seeking retribution. Mantis halted the woman dead in her tracks, high-kicking the knife out of Rosie's needle-scarred hand and flinging it out onto the garbage-strewn asphalt. Rosie stood straight, stunned and received a brutal punch straight to her own face as Mantis decked her.

The other prostitute wrapped her arm around Dylan's throat and wrenched him down.

"*Enough!*" Betty roared into the air. She stepped forward and grabbed Johnny by the balls in a wholly unexpected motion. Johnny coughed at the crushing grasp she had on his jewels.

The fighting halted around her. Dylan struggled to free himself from the hooker's fierce grasp.

Betty thrust her arm down into the waistband of the pimp's pants and retrieved the flat-black pistol he always kept tucked in the waistband.

"Tea!" Betty lobbed the gun over her shoulder, and Sweet Tea clumsily caught it in the air.

"Girl, you done fucked up," Johnny threatened through the pain.

"Give him back, and you never have to see my face again," Betty growled through gritted teeth.

"Who?" Johnny's mouth was inches from hers, eyes boring holes through hers as the pressure in his testicles increased. The dull points of her gel nails ground into his sack.

"Gabriel, you idiot!"

"*Who the FUCK is Gabriel?!*"

The genuine tone of his question stunned them all.

"Don't play dumb! God knows you're anything *but!*"

"I don't know any fucking *Gabriel.*"

Betty felt a surge of guilt course through her.
He was telling the truth.

"I'm gonna let your prunes go. Call off the hounds." Betty flashed her eyes to Rosie and Honey and squeezed harder.

"Oh my God! I fuckin' *promise,* you stupid bitch."

"Say it *nicely,*" Mantis ordered, nearing his face.

"Honey, Rosie," Johnny managed with a nod to them, on the verge of throwing up from the pain. Being an ex-lover, the bitch knew precisely where to grab him.

Betty released her grip on his testicles, and he bent over, gasping deep breaths. He clutched his crotch and offered Betty a look of agony.

"Who... the hell... is *Gabriel*?!"

Betty folded her arms with tear-filled eyes. "He's your *son.*"

A Real Treat

Mantis, Betty, Sweet Tea, and Dylan followed Johnny through a door in the rear of the alley, marching cautiously to a crypt-like basement below. He pulled a string, and an orange Edison bulb flickered on with a *buzz*, filling the disgusting room with a dim, tobacco-brown ambiance.

"Sit." Johnny motioned to the filthy, mismatched furniture around a table filled with items for intravenous drug use. Used hypodermics. A burned spoon with its handle warped backward. A damp wad of browned cotton. Tiny bags of off-white powder marked with hand-drawn pentagrams.

Johnny smiled up at them. "Can I interest anyone in a lil' *China White*?"

"Rain check." Mantis looked around.

"So," Johnny looked Betty over, "I have a *son*? Last time I saw you, a LOT of men could have fathered your bastard child." Johnny's eyes wandered to the hem of Betty's skirt. "By the way, I'm loving this whole *wholesome* vibe. *Very* hot." he languidly licked his bottom lip.

Dylan's stomach rumbled, drawing everyone's attention to his guts. He looked around apologetically. "Sorry."

Slowly, their eyes drifted back to the pimp.

"Don't you *miss* the good ol' days?" Johnny lifted his gaze, lingering on her breasts. "C'mon. You *know* you were into the lifestyle. The *money*. The sex. Shit, practically *begged* for it all by the end."

Betty scoffed. " Yeah. I begged to become a human punching bag. *Regularly.* Nah, sorry, I didn't beg to be *gang-raped* for greenbacks."

"The kid..." Johnny straddled a chair, "He act like me?"

Betty cackled. Loud and sarcastic.

Johnny rested the side of his face on the top of the chair. The bare bulb above him reflected in his glittering eyes. For a split second, Betty remembered why she once found him so appealing. Or rather, *addictive.* His disarming smile and velvet voice usually cut straight through her defenses, but that charm had no effect on her now. Falling prey to it years before made Betty a bone-hard woman.

She didn't need a man. She didn't *want* one.

Dylan's stomach groaned again like a protesting beast. Everyone craned their necks to face the noise.

"What the fuck, man?" Mantis took out a nearly-full pack of cigarettes and popped one between her cherry-red lips.

"Sorry! Can't help it, I'm starving. I haven't eaten all day."

"You need to get that shit under control," Mantis muttered through pursed lips into the filter of her cigarette.

Johnny walked to a nearby cabinet and pulled out a three-inch squared brick of something brown wrapped in plastic wrap. He tossed it to Dylan.

Dylan looked down at the brownie in his hands, stunned by the generosity, though hesitant to eat food gifted by a degenerate. He unwrapped it and inhaled the sweet chocolate aroma and without giving it any further thought, Dylan crammed the intoxicating treat into his mouth.

"*Oh... my... Jehovah!*" Dylan muttered, lips smacking through the chocolate in satisfaction.

Mantis laughed, exhaling a fog of smoke.

"Jesus, kid. Pace yourself." Johnny sounded concerned.

"Thank you for this." Dylan managed before popping the last bit of chocolate in his mouth. "*That...* hit the spot."

"Holy hell, I've never seen anyone eat that much at one time before." Johnny was impressed.

"I've always had a pretty big appetite." Dylan smiled sheepishly.

"*Moron.*" Mantis spat out another forceful puff. "That was a *pot brownie*, asshole."

Dylan's eyes enlarged with a look of panic. *Was she joking?*

"That was strong shit, too. Medical-grade. Brace yourself, kid." Johnny chuckled. "You're in for an *experience.*"

Dylan stood in silence, horrified. Wondering if he should try to make himself throw up.

"Sorry, Bet. Dunno what to tell ya about your *spawn.* As you can see, my pad still is not exactly kid-*friendly.*" Johnny motioned to the dump around him.

Through the corridor behind Mantis, a female emitted a muffled shriek, and a man's gruff voice hollered out, "Shut up, you stupid little cunt!" A pounding noise followed. The woman yowled.

THWACK-THWACK.

It was a sound Betty knew all too well.

It was the sound of closed fists connecting with flesh. Then the hollow thud of meat against wooden floorboards alarmed everyone, save for the pimp, who acted like the noise was totally ordinary.

Expected, even.

Betty's fists tightened. Her jaw clenched.

The girl's screams were soon muffled. Howls of pain were quickly replaced with hyperventilated breathing.

"What are you letting him *do* to her in there?" Betty flashed Johnny a thousand-yard-stare, stood, and walked toward the source of the sounds.

Johnny snickered as if the activity was all part of some sick, twisted joke.

"You mean *they*?" Johnny smirked. "What'd you expect? You were my *bottom bitch*. But even *you* aren't *irreplaceable*."

As she crept, the door flew open in front of Betty, drawing all eyes to him. He fumbled with the massive buckle on his belt and double-checked that the zipper of his wranglers was up. His laugh echoed off the walls of the dingy den.

Behind him, another man pulled a pair of skin-tight jeans over his white briefs.

Betty burst past the men, bolting into the room. In it, a terrified woman was bound by her wrists to a stained bed, skin rubbed bloody from the struggle. Tract marks riddled the crooks of her bruised arms. An ashtray overflowing with butts sat on the bedside table. Two still burned, emitting dancing tendrils of smoke from their ends.

Betty rushed to her side and kneeled on the floor, heart pounding.

"Jesus!" Sweet Tea said from the doorway, fully ingesting the scene before her.

Betty removed the filthy bandanna tied around the girl's mouth, drenched with spit and tears.

"No! *Don't! Stop!* Oh, God," the girl shrieked.

"*Easy.* I'm *not* going to hurt you." Betty tried to calm her. The girl only howled louder.

"Hey, you're alright. *Shhhh.* Look at me, you're alright." She looked around for something to free the girl from the duct tape around her wrists to no avail.

Sweet Tea tried to look away but could not divert her eyes from the train wreck before her. The girl's skin was irritated by fresh cherry burns throughout her ribs, breasts, and thighs. Her youthful, milky skin was tarnished with a rainbow of bruises. Ribs jutted out from her taut sides like that of a malnourished animal. Coppery blood radiated from the smears near her privates, which were on full display.

Outside the room, Dylan grew alarmed over the unknown quantity of drugs he'd unknowingly consumed.

Mantis carefully calculated her next move.

"You got a *problem*?" Johnny asked.

"How you make your money is none of my business."

Johnny laughed at her response and nodded to the customers. "Good to see ya, Issac," Johnny said, grinning.

Issac pressed a black cowboy hat onto his head and nodded cordially. Then, he pulled three fifty-dollar bills from his wallet and held them out at Johnny.

"Here's a tip for the little lady. Eli and I got a little *creative* in there." Isaac hacked, loud and phlegmy. "Sorry 'bout that."

Johnny scoffed. "She'll be fine."

The men nodded again and thudded their cowboy boots up the stairs and into the alley. As the men disappeared, Johnny approached the area where Mantis stood, shamelessly invading her personal space.

She always hated being this close to Johnny. No matter what, she refused to flinch or move from his path.

"Excuse me, darlin'." Johnny leered, examining her with his lewd gaze.

Objectively, she could see why women were attracted to him. Taking his low V-neck and gaudy gold chains out of the equation, his rugged looks and suave Southern mystique made him somewhat appealing.

Dylan watched the tense interaction. They were like dogs at the park debating whether to bare fangs or mount each other. Mantis finally gave in to Johnny's silent request and stepped aside.

Behind her, Johnny removed a velvet painting with a gold-sprayed wooden frame from the dirty wall, revealing the wall safe behind it. He attempted to obscure her view of the keypad, but she could still see with the extra inch of height her combat boots afforded.

6-1-6-6-1-6.

A green button flashed, and the lock released. A massive stack of cash and a strange, warped hunk of gold sat inside. Johnny stuffed the men's money in and armed the lock. He returned the painting.

Around the corner, Betty scanned the room and motioned to the tape. "I need something to cut this with."

Sweet Tea stuck her head into the hallway and whispered. "Mantis… *knife.*"

Mantis handed Sweet Tea her switchblade without a word, and within seconds, Sweet Tea had freed the girl.

"Stay right here." Betty stroked her hair sweetly. She pressed her face to her knees and wrapped her arms around the backs of her bloodied thighs as Betty rose. Sweet Tea handed the blade to Betty.

Betty stormed out, infuriated. She handed the knife back to Mantis and glared at Johnny.

"What do you think of your replacement?" Johnny joked.

Behind him, Mantis wrapped her arm around his throat and wrenched hard. He struggled to breathe. Betty decked him in the face, smashing his nose with a sickening crunch. A rivulet of blood streamed from his broken nose. Betty winced at the pain radiating through her hand.

Johnny reached down to his belt and felt for his pistol. Panic swelled when he remembered they'd snatched it from him half an hour prior.

"What's the matter? Not such a tough guy without your gun?" Mantis whispered in his ear.

"Funny, I remembered *mine*," Betty said, reaching into her purse. She pointed the barrel of her own .38 special at him.

"Well, would you look at that?" Mantis chuckled, Johnny's face now red from the chokehold.

"Step aside, *Mantis*!" Betty glowered at the pimp as he raised his arms in submission. Mantis released him and backed up. With her eyes locked on Johnny, Betty inched closer to the wall and straightened the velvet painting.

"*Bet*, put the gun down." Blood trickled over Johnny's twisted smile.

"Wait!" Mantis shouted. "Betty, *don't shoot.*"

"Why not?!" Betty screamed out, staring into Johnny's cold eyes.

"Trust me. Just stay there a second."

Like a bolt of lightning, Mantis shot up the stairs, clomping up two steps at a time until she burst through the door into the alley. She galloped through the crimson fog toward an idling pickup truck.

"Isaac! Eli!"

The cowboys looked at her. One cracked a smile. Eli rolled down the truck's window and, with his thick, West Texas accent, said, "Hey there, darlin', whatcha' need?"

"Thank God I caught you!" Mantis panted. "Johnny asked me to come get you guys. Said he totally spaced it while you were down there, but he's got a brand new girl he wants to show you for next time. Said he'll give a discount to y'all if you'd be the ones to break her in. Asked me to try to catch you before you left."

"Well, shoot. Alright!" Issac shut the truck off and headed back inside. Once they reached the door, Eli held it open for her. Mantis waved her hand in the air. "No, it's okay. You guys first. I insist."

"Well, that wouldn't be very gentlemanly of me, now would it?"

Mantis wanted to punch him in the throat as soon as the words hit her ears. These men were anything *but*.

"No, really, I insist." Mantis motioned for them to go down first.

Eli shook his head. "This is what's wrong with the world today. You bitches say chivalry's dead, and you're the one's pullin' the trigger."

Isaac sighed, shrugged, and headed down. Eli followed. Mantis pulled the switchblade from her pocket and triggered the blade quietly. She grabbed Eli by the hair, yanked him forcefully toward her, and slit his throat with one savage motion.

Eli gurgled as blood filled his airway. Isaac turned to see the commotion. Mantis grabbed the wooden handrails, lifted her slight body, and kicked Eli with both feet with the force of a mule.

Both men clattered against the concrete. Isaac shrieked, covered in his buddy's viscous blood.

Eli rolled onto the floor and clutched his throat, his body growing increasingly limp.

"Stand up, asshole!" Mantis spat at Isaac.

Isaac looked at the pistol in Betty's hand, then up at Johnny, who had all nine fingers up in a display of submission.

"Stand by Johnny over there where Betty can see you." Mantis pointed with her bloody knife. Isaac scrambled to get up, and Mantis kicked him forcefully in the ribs. He fell to the floor again, and Mantis stepped back. Isaac timidly made his way to the spot beside Johnny.

Mantis hurled the velvet painting onto the floor and punched in the six-digit code. After the long beep, Mantis grabbed the stack of cash and the golden object inside.

"*Strip.*" Mantis looked at the male hostages, hands stuffed full of green and gold.

Neither moved.

"Did I *stutter?*"

Johnny finally pulled off his black shirt, revealing the well-defined abs beneath.

"*Good boy.*" Mantis motioned with her head to the naked, traumatized young woman clinging to the bedroom door frame. "Now, give it to her."

Johnny handed the nude woman his V-neck. The girl flashed Mantis a grateful look before sliding it over her injured form.

"You've made your point," Johnny growled to Betty.

"She wasn't talking to you, *dipshit*." Mantis pointed her switchblade at him like a sorcerer's wand.

She looked at Isaac. "You think you're *exempt* from this? The pants, *dickhead*. Lose 'em," Mantis barked.

Isaac kicked off his Ariats, unbuckled his belt, and peeled off his tight jeans. Mantis carried them pinched between two fingers as if covered in something disgusting. She handed them off to the young woman.

Dylan crept low to the ground and retrieved the man's boots, drawing all the attention in the room to him, inadvertently.

"The *fuck* are you doing?" Mantis looked at Dylan.

"*What?*" He asked, still crouched. "You have any idea how *expensive* boots like this are?" He peered inside the boot and checked the size, quietly rejoicing once he found it.

Mantis rolled her eyes.

Dylan kicked off his tennis shoes and politely offered them to the injured girl. He slid the cowboy boots on his feet and stood, beaming at Sweet Tea with pride. Then, he burst into a loud fit of laughter.

"What's so funny?" Mantis snarled, but Dylan couldn't compose himself long enough to get out a complete thought. She swiped a fallen chunk of black, shaggy hair from her face. Dylan pointed down to Eli's corpse, giggling like a cartoon chipmunk. "He's *dead.*"

There was a moment of silence after the morbid comment.

"That brownie's kickin' in." Johnny tried to hide his smile.

Mantis rolled her eyes again as Dylan's laughter grew louder.

She'd forgotten about the brownie.

"No, seriously," Dylan struggled to compose himself but couldn't, "that guy is like… *really* dead."

"*Now?*" Betty anxiously adjusted her stance, putting both hands on the .38. The muscles in her forearms flexed.

Mantis approached with caution. She knew that Betty's manicured finger was itching to pull the trigger. She also knew *Betty would never be able to forgive herself if she did.*

Mantis slid a slender hand over the revolver and gave the gun a tug. Betty finally loosened her grip on it. Once Mantis had it in her possession, she handed off the stack of cash and hunk of gleaming metal. "Trade."

Betty took it, nodding with a lost look in her teary eyes.

"Hey, *Tommy Chong*, take Betty and her upstairs," Mantis ordered.

"But what if those demon things come back?" Dylan asked.

Mantis pointed the revolver at him.

"Sure thing! You got it. You can put your trust in *me*, Mantis. I *assure* you—" Dylan scrambled over the bloodied corpse at the bottom of the stairwell.

"Sweet Tea's got John-boy's gun. I'll be right behind y'all." Mantis locked her eyes on the shirtless pimp and pant-less cowboy.

Dylan escorted Sweet Tea, Betty, and the wounded girl outside.

Mantis rolled her shoulders back and swung her head around in an unsuccessful attempt to crack her neck. "Anyone got a cigarette?"

Johnny patted his pockets. She pointed the gun at Isaac and smiled. "I know *you* do. Unless you put them all out on the girl. Got any left?" Isaac didn't budge. "*Lemme guess*. They were in your *pants*?"

"*Here*." Johnny offered up a dented pack of cigarettes. She splayed one of her bony hands, and he lobbed it to her. She caught it, plucked one of the white sticks from the little paper box, and shoved it between her lips.

"Lighter's inside," Johnny added.

Mantis fished it out with her nimble digits. She flicked the lighter with her free hand and sucked hard as she lit it. She blew a puff of smoke out and jammed the lighter in her pocket. She looked at the paper container and made a sour face. "Ugh. *Menthols*? Johnny, you really are the *worst* kind of person."

Without another word, she raised the revolver and emptied three well-placed bullets into the brains of each of them.

Muffled gunfire erupted through the brick building. Betty stood with the young woman, now clad in ill-fitting men's clothes, grateful for a shred of salvaged modesty.

Sweet Tea stood worried, eyes tinged pink by the vibrant alley lights. With crossed arms, she tapped her acrylic nails on her blue, leather, unzipped jacket. Long, natural-blonde hair draped across her bountiful breasts, framing her tin-foil gray bikini top. Dylan's enlarged pupils were locked on her.

Mantis emerged from the building, skin ruby-spattered like a Jackson Pollock painting. She blew a meditative gust of cigarette smoke into the humid air.

"Is he…" Betty couldn't bring herself to say the word.

Mantis stuck the cigarette between her lips again and spoke, ignoring the question. "How much money do you think's in that stack?"

Sweet Tea stuffed her hands in the tight back pockets of her shorts, forcing her tits out further. "There's gotta be close to ten grand there."

"Probably closer to *fifteen*. It's all hundreds," Betty said, shaken by the too-familiar brutality.

Dylan stared at his hand, fascinated by its shape and texture. Mantis watched as he flipped it repeatedly, examining every angle.

"You okay?" Sweet Tea turned back to the women.

Mantis nodded. The unapologetic look in her eyes was right on-brand.

Betty turned to the tortured prostitute. She took a hunk off the top of the massive stack of cash and placed the remainder into the girl's trembling hand. "Here. Please. Take this. Get as far from here as you can, and don't ever look back."

***

Mantis and Sweet Tea sat in silence in the back seat of the parked wagon. Mantis stared at the glowing yellow sign before them that read: *El Paso Supercenter.*

Sweet Tea spun the hand crank on her door and brought the window down with a squeak. She gazed up at the breathtaking blanket of stars and spoke, eyes never leaving the sky. "Wanna talk about it?"

"Nope." Mantis examined the bizarre hunk of metal from Johnny's safe. The design on it looked oddly familiar, but she couldn't quite place it.

Soon, Betty and Dylan emerged from the store, arms full of plastic bags. Mantis hopped out the moment they came into sight. Sweet Tea followed. The group convened at the front of the vehicle, where Betty dumped the contents of the first bag.

"Mantis, this is for *you*." She dropped a stretchy, long-sleeved black shirt that said, "*I like it moist,*" with a cute drawing of a slice of cake below it. Then she laid down a pair of black high-waisted shorts and fishnet tights in front of Mantis on the hood. She carefully laid a new pair of scissors beside it.

"Holy shit. You almost know me *too* well." Mantis smiled and kissed Betty on the cheek.

"Yeah, well, your wardrobe hasn't changed in the last decade."

"*Yours* has. You used to dress *cool*. Now you dress like a lady banker," Mantis joked. "Not like that sexy little strappy number you used to don in the old days."

"You may be able to get away with perpetually dressing like a goth teen who is trying to piss off her parents, but I *grew up*. I got a *kid* to think about."

Dylan dumped the other bags on the hood and sifted through the items. He grabbed a three-pack of solid-colored t-shirts and ripped the bag open with vigor, unfurling a gray one.

"For *you*." Betty handed Sweet Tea several colorful items of clothing. The gleeful stripper bounced. Dylan and Mantis were both mesmerized instantly by her generous, jiggling cleavage.

Mantis cut the sleeves and bottom half of the shirt off, leaving a custom crop top that now read simply: *I like it moist.*

Mantis stripped off her old clothes. Betty lurched in front of her, modestly covering her from the strangers exiting the building. "*Really,* Mantis?"

"*Yes*, really," Mantis pulled her top off, drawing Dylan's reddened eyes to her bare, bleach-white breasts. Above them were two small words in cursive.

"They're just tits. You see 'em all day at work." Sweet Tea elbowed Dylan in the side. He looked away.

"Couldn't help but notice you got a few tattoos on your, um," Dylan gestured to his chest nervously, "I couldn't read 'em though."

"Yeah, sure. You were looking at my *tattoos*." Mantis wrenched the crudely cut neckline of the shirt down so that Dylan could see the bony tops of her chest.

"It says *Milk*... and *Milk*."

She unbuttoned her jeans and flapped the front open, revealing another in similar script just above a pink, horizontal scar by her pubic hair that said: *Lemonade*.

"God, Mantis," Betty shielded her eyes. "We don't ever want to see the one over where fudge is made."

Mantis dropped her pants the rest of the way and stood on the asphalt, completely naked from the waist down.

"*Oy vey!*" Dylan muttered.

"I should have gotten you underwear, too," Betty grumbled, mortified, as she scanned the parking lot.

"I don't wear any."

"Obviously," Betty scoffed.

Mantis sat her bare ass on the hood and tugged on her fishnets, followed by her high-waisted black shorts. She slid her feet in her untied boots. "I'm dressed, *prudes*."

Dylan chuckled to himself, moving loose gravel around on the black asphalt with the toe of his new cowboy boots, "*Lemonade…*"

Mantis smirked at his sudden amusement. "You got any ink, kid?"

He nodded, blushing with slight shame. He tugged up his t-shirt, revealing a bold upside-down triangle on his chest about an inch wide.

"That some nerdy fuckin *wizard* reference?" Mantis scrunched her black brows.

"No. It's half of the *star of David.*" Dylan lowered his shirt.

Mantis erupted in a burst of laughter that echoed across the blacktop. "Too cheap to afford the other half? That might be the most Jewish thing I've ever *seen.*"

"I wasn't too *cheap.*" Dylan kicked a rock hard. "It just hurt too much. I had to ask the guy to stop."

"Wow, pussy move. You should have lied and said it was intentional."

"It's okay. Tattoos aren't for everybody." Sweet Tea rubbed Dylan's neck softly.

Mantis tore through the remaining bag of hygiene items for their overnight stay. "Uh, Betty. I don't see—"

Betty reached into her purse and held up a wrapped pack of Iron Pillars.

"Oh, thank *God.*" Mantis tore through the wrapper and placed one of the pristine cigarettes between her lips. She reached in through the open window and retrieved her satchel from the back seat, sifting through the contents.

Suddenly, Sweet Tea got a whiff of the noxious odor originating from inside it. "Ew! What the hell's *in* that?"

Mantis pulled out a decaying demon hand wrapped in painter's plastic. Sweet Tea bolted backward, away from the rancid, clawed hunk of meat.

"It's like an unlucky rabbit's foot," Mantis said, lips pursed around the unlit cigarette. She retrieved her flip lighter and lit it. "Brought it to show Bet. Guess I don't need it anymore." Mantis lobbed the hand over her shoulder onto the asphalt behind her.

"Mantis! *No!*" Sweet Tea shuffled to the severed extremity, picked up the rotting hand, and dropped it in a trash bin padlocked to a cart return. "Don't *litter!*" Sweet Tea growled when she returned.

But Mantis couldn't focus on Sweet Tea.

Her eyes locked onto a fiery object hurtling through the black sky.

A massive blast of light flared through a breach in the earth's atmosphere before dimming. Something hurtled from the center of it, smashing into the ground in the adjoining parking lot, rattling the ground beneath them.

BOOM!

Hunks of asphalt exploded up into the air. The trees between the lots shook. Items bounced off the wagon's hood like they were made of rubber.

"What the fuck was *that*?!" Mantis hollered.

Moments later, the group approached the smoking crater in the asphalt and leaned over the edge of the newly-created gorge. Ten feet in diameter, the hole smoked, wafting a pungent gust of sulfur up into the air.

"Is it… a *meteor*?" Betty asked, fear creeping into her voice.

***

The stuttering sign outside reflected unattractive lemon-colored light through the murky windows of *Sparky's*.

They were lucky to stumble upon a greasy all-night diner on the lonesome stretch of I-10. It was the first restaurant they'd seen since they'd crossed out of El Paso.

A mere moment after their waitress placed the food down, Dylan crammed a fistful of french fries into his mouth. Sweet Tea giggled. Dylan glanced up, flashed them all an apologetic glance, and continued.

"Slow down, kid. You're not training for a fry-eating contest." Mantis played with the lipstick-smeared rim of her coffee cup.

"Sorry, I'm just so hungry," Dylan managed between swallows so big they made him wince.

Mantis motioned to the waitress, "Another plate of fries for the kid here."

The waitress nodded and disappeared into the back.

"Someone's got the munnnnn-chies," Sweet Tea sang into his ear.

Her honeyed voice made his heart race. "Dude, that was so crazy when you kicked those dicks down the stairs. They went down like *dominoes*. And at Classy's, you guys were all, like…" He swung his elbows and faked punches so savagely that he nearly wore his soda. "And then Sweet Tea was all—"

Sweet Tea put her hand on his arm and shoved it back down to the table. "Sweet Tea is *aware*. She was *there*."

Dylan took a massive gulp of his soda, unable to kick his terrible cottonmouth. "Can you guys teach me to fight like that?"

"Hey, he's asking you a question." Betty motioned to the hopeful tag-along.

"Huh?" Miles away, Mantis looked up.

"He asked if you'd teach him how to fight." Betty took a break from separating her salad toppings into neat piles to savor a dainty sip of lemon water.

"No." Mantis glanced up at a crack in the ceiling, no doubt from the recent earthquake.

"Why not," Dylan asked through a mouth full of potatoes.

"Because I said *no*. Eat your food, kid." Mantis pulled out the hunk of gold from her pocket and rubbed it.

Dylan sighed, "Hey, how'd you know what to do when those *things* showed up at the club?"

Betty put her fork down. There was gravity in her voice. "Seven years ago, the day Gabe was born, those things attacked us. There were ten, maybe twelve of them. Gabe was in the NICU on a ventilator. He was premature. Those things came out of the *woodwork*. We killed a few, and then, suddenly, they just… *stopped*."

"I took down four of them in the hallway outside his room," Sweet Tea added, smiling with pride. "Decapitated one with a broken clipboard, killed the other three by exploding some old lady's oxygen tank. It was frickin' *amaze-balls*."

Mantis slammed the gold onto the wobbly table with a loud clatter. "Jesus, you want a fuckin' *medal*?"

"Mantis! We are in a *restaurant*," Betty snarled quietly.

"We're in some greasy spoon in of bum-fuck West Texas. Our waitress is probably out smoking crack in the alley, and you're giving me shit about *my mouth*?"

Sweet Tea folded her arms in front of her chest. "I don't know why I came. *This* is why I couldn't be around you, Mantis. You're only happy if everyone's as upset as *you* are."

From seemingly out of nowhere, the waitress arrived at the table with a steaming silver pitcher of coffee.

"Sorry to burst your bubble, but I was *not* smokin' crack. I was makin' fresh Joe." The waitress looked at Dylan. "I got your second order'a fries on right now, hun."

The table was tense after the waitress left. As the others ate in silence, Mantis examined the golden object, running her fingers across the ornate etchings on its surface. One of the ends was shorn off, leaving a jagged, porous edge.

It was an incomplete artifact of some sort, she concluded while tracing the scrolled design with her fingertips.

Then, it struck her like a bolt of lightning. She jolted, jarring Betty.

She knew where she had seen the design before. *The recent dreams. The strange patchwork creature. The crowned horsemen…*

It was the burned soil cross from her dreams.

"What?" Betty set her fork down, arranging it meticulously against the edge of her napkin.

"This design was in my *dream*. This ugly ass creature showed it to me. It was a drawing on the *ground*." Mantis held up the hunk of metal. "This is the top of a cross." She shook it. "What are the chances I dreamed up this thing *hours* before we found it in Johnny Dickweed's safe? That's *more* than just a coincidence."

"Ugh!" Betty roared in frustration and slammed the side of her fist on the table. "But how does this help us find my *son*?"

Lucy draped her lovely form across the oak pew. Her creamy breasts heaved out from her corset, one made of hand-sewn patches of human skin. Black, Caucasian, Asian, and Latino pieces all intermingled in a symphony of tones stitched with lustrous, braided locks of Native American hair. It seemed fitting, as witnessing her first scalping was what gave her the idea to turn sinners into the statement piece of her wardrobe.

A satin brimstone-colored skirt cascaded down her curvaceous legs over footwear fashioned from brain-tanned bits of flesh and human bones.

Gabriel eyed the empty rows, his gaze landing on the massive, gleaming cross in the center of the church. "When do I get to meet my dad?"

Lucy looked up at the painted ceiling. The biblical images depicted on it made her want to belly-laugh.

How could history have gotten it so wrong?

"Your dad does things in his own way, in his own *time*. Everyone's on *his* schedule."

"What's he like?" Gabriel's azure eyes glittered beneath the chandelier.

There was only *one* word Lucy could use to describe the boy's father:

Unforgiving.

Grace

The motley group waited patiently for their check. Betty's mood had them all on edge.

Mantis chewed her mangled thumbnail. Betty swatted at her. "*Stop that.*"

Mantis's expression soured, nostrils flared. "Alright, *mom.*"

Mantis looked out the wall of diner windows. An attractive woman approached the bus stop across the street. Mantis stared at her like a starving dog would eye a pork chop.

"I'm gonna go take a shit," Mantis mumbled casually, shoving Betty out of the booth with her knee. Betty rolled her eyes and threw her hands in the air before standing to oblige. Mantis pulled out an Iron Pillar between them. "When you and the children here finish, meet me outside."

"I thought you just said you were going to the bathroom."

"I lied."

Betty followed her eyes across the street to the woman on the bench and rolled her eyes so hard she thought she might strain a muscle. "Oh God, you really haven't changed a bit."

Mantis grinned at that and stepped outside into the steamy night air. West Texas felt like a wet blanket. *Smothering.*

Once outside, she lit her coffin nail and took a deep drag. She exhaled, staring at the stunning female, and casually strolled across the lonely-looking highway.

The woman's perfect, inviting legs crossed at the ankles. Her face was obscured by a magazine.

A halogen flickered above her. A cloud of moths fluttered with suicidal abandon against the encased bulb.

Around the corner, a bus halted at the four-way stop sign and peeled onto the highway toward the bus stop.

Fuck. Too late.

The woman put down the magazine.

Mantis stopped in her tracks. The blood evacuated her face. Her veins filled with ice, contrary to the unforgiving Texas heat.

She knew the woman well.

But it wasn't possible.

Grace had been dead for years.

The bus was startling as it flung open its doors. Mantis raced toward the bench, positive her mind was faulty. It had to be a doppelganger. There was simply no other explanation.

"Grace?!" Mantis hollered as the doors closed. The vehicle thundered as it tore out onto the highway. The woman stepped to the window and looked right at Mantis. She placed her hand on the glass. Blood trickled from the gashes in her forearms, streaking it with crimson stripes.

Mantis knew those eyes. That look of pain...

The others raced to her side as the bus barreled away

"What's going on?" Betty had fear in her voice.

Pacing, Mantis furiously shot the butt of her cigarette into the ground like a tiny, smoking rocket.

"Apparently, *Dyl-do* over here isn't the *only one* tripping balls tonight." Mantis flashed a venomous look at Dylan.

"My name's not—"

Sweet Tea put her hand on Dylan's shoulder to politely indicate that he should shut up. For that fleeting moment, he reveled in the contact.

Mantis looked at the bus that had shrunk to two minuscule tail lights. The magazine was the only thing left from the bizarre encounter with the deceased love of her life. Mantis picked it up and hurled it into the road with a roar, and marched back to the Volvo.

Sweet Tea stomped out into the road and mumbled, "*Ugh!* Litter! Don't you care about this fuckin' *planet* anymore?"

Bending down to pick it up, she widened her stance and bent at the waist. Dylan stared at the perfect, round ass stretching her shorts to the max, wild blonde hair flying through in the air. It was a maneuver that Dylan had seen her do on stage more times than he could count.

***

Dylan pressed his head into a flimsy pillow and sprawled across the acrid flower-patterned comforter of the fleabag hotel room they'd rented. Oddly enough, the only room that wasn't occupied or closed for mold removal was a smoking room with two queens. The old, boxy television was on the fritz, but it didn't matter. They were too drained to watch.

Sweet Tea relaxed on Dylan's bed, facing the footboard, enthralled by the glossy pages of the trashy celebrity magazine Mantis had discarded just an hour and a half before.

Cocooned beneath a sheet she'd stolen from Betty's bed, Mantis reclined on the itchy sofa, naked beneath the fabric, rolling a lit cigarette between her fingers. She stared with concern out their second-story window at the empty pool below. She pressed her thumb into her temple hard.

It made Betty nervous to see Mantis hold something flammable so close to her mess of matted black hair.

In her other hand, she fidgeted with the hunk of gold as if it were a stress ball, offering an outlet for the pent-up anxiety.

She craved a stiff drink or rough sex but, unfortunately, knew night held neither in the cards.

Betty read from the bible she'd found in the bedside table, searching for comfort in the passages and distraction from thoughts of whether her son would be found alive. She smoothed the white T-shirt borrowed from Dylan and turned the page with a quiet crinkle.

Dylan flipped, propping himself up next to Sweet Tea, peering at the magazine over her shoulder.

"Anything interesting in there?" Dylan pressed his stubbled cheek to her freshly showered shoulder. She still had an almost imperceptible mist of fine glitter on her from *Lassie's* and smelled like wildflowers, a scent that had become his favorite smell in the world.

"Yeah. There's a spread in here on *Hollywood Hank.*" Sweet Tea never looked up from the page.

"I'd break off a piece of *Hollywood Hank.*" Betty muttered quietly.

"*Betty!*" Sweet Tea's head popped up.

"What? I'm *human.*" Betty went back to reading. "He's adorable."

"*Girl,* same," Sweet Tea agreed.

Dylan felt a wave of jealousy rise within him. "Who's Hollywood Hank?"

Sweet Tea slammed the magazine shut, leaving her thumbs inside as placeholders. "WHAT?! You don't know who *Hollywood Hank* is? Jesus, he's been in *so* many *movies*! He was in that weatherman rom-com about the hot air balloons."

"Cloudy with a Chance of Love," Betty mumbled.

Dylan snickered. "Sounds like the name of an *Alan Parson's* album."

Sweet Tea scrunched her brows. "I don't even know what that *means.*"

"He's a *musician,*" Dylan chuckled. "Wait," Dylan had an epiphany, "was he on that one about the girl that, like, she got shot in the heart or something?"

"Awww, *Love is a Loaded Gun.* That one's so sad!" Sweet Tea pouted.

"Oh, Bet, what was that one where he wrote her the—"

Betty interrupted as if they shared a brain, *"Poet of Philadelphia."*

"Yes! That one's my faaaaave!"

"Sounds like a total *chick flick.*" Dylan grimaced.

"It is. He's like the KING of chick flicks." Sweet Tea rolled on her back, draping the magazine across her voluptuous chest.

"That's why I don't recognize him. See, I have something called *taste* when it comes to films," Dylan joked. "I can talk to you about the Three Colors Trilogy all day or tell you why Gaspar Noe's films offer more to the world of cinema than Christopher Nolan's—"

"You should watch the poet one. He's dreamy in it," Sweet Tea cut him off, staring up at him. Dylan looked down into her hazel eyes, ones that made him feel better than any drug ever could.

"He's in love with this girl, right, chasin' her around Philly helping her find some guy she met on a bus. The whole time he's helping her find this guy, he falls totally in love with her. For some reason, she just doesn't ever give him serious thought at all. So, he writes her this poem—"

"Oooooooh, the *poem*," Betty interjected. "I cry at that part *every time!*"

"It's so good." Sweet Tea poked Dylan in the chest. "You gotta watch it."

Dylan smiled down at her. "I hate to burst your bubble, but I'm like 90% sure that in real life, that guy's a Satanist."

"What? *No!*" Betty's eyes flit like a lightning strike.

"He doesn't need to worship a God. He *is* one." Sweet Tea tapped her finger on an almost life-size photo of the smiling, hunky actor. "Dylan, look at that face!"

But Dylan could only focus on the intoxicating sound of his name rolling off her tongue.

"Gabe isn't a fan of Hollywood Hank. Refuses to watch his movies with me," Betty added to no one in particular.

The moment his name came up, worry about Gabriel filled her stomach with anxiety and bile. She checked her cell phone on the nightstand. She'd done it two dozen times since they'd checked in. The result was always the same: No calls. No messages. She prayed that he was safe.

Sweet Tea propped on her elbows. "Mantis, you've seen his movies, *right?*"

"I don't watch sappy bullshit." Mantis chewed on one of her gnarled nails and nodded to Betty. "But he must be hot if he makes *this* prude moist."

"Ew, don't say *moist*." Betty cringed.

Sweet Tea rolled the magazine. "Pages 23 through 27." She tossed it. Mantis caught it by the cover, ripping it a little. She flipped to the pages and looked at the celeb's face. "Eh, he's not horrible. I mean," Mantis angled the page in various directions, "yeah, I'd sit on his face."

Sweet Tea snorted. Dylan burst into laughter and laid his face against Sweet Tea's arm.

Mantis flipped through the rest of the article's pictures. Her smile faded.

"What?" Betty seemed curious about the reaction.

Mantis rose from the couch and let her sheet fall to the floor, revealing the naked form beneath. "Holy shit…"

Dylan reacted to her nudity, whipping away. "She's, uh, *naked* again. Very, *very* naked."

Mantis sat next to Betty and pointed to a page in the magazine. Betty examined the photo. *Hollywood Hank* was sprawled confidently across a couch in his mansion in front of a large display case containing various items.

Betty didn't know what she was supposed to see. "I, uh, see… a man whose body I'd like to eat a *meal* off of."

"Do you want a robe?" Dylan chimed in, face still turned. Mantis and Betty ignored him.

"Why don't you just *tell me* what I'm supposed to be seeing."

Mantis jammed a nibbled-down fingernail at the display case behind the celebrity's head.

Betty gasped and stood up with the magazine.

"What is it?" Sweet Tea sat up.

"Is she still naked?" Dylan shielded his eyes.

"Yeah." Sweet Tea confirmed.

Betty could see it now.

It was another gold fragment nearly identical to the one from Johnny's safe.

"Fans get an inside look at the home of rom-com sensation, 'Hollywood' Hank Targus. The notable actor possesses an impressive collection of artifacts and memorabilia from past films in his Midland mansion." Betty looked up at Mantis.

"You know what this means, right?" Mantis fought a grin. "We have to go to Midland."

Sweet Tea perked up again. "Oh shit, hell yes! I would, like, die happy if I got to meet him."

Dylan rolled his already-shut eyes.

"I'm not driving all around this state on a *hunch*. Gabriel is out there. He is all alone! We need to *find him*!" Betty seemed frantic and on the verge of tears.

"Betty, what the fuck do you think I'm trying to do?!" Mantis paced, running a hand through her shaggy, black hair. "Bet, I'm telling you, this has something to do with Gabriel being taken. You saw the cross that was burned into Gabe's carpet. It's the same as this bullshit." She raced over and picked up the hunk of gold, shaking it feverishly. "I feel it in my *soul*. That girl on the bus… finding this magazine she left, it's a *sign*. Don't you see that?"

"I should have called the cops." Betty shook her head. " I should have let law enforcement handle this."

"Oh yeah, because the Arizona PD would have *totally* solved this by now, based on a flaming insignia burned into the carpet and an open window," her voice seethed with sarcasm. "I'm sure they were just one *Amber Alert* away from having your boy back at home safely." She scoffed. "You know they can't tell their ass from a hole in the ground. They didn't help you when you were trying to get free of Johnny, and they wouldn't have done shit for you now. They'd be tied up dealing with all the aftermath bullshit from the earthquake." She looked at the magazine again. "Betty, you're a *Christian*. Your religion is, like, *founded* on you following someone on blind faith."

"And you see how *that* turned out." Betty motioned to a wooden crucifix nailed to the wall above the end table with an emaciated Jesus on it.

"Betty, I'm telling you," Mantis held up the gold piece in one hand and the magazine in the other, "this is our *sign*."

"A statewide curfew is in effect following a third night of violence and a recent surge of animal attacks following yet another earthquake," the reporter blurted in a panicked tone on the TV screen. Magdalene Jones was stunning, with light brown eyes that sparkled in the on-camera light. "Police urge locals and tourists to avoid the historic French Quarter of New Orleans at all costs after a recent rash of riots in the downtown area. National Guardsmen have been dispatched to both Jefferson *and* St. John Parishes today to impose restraint on rioters as deemed necessary." Rapid shots of violence flashed on the screen, each in the state of Louisiana.

Magdalene continued over mute clips of the President speaking, "The President addressed the nation today, outlining the impact of the meteoric destruction that multiple space programs have predicted to hit later this week. He went on to discuss the very real possibility of the collapse of nationwide communications and damage to several major cities' infrastructure."

The report cut to another angle of the President, this time with audio. He said, "While we have not yet declared a state of emergency, we *have* raised the threat level, and many states have imposed statewide curfews in an effort to manage the situation safely. We *will* get *through* this."

The feed cut back to the reporter.

"This is Magdalene Jones with LNN news. Back to you, Albert."

"Thank you, Maggie," the male reporter said, tapping papers on a glassy studio desk. "In other news, another asteroid—"

The TV powered off.

Jeremiah Munsey set the remote on the dressing room table, pulled off his makeup bib, and basked in the beam of morning sunlight seeping through the window of the station. He had a smile that said *trust in me* and was a classic — *almost stereotypical* — southern televangelist, all the way to his crisp, white suit.

"My, I *do* love me some Magdelene Jones."

Nina Hartley slumped in the cushioned chair nearby, unimpressed, "Never been a fan."

"Of course not, Nina." It didn't surprise him in the least, as she wasn't a fan of most people. And although Nina was Black, she had a touch of the stereotypical racism and ethnic mistrust that old people from the South were infamous for. But he liked her fiercely loyal attitude toward religion. Since the day they met, she spouted memorized biblical passages with a fiery passion and had iron-clad religious convictions. Religion was her life. *Judgment* was her hobby.

It's why Jeremiah was drawn to her. He'd built their Evangelical empire on a strong foundation of fear. Nina was the Bible-thumping zealot who helped him *instill* that fear.

A nerdy man in his twenties knocked on the open door. He listened to his headset, nodded, and spoke. "Mr. M-Munsey and Ms. Hartwood—"

Nina cut him off, correcting with a growl, "*Hartley.*"

"*Hartley.* Sorry, I'll make a note of that. They're ready for you both on stage. Live in five."

Munsey smiled at Nina. "*Showtime!*"

It was a sunny, sweltering morning in West Texas. Dylan hobbled through the aisles of the convenience store near the hotel. He felt as if he'd slumbered on rocks instead of the filthy floor.

"What do you think of this one? It matches my shirt." Sweet Tea modeled a mesh trucker hat and posed, breasts stretching her royal-blue racer-back to the max. He nodded in approval, though he was not in the mood for a fashion show. Or conversation. Or walking. His back throbbed like that of an old man.

"I don't see any ibuprofen." Dylan rummaged through the over-the-counter stool softeners and antacids. "They've got condoms, cough drops, trucker-speed, and laxatives, but no *ibuprofen*?"

"Oh-my-freaking-God. *Bingo*." *She'd found it*. Sweet Tea leaned in, mesmerized.

Dylan followed her eyes and laughed. "*Please* say you're joking."

"Ain't nothin' funny 'bout *this*." Sweet Tea plucked a cowboy hat, garishly dyed with the design of the American flag, off the top of the metal rack, placed the star-spattered indigo crown of it on her head, and smiled. Her pigtail braids flowed out of the red-and-white-striped brim, resting on her large chest.

Dylan snickered and nodded at the hideous treasure. "How much is it?"

"Don't matter. Could be a thousand bucks for all I care. I'm buyin' it." She waltzed away.

Near the register, Betty leaned against an ice cream freezer, looking at an unfurled paper map of

Texas as the cashier ogled the way her ass looked in her skin-tight, red capris and black pumps. She traced a highway with an acrylic fingernail and then used it to itch the paisley bandanna tied behind bangs wound into a victory roll.

At the register, Sweet Tea grinned at the cashier.

"Can I help you, miss?" He stared blankly. The job had clearly sucked his soul dry.

"One hat, please." Sweet Tea was ready to burst from excitement.

He fumbled for a plastic bag, and she rose to her tip-toes.

"Um, I don't need a bag. I'd like to wear it out. One less piece of garbage cluttering up the landfills. Every bit helps, you know?"

Without responding, the cashier grabbed the hand scanner with zombie-like movements and aimed it at the tag on the brim. The machine beeped. "$22.74."

"What a *steal*." Sweet Tea jammed her hand in the pocket of her ultra-tight shorts and produced a wad of crumpled singles, counting them out. "Oneeee, twooooo, threeee—"

Mantis walked up beside her with a six-pack of beer and set it on the counter. She gnawed her bubblegum, accentuating the hard lines of her jaw, and nodded lazily. "Sweet hat."

"Thank you!" Sweet Tea was giddy.

"Bet could pay for that, you know. You could hold onto those hard-earned singles. Put this *beaut* on ol' *Johnny's* tab."

Sweet Tea continued peeling out bills on the counter. "No, it's okay. I got it."

"Twenty-six cents is yer change." The cashier's accent was twangy and thick. He handed her some change, and Sweet Tea dropped it in the charity jar without hesitation.

Betty made her way to the register with the puffy, ill-folded map. "I'm here. Stupid thing wouldn't—"

She looked up and took a deep breath. She slid the map politely onto the counter, obscuring rolls of colorful lotto scratch-offs in the glass case below. "We'll take the map, thirty bucks on pump two, and," Betty tilted Mantis's six-pack of beers back and looked at the label, "these."

Before the man could ring it up, Mantis interjected, "Gimme a pack of Iron Pillars there, too, *Tex*. Blue label." Mantis loudly chewed her gum and smiled.

Dylan spotted a stack of newspapers by the front door. The daily headline, emblazoned in huge, black letters, read: "The End of Days." The chilling title was nestled above terrifying photos depicting global earthquake damage, meteoric fireball craters, and worldwide devastation.

Dylan set a copy near the register. "This too, please."

Betty paid the total, feeling more guilty about Johnny's fate with every bill peeled from the stack. The gang trickled out, Mantis following in the rear. Near the exit, she leaned in toward a magazine with *Hollywood Hank's* face on the cover.

"We're comin' for ya, Hank," she whispered.

Odessa... Almost

One mile of flat, dusty land rolled into the next. Oil derricks and sun-bloated roadkill were all that broke up the visual monotony. They'd been in the wagon for hours with nothing but counting sporadic tumbleweeds for entertainment. The only radio station that would come through clearly was an AM channel. On it, Reverend Jeremiah Munsey raved passionately about how the Rapture was upon them. It hadn't been on more than two minutes before Mantis asked for it to be turned off.

The fact that Betty's air conditioning hadn't worked since the 1980s didn't help morale either. All four windows had been rolled down as far as they'd go, but the scorching heat made it hard to exist.

Dylan chewed the last of the ice from his fast food cup and offered some to Sweet Tea. She reached into the cup, retrieved a single cube, and rubbed it across her pert lips. Dylan watched so intently that he had to remind himself to breathe.

In the distance, a green sign came into sight. Mantis lowered her black sunglasses and squinted. "*Odessa.* Fourteen miles."

"Oh good, we're getting close." Betty looked out the window. It was destitute on these dusty plains. No other cars for miles.

"Probably would have been there two hours ago if you'd have taken the interstate." Mantis felt for her smokes, patting her body, jostling her satchel through the floorboard clutter: two full beers, four crushed empties, and a wadded burger wrapper.

"This ol' girl is getting up there in the years." Betty ran her hand along the dashboard. "She does better on the back roads. Can't quite keep up on the interstate. You got the scenic route instead."

Mantis eyed the panorama of barren, orange land pocked with mangy sprigs of foliage and chuckled. "How could I have died without seeing the *splendor* of *West Texas*?" She scoffed. "And, for the record, this shit-wagon's not just *getting up there*. This pile's a goddamn *artifact*. If it were a horse, I'd use your .38 to put it out of its misery."

"Watch your *mouth*," Betty ordered. "You know I hate it when you take the Lord's name in vain. Plus, this girl's a *tank*."

"It's sure as fuck *slow* as a tank." Mantis searched for her cigarettes. "Actually, it's *slower*. Shit, I *know*. I was a Marine."

"Yeah, yeah."

"Hell, I could probably *walk* to Midland faster."

"Keep talkin' smack about the crap-wagon, and you *will be*," Betty warned.

Mantis laughed. She loved it when Betty stood her ground.

Mantis contorted to retrieve the mashed pack of Iron Pillars that had fallen between the seat and console. She plucked one from the pack, placed it between her lips, and lit it.

"Mantis, *please* stop smoking in the car," Betty nagged.

"The window is *down*." Mantis glowered at Betty and exhaled a large gust out the wide-open window.

Betty gazed out at the miles of arid scrubland and shook her head.

In the distance, a simple white billboard said in bold letters: HELL IS REAL.

Dylan offered up another ice cube to Sweet Tea.

Mantis turned the rearview so she could see them in the back. She popped the tab of another warm beer and sucked back several heavy chugs while staring at them. She burped. "So, what's the deal with you two? You *boning*?"

Sweet Tea scoffed a sound that pierced Dylan's heart like an arrow. "We're friends." She threw an arm around him and pulled him tight, squeezing him to her breasts.

The words *just friends* burned more every time he heard them. He never intended to be just a *friend*. In the year he'd known her, she'd slowly grown to be his everything.

"Ahhh, the ever-shitty friend zone. Bummer, kid." Mantis raised her unkempt eyebrows to look at him in the rearview. Sun glinted off her silver eyeshadow, making her light-colored eyes appear vampiric. "You should try being an asshole, Dyl-do. Tea's definitely got a *type*."

"That is *not* true," Sweet Tea protested.

Mantis's eyes drifted back to the road. She chugged the last of her beer, crunched the can, and tossed the empty to the floorboard.

"You're killin' me. Use the trash bag!" Betty ordered.

"Chill. It's not going anywhere."

BAM!

Without warning, a thunderous noise pounded beneath the hood.

Everyone jolted. Betty mashed the brakes and whipped over to the side of the road.

Silence all around them. The passengers were shaken.

"Everyone okay?" Betty's heart was in her throat.

Violently angry, Mantis grabbed the can from the floorboard and hurled it out the window.

"MANTIS!" Sweet Tea screeched. "You're *better than that*! Go pick that up!"

The crinkled empty lay in the dusty orange dirt against the sparse roadside foliage.

"Hell no. Fuck that," Mantis growled.

Sweet Tea furiously bolted out of the wagon and marched through an ankle-high patch of prickly weeds to retrieve the trash. She shook it at Mantis. "We only get one earth, and *this* is how you treat it?"

"It's *trash*. Jesus, it's not the end of the world!" Mantis grumbled, and then fought the urge to smile at the irony.

"You only think about *your-fucking-self.* What kind of a world are we leaving for kids like *Gabriel*, huh?" Sweet Tea hurled the can at the side of the wagon. It hit with a tinny *clink*.

"Now, technically, *you* just littered." With a smug expression, Mantis got out of the car.

"Mother Earth is not your personal *trash can*." Sweet Tea crushed the can flat with one of her acrylic high heels.

Filled with dread, Betty stepped out to examine the engine. Mantis popped the hood.

Dylan held his hand out of the window. Sweet Tea handed him the crumpled can. He bagged it and smiled. "You're so damn cute when you're angry."

103

As soon as the words escaped Dylan's mouth, he regretted saying them. He didn't want to come off like the guys at *Classy Lassies*. Now, he feared he was grouped in with the other ogling horn dogs.

Mantis eyed the engine with half an Iron Pillar dangling from her lips, dropping ashes onto the searing metal below. "*Fuck.*"

"What?" Betty was worried. She anxiously crossed her arms.

"Serpentine belt snapped." Mantis ripped out the shorn black strip of rubber. "Jesus, it's cracked *all to hell*. When was the last time you had this thing replaced?"

"I didn't know those *needed* to be replaced." Betty's eyes were panicked.

"This pile's probably older than I am. For someone as OCD as you, you think that'd extend to your whip, too. You ever get maintenance done on this thing?"

"Yeah. There's a guy in my neighborhood that tops off the fluids, and I toss him a few bucks," Betty's voice quivered.

"It's a cheap fix, but I can't do shit 'til I get a replacement."

Betty's eyes filled with tears. She laced her fingers behind her up-do and stared off into the flatlands. Mantis wiped the black soot from her fingers onto her crop top and motioned to Dylan. "'Ey, kid, get on your cell. Find the nearest auto parts store. If it's far, we're gonna need a tow truck, too."

Betty walked across the highway and took in the sun-bleached wasteland, wondering if she would ever see Gabriel again. Every moment they weren't on the road felt like a million years. His fate weighed heavily on her soul.

Dylan drifted out of the vehicle, phone raised in the air. "I'm not getting any bars."

Mantis expelled a disappointed sigh and flicked her ashes onto the sizzling blacktop.

The concern and fury in Betty boiled over. She couldn't take any more…

She screamed out into the field at the top of her lungs. Everyone watched in silence as Betty melted down.

After the long, guttural noise, she marched to the wagon with purpose. She took off one of her shiny heels and whacked it against the car repeatedly. Through a stream of tears, she dented the wagon in several places. She belted the side mirror so hard that shards of silver fell to the ground.

"I just," Betty attacked the door with full force, "want… to get… my *son* back! Is that too… much to… ask?!"

Betty dropped the mangled pump and stomped to the passenger side, reached into the glove box through the window, and retrieved Johnny's gun.

"No!" Mantis hollered.

BOOM!

Betty fired at the car.

BOOM! BOOM!

The others shook with every squeeze of the trigger.

"Bet, *stop*!" Sweet Tea squealed, covering her ears. The pleas were useless. Within seconds, Betty had put two bullets in the windshield, one in the front tire, and had emptied the remainder of the clip into the engine.

Betty pulled the trigger, dry-firing, long after the bullets were gone.

Dylan tucked his cell phone away. "I think we're gonna need more than a tow."

Every minute of the twenty they'd waited for another vehicle to pass down the long stretch of highway felt like an hour. Betty sat in the driver's seat in silence, staring through the bullet-riddled windshield with a blank expression. She tapped her busted high heel rhythmically against the steering wheel. It sounded like a strange clock ticking, draining away precious seconds that should have been spent finding her son.

Sweet Tea sat on the bullet-riddled hood, picking at one of the holes. She'd volunteered to be the lookout, but they could see someone coming from half an hour away due to the flat terrain.

Dylan and Mantis stood outside, leaning up against the car's rear. Dylan read through the newspaper.

"Asteroid impacts in Pyongyang, North Korea. Death count nears four million." Dylan flipped to another page. "Toxic Meteoric Firestorm Converts Lake Baikal into Swampy Wasteland." Another pause. "Scientists estimate over 2000 bowling-ball sized fireballs hurled to the earth at 2 p.m. yesterday, potentially killing nearly all aquatic life, and tainting the world's largest freshwater supply of drinking water."

Mantis peered over his shoulder at the photos. "Global quake disrupts travel infrastructure as tectonic plates shift." And at another... "Seismic blast collapses Midwestern communication towers. God, this is grim as hell." Mantis lit a fresh Iron Pillar with the butt of her old one in true chain-smoker fashion.

"There's one in here about that religious guy Betty likes." Dylan flipped through the pages and found the article. "*Munsey.*"

"What's it say?" Betty spoke up, nerves shot.

Dylan read from it. "Says two days ago, the Christian network unveiled a statue of him outside their headquarters. Apparently, a couple people used it for target practice and dribbled red paint from the bullet holes."

"Of *course.*" Betty mumbled.

"Network says they're not going to remove or repair the statue. They said, 'We, at the network, feel the statue now promotes a more everlasting message. One that illustrates that our Christian faith will never die.'"

Mantis leaned through the passenger window until her hand located the final can of beer on the floorboard. She pulled the switchblade from her pocket, flipped the blade open, and jammed the tip into the can's bottom. Warm beer sprayed through the hole. She popped the tab and shotgunned the contents in seconds, dripping at least a quarter down her black shirt. Upon completion, she crushed the can with her boot and belched inside her closed mouth.

Sweet Tea watched her like a hawk, and Dylan walked around to the other side of the vehicle to take a piss.

Mantis hurled the aluminum puck through the window onto the floorboard. "Happy, Tea? I didn't leave it on the *ground.*"

Sweet Tea just stared at her.

Dylan was still pissing when Mantis arrived back at the rear without any form of announcement. He pinched the stream and fumbled with his underwear. "*Shit*, I didn't hear you come around."

He prayed she hadn't seen much, but the grin on her face said she'd seen *everything*.

"Daaaaaaaaamn, kid!" Mantis bobbed her head. "You really *are* Jewish." Mantis looked at Sweet Tea and pointed at Dylan's nether region. "You seen what this kid's packin', Tea?"

"Nope." Sweet Tea said, peering off into the plains in search of life.

"I believe you. If you *had* seen this kid's beaver-basher, you'd be married by now."

"*Mantis.*" Dylan's voice begged her to stop.

"You got a fuckin' *kickstand*, kid. That's all I'm sayin'." Mantis headed away from the blacktop and motioned for Dylan to follow her into the brush.

"What's up?" Dylan looked around. "If you're gonna murder me, just do it already." Dylan was joking, but deep down, he knew she had it in her.

She snorted. "If I was gonna kill you, I'd have shot you when you stole those godawful boots." Finally, she turned around, and Dylan slammed into her. "Whoa!" She shoved him off like a brute, and he nearly fell. "Jesus, kid, with what you're packin', you should give women more space. You're gonna impregnate someone that way."

Dylan looked at the sky, fighting the urge to laugh, cheeks pink with embarrassment.

"Okay. If you're gonna be taggin' along, we can't be constantly saving your ass, so I'm gonna show you some moves."

"No way!" Dylan was awash with excitement.

"Just some basics." She grinned a little. "Plus, I want you to be able to look at least a *little* cool in front 'a Tea."

"Why?" He asked, confused.

"Because." It was a statement. "She dates fuckin' *assholes*. Since I met her, it's been one douche-canoe after another. I hate it. It's time to break that cycle, man. You gotta show her what you're made of, or you're gonna be stuck in that friend zone 'til your balls turn to dust. Do you wanna *be* the pussy? Or do you wanna *get* the pussy? With a dick that big, you *gotta* have some balls in there somewhere."

Dylan lunge-hugged Mantis. "Aw, you think I'm a nice guy!"

As he pulled away, Mantis furiously snatched him up by the front of his gray tee. "Hug me again, and I will reach in those jeans, rip off that big ol' disco stick, and choke you to *death* with it." The look in her eyes assured him she'd do it.

"Copy that." He put his hands up in surrender. "You're not a hugger. Understood."

Mantis released him. "So, what *do* you know?

"Like fighting-wise?"

Mantis's brain hurt. "Yes, dill weed, *like fighting-wise.*"

"I took a year of *karate*." Dylan smiled.

"Karate's a start. I can work with that."

"But I *was* seven at the time," Dylan added.

"Okay. Nevermind. Karate's out." Mantis sighed. "So, let's talk target areas. When you're hand-to-hand, you wanna focus on the head, neck, and groin. And if you get a chance to get one of those fuckin' creatures in the eyes… do it."

***

Dylan pridefully beamed, exhausted from his first lesson in basic combat. It was the least annoyed he'd seen Mantis since they'd met. Fighting made her glow.

"Where'd you learn all this stuff?" Dylan asked, circling with her as she threw slow-motion practice swings at him.

"Military."

She swung again. He felt the air off it. He dodged and retaliated with a half-speed knee to her groin. "What branch?"

"Nice." She smiled, thrilled he was picking up the skills like a sponge. "USMC, baby."

"Marines?"

She nodded, pretending to kick him in slow motion. "Four years. I was a Devil-Dog MP."

"Well, thank you for your service." Dylan's focus broke when he saw Sweet Tea pacing nervously in the street some thirty yards behind Mantis in all of her curvaceous glory. He was helplessly mesmerized by her sexy stride, whether in the strip club or on boring Texas plains.

Mantis swung at him, popping him hard in the shoulder with a fist.

"Damn, girl, you've got some *guns*."

"Or… you're a pussy. Distraction can get you killed. *Focus*." Mantis bounced around, light on her feet. "Now, show me the chin jab again."

"Maybe you should tie your shoelaces if you're gonna bounce around like that. That's a good way to end up on your face."

"Thanks, mom. Now, chin-jab. We ain't got all day."

Confused, he slowly crimped his hand, clumsily trying to recreate what he'd learned. Mantis shook her head.

"No. Open your hand. It's not a punch; it's a jab." Mantis drove her open palm up into his chin at a fraction of the intensity she would on a real enemy. His teeth clacked together.

"Son of a bitch!" Dylan covered his mouth. He pulled his fingers away slowly to reveal blood on his lips and teeth. His now-ruby lips twisted into an impressed smile. "*Cool.*"

The Red Pickup

As Dylan and Mantis approached the wagon, a sudden, icy wind ripped across the plains. The temperature dropped at least twenty degrees in mere seconds. They all paused in place to scan the cactus-ridden prairie. They hadn't felt a breeze all day, and now... a freezing wave? In the blazing midday sun?

Mantis looked at the sky, then peered down the empty road in the direction of Odessa. A smile spread across her pale face.

A truck barreled down the highway. Fire-engine-red, rumbling with horsepower, the pickup bowled down the sizzling asphalt toward them. It was their ticket out of this dusty Hell.

"Guys!" Mantis pointed at the truck and raced toward the road, heavy boots kicking up dust clouds. She waved her arms wildly but grew bewildered as the truck only sped up.

Betty stepped out of her bullet-ridden vehicle into the road.

The truck had not slowed. In fact, it was now drifting slowly off the road.

"This asshole *asleep*?" Mantis shouted.

The red Chevy drifted onto the shoulder. They could see the spinning rims covered in a layer of orange dust and a silver cross-like emblem on the grill... but no *driver*.

"Get out of the way!" Mantis shoved Betty away as the truck went off the asphalt and jolted onto the arid plains. The change in terrain slowed the truck, and it lost momentum with every revolution of its balding tires. It crept to a complete stop in front of the white billboard:

HELL IS REAL.

Mantis could only laugh. Hell *was* real. And they were already *there.*

The engine rumbled.

"This is a sign!" Betty exclaimed, clasping her hands to her face. "I prayed to God for a way to get to Midland so we could find Gabe. *This* was His answer."

"You're fuckin' kiddin', *right?*" Mantis scoffed.

Betty jumped joyfully and raced toward the truck. "Oh, ye of *little faith!*"

Mantis laughed, certain that miracles didn't exist. Faith was for the *gullible.*

She'd had faith once. *Strong,* even. But Grace had cured her of *that.* Mantis was done with the notion of an omniscient old man in the sky, constantly outsmarted and thwarted by an angry red man with horns and a pitchfork. She was done fearing Hell. She'd already experienced it the moment she'd found Grace limp in their blood-filled bathtub, wrists gouged deep enough to expose bone.

As she rocked Grace's wet, naked corpse in her arms, any semblance of faith she'd had slipped away.

There's no way any God could allow such pain and cruelty in a world *already* riddled with such ugliness and tragedy.

The others galloped toward the Chevy. A twangy, upbeat country song played inside the cab.

Dylan reached the truck first, popped the handle, and pulled the door open. Sweet Tea let out a horrified scream. Betty stumbled backward into a knee-high shrub.

Inside the cab, a black demon burst forth at Dylan, knocking him back onto the ground. He curled his fist tightly and punched the creature in the side of its face. The force knocked a few of its slimy teeth onto the dry earth near Dylan's face. His hands wrapped around the creature's throat. He squeezed hard, but his hands sunk into the soft tar-like substance the demon was made from. His trembling fingers couldn't feel bones or any semblance of structure beneath.

Sweet Tea frisbee'd her new cowboy hat into a brush-free clearing and leaped on the beast's back.

By the time Mantis reached the Chevy, she knew for certain the truck wasn't a miracle. She caught a glimpse inside. There was a horrific mess of glistening blood and a tangle of intestines across the seat.

It seemed the creature eviscerated the person driving the truck, leaving very little intact to identify them. A smashed black cowboy hat was upturned on the floorboard by a severed slab of face. The interior was coated with thick hunks of mangled meat. The driver's alligator skin cowboy boots dangled limply out the open door of the pickup, still attached to the man's shorn lower half.

Mantis raced up with half an Iron Pillar still dangling limp from her lips.

"DYLAN! Watch out!" Sweet Tea pointed to a patch of cacti on the ground beside the creature's lower extremities. Dylan struggled hard to free himself.

Sweet Tea roundhouse-kicked the demon in the face.

REEEEEEEEEEEEEE! It reared back, screeching at an ear-damaging decibel.

"No, Tea! I don't," Dylan wrestled it with all his might, "need you to save me."

He rolled the demon on its back and punched it in the face, caving its pliable skull inward. The strike only angered the thing. Its puckered face swallowed Dylan's fist, digging its fangs into the soft flesh of his hand.

Dylan screamed and yanked. The substance pulsing beneath the surface grew hotter until his hand was burning. Sweet Tea rushed to his side and pulled Dylan backward. But as much as Dylan wanted the pain to end, he wanted to save face with Sweet Tea even more.

He was going to impress her even if it killed him.

"No, I got this!" Dylan forged on through the pain.

Dylan reared back, placed his boots on the creature's throat, and shoved as hard as he physically could until his hand tore out from between the jaws of the beast. A trail of long, jagged teeth marks tore down his arm as nail-thick teeth raked across it.

Mantis yanked the remaining half of the slaughtered cowboy from the seat of the cab and tossed him carelessly on the ground with a wet *thunk*. She casually walked around to the tailgate as if she had all the time in the world. In the bed, a stack of wooden boards wrapped in an aquamarine tarpaulin was bound with thick ratchet straps and a red strip of plastic. She unlatched the tarp and removed it, moving at a glacial pace compared to the brutal struggle going on beside her.

Betty's gaze flitted back and forth between the creature, the stubborn young man, and Mantis.

REEEEEEEEEEEEEE!

The monstrosity screeched again. The beast pressed Dylan flat on his back, craning its neck down, chattering its hundreds of teeth like a wind-up toy. Glowing, orange liquid oozed from its now-concave mouth. The goo burned through Dylan's gray tee as though it were a highly corrosive acid.

Mantis halved the tarp taco-style and placed it across the blood-soaked front seat of the cab, covering glistening entrails and mangled hunks of lungs and liver.

"Fuck that thing *up*, Dylan!" Sweet Tea bent at the waist, yelling like a wrestling coach.

Dylan responded with a burst of energy, kicking hard against the beast as it gnashed at his throat. Suddenly, its torso rumbled loudly. From beneath the creature's tar-covered chest, bug-like legs forced their way through magma-colored crevices, sliding out into the hot, dry air and stamping down on the ground. They were hairy, resembling the legs of a too-massive grasshopper.

Sitting on the tarp, Mantis slammed the truck door shut, jut her arm out the window, and reversed. After rolling a few feet, she yelled to Dylan.

"'Member what I showed you?"

The creature's internal structure crunched loudly as it transformed into something even more hideously bizarre.

The demon squealed as it turned inside-out through one of the widening crags in its torso.

Mantis revved the engine of the pickup and nodded to Dylan. The creature crept onto its newly developed insect feet, assuming a wide stance, and vaulted toward Dylan.

But Dylan was ready for it *this* time.

Before the horrific monstrosity made contact, Dylan executed the chin-jab, slamming the butt of his palm into its sunken face and fiercely knocking it back into the bunching of cacti.

RAWWWWWWWWWWRRRRRR!

It howled in pain and swung a huge grasshopper-like leg.

Mantis mashed the accelerator to the floor and gunned the pickup straight into the beast, smashing into its strange body.

As the pickup made contact, the demon exploded like a water balloon full of noxious black-and-orange goo, splattering a mess of tar, grayed innards, and insect limbs like shrapnel from a gnarly, detonated pipe bomb.

Mantis coolly flicked her ash out the window and nodded proudly at Dylan. She flicked on the windshield wipers. But it was futile. The rubber blades only smeared the oily substance.

Sweet Tea cheered, helping Dylan to his feet. "Oh my God, you kicked that thing's *ass*!"

Spattered with bits of creature, acting on pure adrenaline and instinct, Dylan pulled Sweet Tea close and tried to kiss her.

Sweet Tea pulled back and slapped him in the face. The mood had shifted in an instant. "Are you *kidding* me?"

The slap was so hard it almost made Dylan forget where he was. He looked at her, stunned and apologetic. "I'm sorry! I was just feeling the moment!"

"You did great, Dylan." Betty smiled with gratitude and dusted the dirt off his back.

Mantis leaned back in the driver's seat and patted the crinkling tarp beside her in the blood-soaked cab. Through the filter, her muffled words rang out, "Get in. Your *chariot* awaits."

The bright red pickup sailed up Highway 385 and cruised right into the Odessa city limits without a hitch. Betty squirmed in the passenger seat on the lumpy tarp. She muttered up into the blood-freckled roof of the cab. "I just pray I'm not sitting on this dude's face."

"Savin' yourself for ol' *Hollywood Hank, are ya'?*" Mantis joked. The traffic light turned from amber to red, streaking its colors through the murky windshield.

"I'm glad *someone* finds this funny," Betty grumbled. "Every fiber of my being is begging me to scrub this plasma-smeared *cesspool*."

Mantis looked over at the white sedan in the next lane that read *Odessa Police* on the side. Inside the squad car, two officers sat studiously. The one in the passenger seat was firm and stocky. His biceps rippled as he tapped his palm rhythmically on the side of the car through the open window. He scanned the street and peered up at Mantis through his window.

The back of her combat boot squished against what she could only assume to be a gory hunk of cowboy. She nodded, "Howdy."

He nodded back, observing their disheveled vehicle. An alarming code came through the policeman's radio. He responded into the handset quickly. As the light turned green, the cop car peeled out. The siren turned on, and the sedan sped away.

Mantis accelerated slowly. "Nothing to see here, boys in blue. Not like we're four people driving around in a crime scene on wheels. No, sir, those aren't the guts of a giant demon grasshopper on the hood."

Dylan joined in. "No, officer, that guy covered in black goo in the back is definitely *not* in possession of two dead men's cowboy boots."

"What?" Mantis peered in the rear-view.

Dylan held up a bloody pair of black alligator skin boots taken from the truck owner's feet. "These babies' r gonna shine up reallllll nice." Dylan danced in his seat. *"Gots me some allagatah' boots."*

Betty turned in her seat to flash Dylan a very disapproving look.

"It just so happens they fit like Cinderella's slipper, too."

"Well, aren't you the belle of the ball," Mantis said, rolling her eyes.

***

Mantis and the gang arrived at Hollywood Hank's Midland mansion as the evening sun set. The fiery orange ball colored the atmosphere a shade of red that made Mantis crave a big glass of pomegranate sangria.

The house on Dunbarton Oaks looked just as impressive from the outside as it had in the magazine. Full-size cow skulls were mounted on either side of the front door like morbid welcome wreaths, and the home's mixed stone veneer screamed *Texas*. A perfectly pruned row of seven possumhaw holly trees was rooted firmly in a dirt oval, shaping the drive into a concrete horseshoe. Massive Live Oaks loomed near the stone gates, marking the start of the vast acreage beyond.

The address was surprisingly easy for them to acquire. In the small town, everybody talked. Hank's address was a topic people spoke freely about. Sweet Tea had asked around at a gas station where Mantis pulled in to top off the dead cowboy's pickup with unleaded. It took Tea less than three minutes to get an address *and* a hand-drawn map on the back of their receipt to the home of the town's only notable actor.

Mantis was nearly finished with her cigarette as the group stared out the smeared windows at the colossal dwelling. Mantis shook her pack and eyed the single, lonesome remaining Iron Pillar, irritated she would soon be out.

"How do we get in?" Sweet Tea eyed the house through the narrowed eyes of a spy, twirling her long braid of golden hair.

Mantis chewed her thumbnail, deep in thought. Dylan perked up with a suggestion and pointed to one of the willowy Live Oaks. "Someone could give me a boost up the tree, and I could—"

Betty cut him off. "What? Shimmy down the gate and come in the back door?"

"*Yeah.*" Dylan was unsure if she was mocking him.

"You don't think *Hollywood Hank* is going to have security cameras? And *alarms*?" Betty raised a perfectly plucked brow.

"You've seen too many movies, Dylan." Sweet Tea shook her head. "Maybe we could—"

Sweet Tea was interrupted by the loud creak of the driver's side door slamming shut. Mantis's messy, black hair bobbed with every mannish step as she lumbered toward the drive. She sucked the final puff of her cigarette and flicked the butt at one of the berry-filled hollys.

She turned. "You guys comin'?"

"You got a *plan*?" Betty asked quietly, though their presence couldn't possibly be more conspicuous. The fire-red paint spattered with demon residue was like a billboard announcing their presence.

"Yeah, I got a plan. The plan's to go to the fuckin' front door and ring the goddamn bell." Mantis rolled her eyes. "Not everything's gotta be all *Charlie's Angels* with us."

"*Then* what?" Betty asked, always the voice of reason.

Mantis spoke slowly to insinuate that Betty was being dense, "*Then*, we're going to get that *gold thing* in his *trophy case*."

"*You* can't just walk into a movie star's mansion and say, '*Gimme that thing you care enough about to encase in glass.*'"

"Why not?" Mantis shrugged.

"Because that's how you go to *prison* or get *shot*." Betty whispered tensely.

"So… we just get Sweet Tea to ask for it then," Mantis said, still not understanding the problem.

"Wait, what? Why *me*?" Sweet Tea asked.

"Because guys give you anything you *want*. You bat those eyes, and they bend over backward."

"No, they *don't*!"

"Yes, they *do*." Dylan retorted, having similarly fallen prey to her feminine wiles for a year himself and had seen patrons at Lassie's empty wallets of hard-earned cash for her nightly.

Betty interrupted, "We aren't gonna make it past the front door! That is *Hollywood Hank's* house!"

"You say that like people are supposed to *give a shit.*" Mantis chuckled. "I don't give a fuck if it's the home of Jesus *himself.* So, you guys comin', or not?" Mantis was already at the stone stairs.

Betty grunted angrily and left the vehicle in a huff. "Always goin' off half-cocked. Never thinking *anything* through." Betty smoothed her clothing and hair and hobbled toward Mantis on her busted high heel. She stopped in her tracks, growled, yanked her shoes off, and tossed them into the truck bed.

"The fuck are you doin'?" Mantis knitted her over-grown black brows.

"Well, if you don't need a *plan*, *I* don't need shoes." Betty stomped up the drive toward the porch. "Let's get my son back."

Overhead, a booming male voice spoke, "Can I *help* you?"

The abrupt noise rattled them in an instant.

"What the *hell*?" Mantis looked all around the porch.

Betty pointed to a loudspeaker near a small, swiveling security camera on the porch's roof. They peered up at it. Dylan and Sweet Tea finally joined them.

"Yeah. Um, hi." Mantis's demeanor was relaxed. "Hollywood Hank ordered us."

"I *ordered* you?" The man was confused. Betty and Sweet Tea's demeanor changed immediately as they were plunged into fan-girl mode.

"Oh, wow. Hank, *huge fan*!" Betty raised on the balls of her bare feet.

Mantis glared at her. "Sorry about that. She's new to the agency." She stared at the camera, posture atrocious.

"What do you *want*?" The voice grew impatient. "I didn't order anything."

Mantis rubbed her ear and winced at the volume of the loudspeaker. "That's what we're here to ask *you*, actually. You only have us for the full hour."

"*Excuse* me?" The voice boomed again.

Mantis sighed, "Ugh! C'mon, dude. Do I have to spell it out for you? We're from the..." she whispered, "*escort service.*"

Silence.

"You called and said you wanted, quote, 'three white bitches' for an hour.' You gonna let us in or not?"

The little gears spun, and the tiny camera pivoted to look them over.

"I didn't call any escort service," the voice barked.

"Yes. Boss said your assistant prepaid with a gold card. Said you wanted us here right away. I promise we're not the fuzz. We're just here to *love you long time*," Mantis spouted playfully in a slightly racist Asian voice.

Silence again.

"Who's the dude?" The camera panned to Dylan.

Mantis was momentarily at a loss for words and then spouted the first thing that came to mind. "Our *pimp*."

Betty looked at Mantis with an expression that said: *Are you crazy?*

"*That* guy's your *pimp*?"

"Oh, so now we're *liars*? Spin your stupid little camera down at the ground and take a good look at this asshole's shoes." She pointed to Dylan's cowboy boots as the camera's tiny motor whirled again. "That's *right*. That's *alligator skin*, motherfucker. *Genuine*. What kind of idiot just walks around wearing those for *fun*?"

Dylan didn't know how to react. He looked up at the camera, crossed his arms, and tried to sell the ridiculous lie.

"Fifty-five minutes left." Mantis tapped a finger against her bare wrist.

"Hmmm. Blondie, do a lil' turn for me." Hank's voice made Sweet Tea blush. She twirled so he could see every angle. The overhead voice contemplated with another, "Hmmmm."

Click!

The front door unlocked.

"I'm in the den. Your... *pimp*... can wait in the foyer."

Mantis tried to hide the shit-eating grin on her face as they shuffled in.

Betty mouthed, '*I can't believe that worked*' to Sweet Tea. Dylan shut the door behind them. Mantis slapped the truck keys into his sinewy chest. "You're on getaway-vehicle duty, Dyl-do. Be prepared to get us rolling fast if shit goes south."

Dylan nodded obediently.

Mantis led the others through the formal living room, which seemed like the most logical path to a den. Celtic woodwinds played on the built-in speakers overhead. Betty and Sweet Tea grew giddy.

"I can't believe I'm in *Hollywood Hank's* house right now!" Betty whispered.

Sweet Tea's breasts bounced as she jumped vigorously. "We're in the promised land!"

Mantis rolled her eyes and went back to scanning the room for the hunk of gold so they could get the hell out of there.

"In *here*," a man's voice bellowed from down the hall. Abruptly, Hank's voice boomed over a whole-house intercom. "Maria, get your ass in here. I need a drink!"

The hallway opened up to a massive caramel-colored den with vaulted ceilings. A granite wet bar sat in the back, brimming with high-end bottles of booze. A gigantic flat projector screen was mounted to one wall. Near it, a baby grand piano reflected lights from a crystal chandelier dangling overhead. Several stylish couches were carefully peppered throughout the colossal room.

Hollywood Hank was draped comfortably across one of them with a tablet in his hand. He pressed a button and spoke into its built-in mic. His voice oozed out of the intercoms in every room. "*Maria!*"

As the girls entered, Mantis spotted the display case from the magazine on the wall behind Hank. It was full of international knickknacks on decorative stands, just like it had been in the photograph.

One stand was empty.

Mantis's heart sank in her chest as she realized the void in the display case was where the golden should've been.

Hank tapped the screen, and the music shut off. He pushed another button, and a buzzer rang out through the house, echoing through the cavernous space. "MARIA! For fuck's sake, get me a goddamn drink!"

Hank shook his head and looked at Betty. "I'm 'bout to have this bitch *deported*."

"Thank you for allowing us into your home, sir." Sweet Tea politely clasped her hands behind her back, forcing her boobs front and center.

Betty burst forth, unable to contain her adoration. "Hank, it is SUCH a pleasure to meet you. I've seen *all* of your films. Multiple times. You are just," Too overcome with excitement, Betty couldn't find the words." You make women like me feel like there's always a chance to find love, you know? Like you and Starla Dwight did in *Cloudy with a Chance of Love*."

"Ugh, Starla? That wrinkly bitch fought me for every scrap of screen time she could. Friggin' *hog*. I heard the fucking gaffer gave her *the clap* after the wrap party."

Mantis already hated him. All of the on-screen charm and charisma he could *possibly* have couldn't make up for the fact that he was a dickhead in real life.

"MARIA!" Hank shouted into the tablet.

"You know what? I got it, Hank. What'll it be?" Mantis crossed the room and shimmied behind the bar.

"You don't have to do that. That's what I pay *Maria* for," Hank said, not bothering to look at Mantis behind him.

"It's cool. What's our poison? Martini? Whiskey sour? You look like a whiskey-sour

128

guy." She leaned over the bar, waiting for a response.

"Bourbon, neat," he said firmly.

"Cake-walk. Brand?" Mantis plucked a bottle with a white label from one of the shelves and poured some straight into her mouth from the jigger. She swallowed, making a horrid face in reaction to the taste.

Betty looked at Mantis. Her eyes grew large as if to say: *Don't screw this up for me!*

"Dealer's choice." Hank shrugged lazily.

Mantis took another large mouthful of the booze and, instead of swallowing, she dribbled it back into a tumbler over some ice cubes, grinning mischievously at Betty with wet lips. She plopped the bottle on the bar top and rejoined the others.

Betty stared in horror as Mantis handed Hank the short glass of back-washed bourbon.

Hank sipped it greedily and moaned, "*Nailed it.*" He glanced up from his tablet. "So what is it that you *really* want, ladies? Clearly, you're not escorts." He motioned to Sweet Tea. "Well, maybe *you*."

"Wait, what makes you think we're not *hookers*?" Betty put her hands on her hips like the angry mother she was.

Hank pointed to Mantis. "She said I had an hour and looked at her wrist, but she's not wearing a watch."

"So what?"

"Plus, your pimp looks like he couldn't *whip cream.*"

Mantis chuckled. "Well, he's not wrong."

Hank pointed to Betty's feet. "Plus, prostitutes may not have had much in the way of *dignity*, but they typically at least have *shoes*."

"Why'd you let us in?" Betty chewed her lip.

"Curiosity." Hank smiled. His gleaming teeth made Betty's heart pound. His hair shimmered, the color of a new penny. It was the kind of hair she dreamed about running her hands through.

He was the total package. And he *knew* it.

He scratched his meticulously trimmed beard and laid the tablet down. "So what's this all about? You ladies looking for an autograph or a selfie or something?" Hank flashed a sly grin to Betty. "You're not here to, like, steal my *underwear* or somethin', are you?"

"No." Betty blushed.

"We saw somethin' in your display case in a magazine, and we are prepared to offer you money for it," Mantis blurted.

"Oooh, *collectors*? Intriguing." Hank took another sip of his drink. Betty winced. "I like how direct you are. It's refreshing."

"The thing we're lookin' for is metal." Mantis walked to the display case, brimming with film props and collector's items. She pointed to the empty stand in the case.

As her finger was pressed to the glass, she noticed a miniature bronzed statue of a bizarre humanoid creature with a goat head on the shelf above. Its head had long hair and an upside-down star on its forehead between two menacing horns. She was entranced. It had the breasts of a woman and the body of a man. She'd never seen anything like it.

"It *was* right there." She pointed to the empty stand, eyes latched on the goat statue.

"Oh, *the talisman*? You're out of luck. I sold it." He quickly corrected himself, "Well, *traded* it."

"To *whom*?"

"Calls himself the *Tax Man*." Hank took another tiny sip from the tumbler. "He's my accountant. *Super* intense guy. Pretty sure he needs to lay off the coke, actually. The dude's wired 24-7. I can never remember his real name. Promised me an *exponentially* better return this year if I gave it to him."

"You just… traded it?" Sweet Tea asked, pretending she'd been paying attention to his words instead of just his gorgeous face.

"Yeah. Uncle Sam's a real *cocksucker*. What the hell do I need with some useless hunk of metal?" Hank shrugged.

"If you thought it was just a useless hunk of metal, why'd you have it in your display case?" Mantis pressed her chewed nail against the glass.

He sighed. "I put it in there because the broad that gave it to me was acting like it was *all important*. Bitch was cuckoo. Said it was part of some…" he waved his hands in incredulity, "ancient talisman."

"A talisman for *what*?" Mantis wanted answers. She wanted to know why she'd seen it in her *dream*. Or why it felt important when she held the piece they'd taken from Johnny.

Hank shrugged. "I wasn't really listening when she was yammering on about it, to be quite honest."

"Why did the *Tax Man* want it?" Mantis stepped closer.

"He said somethin' 'bout how he had another piece just like it, and he wanted to keep 'em together or some shit. I'll give you his number if you want."

"Got an address?" Mantis perked up.

"Yeah, I do, actually. Got something to write it down on?"

"You can text it to me," Betty purred.

Hank pulled his phone from his front pants pocket and logged into his contacts list.

"Ya' know, keepin' your phone in your pocket like that'll give ya' *ball cancer*," Mantis cheerfully volunteered.

Hank smirked. "I'll keep it in mind. Who am I texting this shit to?" He held out his phone, and Betty snatched it up immediately.

"You're texting it to… Betty… and *that*… is my number." She offered his phone back with a flirtatious smile.

Hank typed letters wildly into a text with quiet little clicks. The phone jingled quietly, and he stuffed it back in his pocket and then pulled it back out again with alarm. He looked at Mantis and tossed his phone to the couch with a slight, grateful smirk.

Betty's phone beeped. A grin spread across her face.

"Anything else?"

"One question. What's with the fuckin' *Riverdance* music," Mantis blurted.

"Preppin' for a new role. Playing a bartender from Dublin in the next flick."

"Aye, well, *gidday mate*," Sweet Tea exclaimed.

Silence.

Mantis sighed. "The public school system failed you so hard. Thank God you're *pretty*."

"Why?" Sweet Tea seemed oblivious.

"That's *Australian,* you asshat, not Irish." Mantis rubbed her temples. "*This* is why other countries hate America."

Betty turned to him. "Thank you for the info, Hank. We'll take *Crocodile Dundee* here and get out of your hair."

On their way out of the den, Mantis walked past a wall with photos of Hank with other noteworthy stars. Hank was posed with politicians, musicians, directors, and movie stars. Mantis jammed her finger against one on the end. It was a picture of him with Betty's beloved Evangelist.

"You know this dude?" Mantis looked back at Hank. "Jeremiah Munsey?"

Hank laughed, "We go *way* back. Used to take acting lessons together in L.A. Back when he was just lil' ol' Jerry Beck."

"Munsey's not his real last name?" Betty scrunched her face.

Hank laughed. "Not even a little bit."

"I love watching him. He's the real deal," Betty cooed, her voice full of hope.

Hank just laughed.

"May I use your restroom on the way out," Betty asked, face pleading.

"Yeah, fine. It's past the foyer. You'll see it."

As they made their way toward the entrance, Dylan looked up, hope in his eyes. "How'd it go?"

Betty breezed past him with a purpose, overshooting the bathroom.

Mantis leaned against a marble statue. "Well, we got to hear Sweet Tea do a *tragic* Steve Irwin impression."

"Did you get the *thing*?"

"No. But we got a lead on where it is now. *Hollywood Fake* gave us an address."

Betty came racing back through the house at top speed, bare feet padding on the cream-carpeted runner. She had a pair of men's boxer briefs in her hand.

"*Go-go-go-go-go-go-go-go-gooooo,*" Betty murmured.

Mantis burst into laughter and grabbed the front door handle. Someone yanked from the other side. Betty tucked the underwear in her purse just in time and pretended to look calm. A Latina woman entered with a mountain of dry-cleaned clothes in her arms.

She looked at the four of them blankly, alarmed by their presence.

"Sorry, doll. We're just on our way out," Mantis explained. "Also, your boss is kind of a dick."

"*Ay Dios mio,* tell me about it." The frazzled woman sighed with relief. "He can't do *anything* for himself."

Mantis and the others politely crept out the door behind her. Mantis glanced at her ass as she walked by.

"Good Lord, keep it in your *pants*," Betty begged, rolling her eyes.

"Thanks for calling me pretty, Mantis," Sweet Tea swooned in the back as the Chevy rumbled down the road. Mantis tapped her thumbs on the wheel of the pickup as they neared a red light. They'd been making great time since Midland and traffic had been almost non-existent.

"She was implying you're ignorant and that looks are all you have. It wasn't a compliment," Betty muttered.

"No!"

"Yes, I did, Tea," Mantis grumbled. "And the fact you didn't pick up on that should tell you it's accurate."

"*I* don't think you're dumb, Tea." Dylan placed a hand on her knee, unsure if she'd allow him to leave it there. To his surprise, she did.

Progress.

"*Take a left onto… South Avenue K,*" the robotic voice chirped from Betty's phone. Mantis pulled into the turn lane.

"I'll take the phone GPS over that stupid paper map any day," Mantis mumbled.

"Yeah, well, paper's good to have. There are a lot of areas that you can't get signal out here."

"That folded monstrosity is only handy in case we run outta toilet paper." She whipped through the turn. "Shit, I'd like to wipe my ass with this whole *state*."

"Lay off Texas. Some of us call the Lone Star state *home*," Sweet Tea warned. "I'm East Texas born-and-bred."

"Really?" Betty turned, crinkling the lumped tarp beneath her.

Dylan smiled. "Where?"

"Little town called Sulphur Springs." Sweet Tea looked out the window. "I was a big track and field star there, believe it or not."

"*Your destination is on the right.*"

Mantis pulled into a nearby parking spot and mocked the app, "Arriving at… shit-ty Podunk town." She looked up at the metal warehouse.

Sweet Tea pointed to the faded lettering on the corrugated wall above. "Guys, the building says '*The Tax Man*: Full-Service Tax Accountant' right there."

"Bet, you got the cash?" Mantis popped her last Iron Pillar behind her ear for safekeeping and searched her tight pockets for her flip lighter. When she didn't feel it, she blindly felt around on the floorboard for it.

"Yep," Betty patted her studded rockabilly purse.

"Let's peel off a thousand and lock it in the glove box. I wanna make sure we have enough for gas and food back to Tucson." Finally, Mantis felt the cold metal beneath her fingers and pulled it up. The lighter was covered in coagulated blood from the mangled remains of the cowboy beneath her. She wiped the blood onto the front of her crop top and jammed the lighter back in her pocket.

"What if someone breaks in and takes it?"

"Bet, if someone breaks into the truck, we got bigger problems. They're going to find a *body*."

Betty had almost forgotten after the excitement of meeting her idol. She jammed some cash in the glove box and looked out at the empty streets. "Does… anything seem *weird* to you?"

"Yeah. The fact that Dylan cut a fart that could gag a maggot back in Midland, and not *one* of you bitches said anything about it the *whole* two-hour drive," Mantis shook her head.

"I didn't *fart* in *Midland*, ladies," Dylan said, "I swear."

Mantis shoved a finger at Dylan. "Yes, you did! And it *lingered*. I thought it was the dead guy for the first two, three miles, and then I smelled the fuckin' *onions* in it."

"Mantis, I don't even *eat* onions!" Dylan's voice went high. "I'm *allergic*."

"No, Dylan, it *had* onions in it." Mantis looked around at everyone. "Who, then? Who the fuck had onions at lunch?"

"Me, okay?" Betty grimaced. "I had a *salad,* and the red onions didn't *sit right. Move on.*"

Silence.

"Betty! I don't know whether I wanna *high-five you* or make you ride in the bed of the *truck* back there with Doc Holiday's lower half." Mantis stared at Betty, dead serious. The others tried not to laugh. "No, *really,* Bet. You need to get yourself checked."

"Can we *go* now," Betty shouted. "*Please*?!"

Post, Texas was ominous. So quiet that their shoes echoed through the silent downtown streets. Daylight was lost. Dim streetlights flickered as they made their way to the building's entrance.

Dylan loaned Betty Johnny's client's cowboy boots, which proved quite large for her dainty feet. But too-large was better than questing barefoot.

The avenue was long and straight. If she looked hard enough, Mantis could see a mile ahead, maybe more. She put one hand on the door handle and fished out a pink switchblade from her pocket, handing it to Dylan.

"Where'd you get this?" Dylan whispered. "Did you steal it from the hooker?"

"Ye who is without sin can cast the first stone," She said, glancing down to his stolen alligator boots.

"Okay, *touche*," he snickered.

"Know how to use this?"

"You kiddin' me?" Dylan grinned. "I'm like Gordon-fuckin'-Ramsay when I'm chopping kale at home!"

"*Great,* so if one of those big-ass demons attacks you, just picture it as a fucking *collard green*, and we'll all be safe." She rolled her eyes so hard it hurt and then removed the black switchblade from her other pocket.

"Wait, could I have the black one," Dylan asked.

"No."

"Why not?"

"Because I said so."

"Can I *keep* this? I wanna name it."

"No."

"No… meaning I can't *keep it,* or no meaning I can't *name* it?"

"*Both.*"

"Too late. His name is already *Excalibur.*"

"*He?* It's fucking *pink.*"

Betty cleared her throat, arms crossed.

Without another word, Mantis shook her head in agitation and opened the door. A look of surprise spread over her face. Though it was still early evening, she expected the commercial building to be closed.

The front door opened. Inside, a wooden desk was placed in the center, dwarfed by the size of the walls and ceilings throughout the rest of the empty warehouse. A filing cabinet sat beside it, paint chipping in several places. On the desk, stacks of papers and receipts were strewn in a giant mess surrounding a laptop. Off to one side, a hand mirror sat with a pile of white powder adorning its shining glass surface, divided into generous parallel lines with a glimmering razor laid at the end of one. Beside the mirror sat a small plastic baggie with a sticker of a black goat's head inside of a red upside-down star.

On the other side of the desk, a stubby sawed-off shotgun rested upright on its butt.

The man at the desk looked up from his laptop. He grabbed the weapon, and Mantis thrust her hands up.

"Easy, *pilgrim,*" she said in her best John Wayne voice. "This ain't the friggin' gunfight at the O.K. Corral and, frankly, I don't actually remember the Alamo."

"Have you ever even, like, *seen* a western," Dylan whispered.

The stocky man glared beneath the single, harsh overhead light, eyes completely bloodshot.

"We are lookin' for the *Tax Man*," Mantis said calmly.

He glared at them for a moment in silence, hands still perched on the gun.

"That you? I imagined you worked in a..." Mantis looked around, "*cubicle* or something."

"You *cops*?" He leaned forward in his seat. The chair groaned beneath the weight of his stocky frame.

Mantis couldn't help but laugh at the accusation. "No, we're not cops. In fact, I'm pretty sure we've broken, like, every law since we crossed the state line."

Silence.

"Want proof?" Mantis pointed to Dylan. "I'll make this kid snort a whole line of your coke if you want. Yesterday, he ate a weed brownie—"

"Tick-tick. Time is money," he interrupted. "Get to the point or leave."

"Okay. Simmer down. *Damn.*" Mantis blinked hard. "We were sent by Hank—"

"I know a lotta Hanks." He spoke fast, but his voice was deep, commanding. His fingers clasped around the shotgun like a python.

"*Hollywood* Hank. The chick-flick actor." She felt like a hostage negotiator.

The Tax Man removed his hand from the shotgun and itched his short, blond hair. He laughed suddenly, loud and hearty. Mantis found his smile more off-putting than the double-barrel beside him.

"Of course. Hank! He's not firing me, is he? Did he send you to do his dirty work? I knew that bastard was too lazy to come here and do it himself."

This guy is a certifiable looney, alone in this dank, brick castle, Mantis thought.

Betty carefully pulled the gold wad from her purse. "We're lookin' for the rest of this. Hank said he traded his portion of it to you."

The Tax Man's eyes widened. "I've been trying to buy that one for some time now. *That one,*" he opened the file cabinet and flicked through some files before selecting one. He pulled out a stack of papers. The top page had a picture of their hunk of the talisman printed on it in black-and-white ink. Handwritten notes were scrawled in the margins. "That, there, was Johnny's piece. The pimp in El Paso. He just... *gave* it to you?!"

"Well, it took some *convincing.*" Mantis cleared her throat.

"How much are you asking for it?"

"No, I don't think you quite understand. We want to purchase *yours.*"

The Tax Man laughed hard. His voice cut through the air like a sharpened machete."You're joking."

"We... have... cash." Mantis smiled.

The Tax Man ground his knuckles into the desk. "How does one put a number on something so *priceless*?"

Mantis pulled the cigarette out from behind her ear and lit it. "You handle accounts as big as Hank's, and your operation is no-frills. *Clearly* minimal overhead. You make your living touching other people's dough, and once you get it, you like to keep it. I respect that." She exhaled. Smoke danced its way toward the singular, alien beam of overhead light. "I have a feeling you're the kinda guy that'd sell his own *mother* if the price was right. We're prepared to pay eight thousand."

"No." He said matter-of-factly.

Betty stepped forward and whispered into Mantis's ear, "Mantis, we only have four—"

Mantis stepped away from Betty. "Nine G's and the boy here'll throw in authentic pair a' gator skin boots, if that's your thing."

"Like *hell* I will," Dylan retorted angrily. "You can pry these off my *cold, dead body.*"

Mantis pinched her eyes shut at the irony.

"No."

Silence again.

"Eleven thousand."

"Eleven thousand?" The Tax Man suddenly flashed a ravenous look, red eyes twinkling in the beam. "*Cash,* huh?"

"Eleven grand in filthy, gorgeous cash."

The Tax Man dug in the front pocket of his jeans and retrieved a small ring of keys. He unlocked the top drawer of his desk, pulled out a rectangular box, and set it on the spreadsheets. The design etched into the box's top looked ancient. He opened the lid as if the fragile hinges were going to fall apart. Inside, a hunk of metal shined almost platinum as the wood revealed it. It was seated in a red velvet base, shaped for a crucifix roughly a foot tall.

Only two small portions of the golden talisman sat inside the grooves.

The second she saw it, Mantis was filled with a pang of frustration. She knew instantly that the piece they already possessed wouldn't complete the shape. "Where's the rest of it?"

"A couple pieces are still out there. I've managed to track a few down, but the others aren't as willing to part with theirs as Hank."

"Like *who*?"

She hadn't driven all around this God-forsaken state for more riddles.

He shuffled through his file cabinet again and produced another image of a different golden piece. "Yarost, that rotten Russian bastard. Finest snow dealer in Texas. Shit's pricey, but it's *stellar*. My ass drove all the way to Temple to try to finagle him out of his portion. Came back with a fourteen-thousand-a-year coke habit, a fractured rib, and a bullet hole in my ass cheek."

"What the hell? We just keep falling further down the rabbit hole trying to find this thing," Sweet Tea exclaimed.

The Tax Man hadn't noticed her, *or her double-D breasts*, until she said it.

"Well, don't *you* look like a million bucks? What's your name, little darlin'?"

"This *little darlin'* will tell you when we get an address for this *Yarost* guy."

"Aren't you just *adorable,* puttin' your little two cents in wherever you can?"

Without thinking, Dylan popped the pink switchblade open by his side.

"How about you tell your little friends to go outside," his voice oozed with desire, "and you stay til' we *work somethin' out*."

"In your dreams, *pig.*" Sweet Tea leaned over the desk, breasts in full view, pretend-cranking her middle finger up like a jack-in-the-box, a foot in front of his face.

Dylan watched the accountant's expression morph from lust into hatred, fingers snaking around the shotgun once again.

"Tea! *Get down!*" Dylan's screams reverberated off the metallic walls. Before he could say more, the coked-out accountant was on his feet, walnut stock against his bicep.

BOOM! Click.

Sweet Tea ducked in the nick of time as he pulled the trigger. The sound *thundered.* Metal pellets exploded from the shell like fireworks, *thwacking* the siding like deadly hail thirty feet behind them.

BOOM! Click.

Betty found herself just inside in the line of fire and tumbled to the concrete as stray buckshot ripped into her skin. Mantis dropped to her knees by Betty as the *Tax Man* scrambled to load more shells in the chamber.

Sweet Tea pressed her back against the desk, eyes wide in disbelief and shock.

Dylan knew he had to act. He whirled the open switchblade with all his might. It flew in a pink blur, end-over-end, stopping abruptly in the accountant's forehead. It sat still, buried in his skull to the hilt.

The accountant wavered in place. He clung to the double-barrel, confusion obvious. Dylan stared in silence. An overwhelming need to vomit overtook him. He hurtled himself toward a small wastebasket by the desk but didn't make it, barf splattering across the cold, gray floor.

Mantis rose from Betty's side and launched herself onto the cluttered desk, receipts wafting into the air like concert confetti. She growled and tackled the stunned man on the other side with jarring force. They tumbled together to the ground.

WHAM!

The shotgun plummeted to the desk, cracking the keyboard on impact. Once on the floor, Mantis stomped her boot into the handle of the lodged knife in his brain. He howled. Blood oozed from the wound. She twisted back, grabbed the sawed-off from the desk, and aimed it at the man's rounded, bleeding face.

From his stupor, he managed a final expression of terror.

BOOM! Click-click.

A soupy mess of bone, hair, and gray matter erupted in every direction. Through the ringing in her ears, Mantis managed a smile, face spattered with bloody blow-back. She laid the weapon on the desk and stepped away from the mutilated corpse.

Boots clomping and sliding through the human stew, she bent down to retrieve the gnarled pink knife. She spun it, examining the marred mess of metal ruined by the buckshot. She waltzed to the puddle of bile and handed it down to Dylan. "Here you go, kid. You earned those naming rights. Give him any moniker you want."

Dylan sat in horrified silence, holding it, in total disbelief at how wrong the last sixty seconds of his life had just gone.

Mantis looked down at Betty, who was on the floor clutching her bloodied arm. "Well," she wiped her cheek, smearing blood up in streaks, "that went well."

Gabriel sat in his cushioned chair near the stained glass window. Even his own *breath* seemed loud in the silent church. It was like a void, cold and quiet, as lifeless as the dead people depicted on the walls like artsy hieroglyphics.

The woman next to him smiled and held a palm. He offered an arm to her willingly.

"You're an old pro at this by now," she said playfully, sliding a large needle into his arm. Red shot through the tubing, filling a plastic container with the garnet liquid.

He smiled, weak and pale, and looked back out through the colored shards of glass fused by snakes of melted metal. Black shadows below danced in the fenced-in park just beyond the steps of the church. One of the black blobs thrust itself on another. Though muffled, Gabriel could hear the undeniable sounds of a man attacked. His blood-curdling scream rang out above the sound of waves and wind. A tugboat tooted in the distance, overpowering the man's wet gurgles.

Another black blob came from around the side of the building at him, and the two living creatures fought over his colorful blur like a game of tug-o-war, growling and gnashing, slurping and tearing.

"Almost done, then you can go play in the rectory, okay?" She smiled, completely unaffected by the horrors beyond the church.

"When will Miss Lucy be back?"

"Soon. She just went for a little walk. She loves this place. It's one of her favorite cities in the world. Well, *this and Vegas.*"

"I don't think it's safe for her out there."

"Oh, she'll be fine. Honestly, I pity anyone who crosses her." She patted his knees. "Plus, she said if that little place over there across from the park hasn't shut down, she's gonna bring us all back some fresh *beignets* and *cafe au lait*."

"Is that the thing with the powdered sugar on top?"

She nodded and looked at the bag of blood, holding it up to the light.

"I love those. My mom makes them for me sometimes."

"She does?"

Gabriel nodded, icy-blue eyes staring off into the swirling black mass behind her. Smoky tentacles danced around the edges of the hollow abyss.

"Well, Gabe, I hope you know just how special you are." She pinched his nose lightly and shook.

He giggled and leaned back. He did. And that thought made him feel content.

Powerful.

Dr. Goldstein Can See You Now

The truck's air-conditioner groaned as the Chevy idled in the parking lot of *Tombstone Drug and Spirits*. Betty clutched the wooden case in her shaking hands. She's seen so much violence since Mantis had come back into her life.

So much *chaos*.

So much *death*.

She opened the box and slid her fingers through the empty grooves where the rest of the hunks of talisman should be. She dug in her purse, wincing in pain, and pulled out the hunk of gold from Johnny's safe. On the edges, there were letters. She spun a hunk, now smeared with the slippery blood on her fingertips.

She accidentally dropped it into the box.

Tink!

It *clanked* against the first piece. Then, something miraculous happened. The pieces glowed and then melded together as if molten, forming a seamless bond between the two, turning them into a singular piece. Betty gasped.

She touched the talisman and jerked away as the metal singed her fingers with its intense heat. Her eyes were wide with wonder as she wrapped her mind around what she'd just witnessed.

Mantis, Dylan, and Sweet Tea emerged from the store with totes filled to the brim with various goods. Dylan and Sweet Tea piled in the back, and Mantis handed her bags back to Dylan. She hopped in the front and slammed the door.

"The guy at the register said there's a hotel a few blocks from here." Mantis pointed down the street, bathed in muddled light from the parking lot's overhead security lamps.

"You're *never* going to believe what I just saw," Betty said, astonished.

"No, I, too, saw the homeless dude over there wanking it while talking sexy to that pigeon. What the fuck is this world *coming* to?" Mantis shifted and made her way out of the parking lot.

Betty turned the box toward her, displaying the singular, long strip of ornate metal.

"Holy shit!" Mantis reached out to touch the talisman. "How'd you get it into one piece?"

"Don't! It's really hot. I dropped one, and they touched. It did it on its *own*," Betty said, her voice barely a whisper.

Mantis touched Betty's pale, clammy forehead and looked down at the blood-soaked swath of skirt tied around her arm. "Let's get you to the hotel, Bet."

***

Betty waddled into the hotel room. Sweet Tea carried the drug store bags to the adjoining room a few feet further down a marigold hallway. Mantis and Dylan brought up the rear.

Betty sat on one of the queen beds. A knock sounded on the door joining the rooms. Dylan opened it. Sweet Tea smiled and entered with two sacks of goods. "The rest of the stuff's in there. Here are your supplies, doctor."

"Care to be my assistant?" Dylan's smile was charming.

"You trying to play doctor with me?" Sweet Tea looked at him out of the sides of her eyes.

Mantis sighed. "Can y'all do this will-they-won't-they bullshit later? She's bleeding."

Sweet Tea tossed her blue leather jacket on the dresser.

"You got two rooms?" Betty looked at Mantis. "I don't know if we can afford—"

"They were cheap as hell. Plus, this went on someone else's card. Let's live a little." Mantis retrieved a wrapped pack of Iron Pillars from one of the totes and tore through the plastic in a flurry.

"Wait, who's card did it go on?"

"*Tex Addley's.*"

"Who's *Tex Addley*?" Betty made a sour face.

"Lady at the front desk thinks it's Dyl-do over here." Mantis bobbed her head toward Dylan, voice distorted by the cigarette between her lips. "But the real Tex, what's *left* of him is in the pickup."

"You stole a credit card from a *dead man*?"

"Of *course* I did! And I saw his license while I was in his wallet. He *was* good-lookin' when he had a face. I'da banged him. So, yeah. Rooms are on Tex tonight. I hear he doesn't really need credit these days." She took a long drag and, on exhalation, she said, "I'm *stimulating the economy*. So was Tea when she *insisted* on *paying* for canvas totes instead of using the *free* plastic bags."

"They're reusable! Do you know how *hard* plastic is on the environment?" Sweet Tea's pitch went high.

Mantis rolled her eyes. "Simmer down, *Norma Rae*; we got you the dumb bags. Plus, I hear those things are worse for the environment in the long run."

Sweet Tea scoffed and glanced at Dylan, but Dylan shrugged apologetically as if to say *I think she's right.* He rose and handed Betty some pills. "Take these."

"What are they?"

"Ibuprofen."

"We got vodka too, babe," Mantis chimed in.

Betty whipped her head around. "What *kind?*"

"Your *fave.* Whipped Cream." Mantis grinned.

"Booze me, baby."

"I wouldn't recommend that." Dylan offered. "Alcohol thins the blood."

"I'm going to thin *your* blood in a minute if you don't get those no-good M&Ms outta my face," Betty threatened. She looked down at her arm and whined, "This is gonna *wreck* my *tattoo!*" She reluctantly snatched the pills from Dylan's hand and tossed them into her mouth, making a face like she was forced to swallow something rotten.

Mantis couldn't help but laugh. She was used to Betty always being *the composed one* with her act together. Seeing her in this infantile state was actually a relief. It reminded Mantis of the actual person she'd befriended long ago.

Sweet Tea placed a pile of hotel washcloths on the bed. "These are all the little ones I could find."

"Alright. Nurse Tea, tweezers." Dylan held his hand out.

"Tweezers." Sweet Tea placed the tool in his hand.

Mantis retrieved the vodka, opened it, and handed it to Betty.

"Is there something I can pour it in?" Betty asked meekly.

"Yeah. *Your mouth*." Mantis chuckled.

"No, that's so trashy."

"Betty, this is gonna hurt. Sorry in advance. I gotta get all the buckshot out so it doesn't fester." Dylan gagged a little at the sight of the wound but composed himself. "Jesus, my ears are still ringing from the blast."

"Have you ever done *anything* like this before?" Betty sounded worried.

"Absolutely. I *specialized* in bullet removal back home."

"Really?" Betty furrowed her brow.

"No, Betty. I'm a lower-middle-class Jew from a suburb in *Tucson*. I'd never even *seen* an actual gun 'till I met you two." Dylan gagged again.

"You're not gonna barf on her arm, are you?" Mantis grimaced.

"*That's it.*" Betty shoved the vodka into Tea's hand, grabbed a towel from the stack, and tamped it down over her buckshot-riddled arm. "I'm going to a *hospital*. I'm not letting Dr. FreshBeats over here dig into my arm with *eyebrow tweezers.*"

Mantis intercepted Betty. "Sorry, Bet. Buckshot is from a *shotgun shell*. Bullet wounds plus hospital equals *police involvement.* And that could lead them to, I don't know, say, the guy whose head I blew off earlier. Or the half-a-cowboy in the truck. Or, say, three dead *dickwads* decomposing in a basement in El Paso."

Betty growled and plopped back on the bed, defeated. She chugged straight from the vodka bottle and wiped her lips with her forearm. "Just get it over with."

Mantis couldn't remember a time she'd ever seen the woman so intoxicated. Betty always was the infuriatingly *sensible* one. She had a way of strangling all of the fun out of life with her overbearing choke-hold. Through their years apart, Mantis hoped Betty'd found happiness. The last she saw her, she'd finally attained the one thing she'd always wanted: *a child.*

But now that Gabriel had been taken, she couldn't imagine the pain and fear the poor woman was going through.

Betty was now sprawled across one of the queen beds, staring at the comforter beneath her. Dijon-yellow. Busy, yam-colored geometric designs. *Hideous.*

The buckshot had been plucked. Dylan covered her wounds with bandages and gauze. If kept clean, she'd heal fast.

Mantis sat on the chair nearby, picking her nails with her switchblade. Dylan and Sweet Tea sat on the second bed, sharing slices of pizza they'd had delivered to the room.

"Bet, it's your turn," Sweet Tea said, ensuring Betty was awake.

"Huh?" The wounded woman rolled over.

Sweet Tea attacked her slice of pizza and spoke, chewing the mouthful. "Truth or dare."

"*Truuuuth.*" Betty moaned into a pillow.

"What's your favorite thing to do with Gabe?" Sweet Tea knew it was a sore subject but broached it with optimism.

Betty rolled over onto her back and smiled. Her words slurred a little. "The *carrrnival.*

He *loves* the carnival. Especially the *carrrrousel.* The one that comes to town always has one black horse. Sssss the only one he ever wants to ride." A tear rolled from the corner of her eye.

She sniffled and wiped her face. "*Dylan.*"

Dylan sat up straighter. "*Truth.*"

"How long have you been in love with Tea?"

"Aw, *come on.*" Dylan tried to sound casual.

"The truth shall shet... *shet...* the truth shall *shet* you free." Betty drunkenly waved her hand like a conductor. "You know what I *mean.*"

Mantis mocked Betty in her best Sean Connery impression. "*Yesh,* do tell *ush,* Dylan. The truth shall *shet* you free."

"I'm pretty sure I said dare, actually." Dylan took another bite of his pizza.

Mantis flipped the blade back in and tapped the knife on her knee, fidgeting absentmindedly.

"So, like, *foreverrrrr,* I'm guessing?"

"Aww, come on. Leave him alone. We're just friends." Sweet Tea playfully nudged his shoulder. *There they were again.* The words made him sick.

"I remember the day I met her." He couldn't look at Sweet Tea but felt her eyes burning into him.

"Shut up. No, you don't." Sweet Tea ate a piece of pepperoni off of the slice in his hand.

"Yep. They had just hired me at *Classy Lassie's.* Told me I could plug in my stinger in a side room. There weren't enough outlets in my corner for everything. So I walked into this room, thinking it was like the janitor's closet or something, and there she was. Naked as a jaybird.

Looked like Lady Godiva with all that blonde hair."

He choked on a piece of crust, and Mantis offered the vodka to him. "Jesus, kid. Slow down on that pizza. No one's gonna take it from you."

Dylan took a large swallow from the bottle and scrunched his face. "Oh dear *God*, whipped cream vodka and pepperoni pizza. *That* is an absolutely *horrid* flavor combo."

"Your turn." Sweet Tea said, taking a swig from the bottle, too.

"*Mantis.*" Dylan nodded.

"Dare," she said without a second's hesitation.

"I *dare* you to give me a *genuine compliment.*"

"Fuck. *Truth.*"

"Okay, why does everyone call you *Mantis*?"

"It certainly ain't 'cause I *pray* a lot."

"Grace told me why people call you that once," Betty volunteered. "She said that when a female praying mantis has sex, she bites her lover's head off afterward." She laughed. Hard. *Too* hard.

But Mantis found nothing funny once Grace's name slipped from her drunken lips.

"Who's *Grace*?" Dylan's question was innocent enough.

"There's a real *truth* for her." Betty's once-giggly tone turned hostile. "Grace was my besssst friend." She peered at Mantis through narrowed eyes. "You treated her like shit."

"Fuck you. *I* was your best friend!" Mantis growled and gritted her teeth. "I've never been anything *but* your friend since I saved you from getting your abused-fucking-ass sold by the *hour*." Mantis's hands trembled from the anger. "Who was *there* for you? Who *bought you* back from the fucking *devil* you sold your *soul* to, huh?"

Mantis stood, pounding a finger into her sternum. "I did! *I* was the one who pulled you out of the gutter and gave you a place to stay!"

"You're a *coward*. You can't even say her *name*." Betty sat up, tears rolling fro her eyes once again. "You're the reason she *killed herself*, you know. I can't imagine how hard you made it for her that it'd be *less painful* to slit her own wrists."

"You ungrateful, self-righteous *bitch*." Mantis grabbed a room key, lighter, and cigarettes from the desk. "You like to act like you're some born-again Christian with *values*. I found you in an alley, like a piece of discarded *trash*. You'd been used and abused by every *piece of shit* with cash and an hour to kill."

"You never treated her right, Mantis," Betty grumbled.

Mantis threw on her leather jacket, yanked a wad of rumpled cash from Betty's purse, and stuffed it in her pocket. She stormed out of the room in a huff.

Dylan crawled off the bed. "I'm gonna go see if she's..." Without another word, he followed Mantis out the door.

"Quit followin' me, kid." Mantis stormed down the stairs of the hotel.

"She was drunk. She doesn't mean any of it." Dylan said, hot on her heels.

At the bottom of the steps, Mantis swung around. "She *does,* though. She blames me. Always *has*."

Mantis plowed through the exit into the parking lot. Dylan followed.

"Just go back up there, Dyl-do. She's probably right. I *am* cursed."

"You're not *cursed.* We wouldn't have made it this far without you."

"Yeah, great. If not for me, you *wouldn't* be in some rat-infested hotel in the middle of Texas chasing down some hunk of metal from a dream that, frankly, might mean fuckin' nothing." She looked down solemnly and lit a cigarette, smoking it hard and fast on the concrete barrier at the edge of the lot. "I should have never gotten her involved. I should have never gotten *any* of you involved."

"Well, I'm glad you did. If you hadn't come for Sweet Tea, I'd probably be dead by now. So," Dylan nudged a rock with his alligator-skin boot, "that's something."

She fought a smile. The little wimp was growing on her.

"I gotta say... when you hit that dude right in his fuckin' forehead today," Mantis drew in a lungful of tobacco and laughed as she exhaled, "that was pretty badass. Where the hell'd you learn to throw a knife like that?"

"I didn't! I just… threw it." He chuckled softly, and then his expression turned grim. "I keep thinking, what if that guy had kids or a wife? I'm a… I'm a *murderer.*"

"Well, technically, I think *I* killed him, so just… take that Jew guilt down a notch. You gave him," Mantis burped, mostly smoke, "a really wicked fuckin' *headache.*"

"Yeah?" Dylan fought a smile.

"Yeah. My opinion: women don't really need all this Hollywood Hank hot-air-balloon grand gesture bullshit. We don't need some putz spouting shit poetry to profess their love publicly. You wanna know the *one thing* that'll land us just about every time?"

Dylan nodded, listening intently.

"*Jealousy,* dude. Make her jealous, and she'll be *done-zo.* Trust me, I get a lot of tail." She laughed again, sputtering smoke like a struggling train.

"Does it always suck this bad to love someone?" His green eyes were transfixed on the shadowy figures behind the drawn second-story curtains.

"*No.*" She looked at the ground, pain flashing across her eyes. "Sometimes it's *worse.* Love can be *misery.*"

"Was she pretty?" Dylan looked at her. "*Grace.*"

"Goddamned beautiful." She reached into the pocket of her leather jacket and fished out the folded picture of her and Grace in Paris. She handed it over. He treated it like fragile rice paper, studying it. In it, the expression on Mantis's face was one of pure joy and contentment, an emotion he'd not yet seen from her. He handed it back.

"Life's short, kid. When you find the one you want, don't waste any time. You gotta fight for what you want in this world." Mantis sniffed and swiveled her head around. "I need a drink. You wanna drink? I saw a bar a couple doors down when we pulled in."

Dylan nodded. Mantis hopped on the wall and walked the edge like a balance beam in her untied combat boots. She lifted her leg up with perfect balance, put the cigarette out on the rubber sole, and flicked the butt into the shrubs. "Shit, I could go for a porchcrawler right now."

"What's a porchcrawler?"

Mantis hopped off the ledge and wrapped a lanky arm around him. "Oh, I still have so much to teach ya', kid."

The city lights outside the hotel sparkled in Sweet Tea's hazel eyes. Gently, Dylan cast a renegade strand of honey-blonde hair from her perfect face and leaned in to kiss her, stopping just shy of her bubblegum-pink lips. "I want to kiss you."

The understatement of the century…

"No, I *need* to," he whispered. His heart thudded like horse hooves against his ribs.

"What are you waiting for?" She leaned in, pressing her pillowy lips to his.

He felt the surge the moment their lips met.

The *spark.*

The electricity that poets spoke of. It was everything he'd ever *dreamed* it would be. Blood surged through every inch of his body.

The rooms were quiet, except for her heavy breathing, an intimate sound that turned him on like nothing else.

He pressed her perfect body against the marigold wallpaper as their kissing grew feverish. The year of desire and sexual frustration had culminated. Warmth resonated from her.

He'd *ached* for her.

Touched himself to the *thought* of her.

And that *body…*

He caressed the sides of Sweet Tea's face, fingers sliding through her long locks. He wanted to melt with her. He needed to be *inside* of her.

He kissed her neck softly at first, then nibbled gently with his teeth. She moaned softly, pleasurably, careful not to wake the others.

She smelled like wildflowers. He couldn't breathe her in fast enough, deep enough. He filled his lungs with Jasmine perfume, unable to get enough of her.

His head swam from the drinks, the kiss, the *moment*.

Sweet Tea shoved away from the wall, and he moved with her, staring at the curvaceous vision bathed in moonlight before him. The feel of the mattress pressing into the back of his thighs sent a shock through him, buzzing with excitement at the thought of finally making love to her, pulsing through him like a drug. She knelt around him, toned body writhing against the material of his jeans.

Sweet Tea smiled down at him. A smile he'd die for. A grin he never tired of.

He gazed at her, eyes wide and full of wonder. "*I love you.*"

The words felt just as crazy coming out as they had being kept *inside* for months.

She pressed him back against the mattress, and Dylan felt a tidal wave of relief wash over him. And suddenly, at that moment, he forgot what had taken him so long to say the words to her.

PART FOUR:
FAMINE

It was midnight. Thick masses of twinkling stars gathered, worshiping the moon like a miraculous prophet, dying the tall wheat a muddled blue-gray.

Mantis knew the dream all too well. But she didn't know how to escape it. Or... if she even *wanted* to.

The gnarled lamb with seven horns sat atop its rocky perch in the middle of the field. It raised its bloody head and glared unflinchingly with its seven pink irises.

The old man shuffled forth in his tattered cloth, offering up the delicate book encrusted with glittering gemstones and metallic trim. The lamb nudged a wad of pages back with a blackened hoof, revealing a new chapter.

On it sat a single word in cursive:

FAMINE.

From behind her, the patchwork beast approached again with haste, snatching her tight with his raven-like claw and dragging her to the smoking tree line in a hurry.

"You're hurting me!" Mantis exclaimed loudly at the creature, but her words didn't register with him. "Where are you taking me?!" Her blood dripped onto the soil. The droplets sunk in like acid, eroding the dirt instantaneously.

He peered down at the scorched holes. The look of horror on his bizarre, stitched-together face twisted into an expression of pure revelation, and he gasped. "It'sssssss *you*! You're the chosssssssen one!"

He dropped to his knees and bowed down as if she were royalty. It wasn't until he dropped that she realized she was completely naked.

Light shone up through the blood-made holes in the earth, dancing on the curves of her milky skin.

"Chosen for *what*?"

"Come and sssssssee!" He stood, brushed off his filthy clothes, and then took off toward the tree line. Mantis trembled, head swimming with confusion. The ground beneath her vibrated. Dizzy and terrified of the quaking, she followed him through a dense layer of drifting fog.

Soon, a rider approached, this one with a slender, malnourished physique and a pitch-black Clydesdale. The rider's scrawny body was not adorned in armor this time. Nearly every bone jutting angrily through his thin skin was visible to the naked eye. His back bowed, weak from the weight of the large brass scales he dangled above the horse's head. He wore nothing but a glossy black mask with a painted expression of sorrow. His black crown was smaller and less ornate than the others, adorned with severed claw-like demon fingers, dripping their magma-like blood down the curves of his sunken face.

The creepy patchwork beast rejoiced beside her. She gazed into the middle eye on his forehead, never blinking.

"*Famine,*" he gurgled in pure ecstasy before scurrying off into the smoke.

Hung Over

The moment Mantis pried her eyes open, she knew she'd hurl. She thrust herself off the homely comforter and raced to the adjoining bathroom, barely making it to the toilet. When the entire contents of her stomach had been heaved into the bowl, she laid her pounding head against the toilet seat and looked over at Dylan, who'd fallen asleep in the bathtub. Mantis's upchucking startled him awake.

He looked over, feeling green himself. "You know you're buck-ass naked, right?" It almost didn't even phase him anymore.

"I don't caaaaaare."

"You feel the quake? We had another this morning."

Mantis shook her pallid face. "Is that why you're in the tub?"

Dylan didn't answer. He only stared up at the ceiling. Mantis thought she might have another round of bile-spewing, but then she caught a glimpse of the massive erection in Dylan's pants.

"That… for *me*?"

"You wish," He groaned and rolled over, facing the wall. "I had sex with Tea."

"Oh shit, son. High-five." She held up a weak, pale hand. He didn't budge.

"In a *dreeeeeam,*" he growled.

"*Oh.*" Mantis limply flopped the hand to her bare thighs.

"And now I get to deal with *this*." He writhed on his back again and motioned to his crotch.

"Shit, *lotta* people'd be glad to have one that big."

He whispered angrily, "Not the *size*. The *hard-on*! I gotta wait until this thing goes away before I can go out there."

"What the fuck even *happened* last night," she asked, sweaty face pressed against its porcelain perch.

"About six *porchcrawlers*. *That's* what happened." Dylan slunk deeper into the tub. "*Each*."

"*Fuuuuck*." The moaned word escaped her lips like a dying man's last exclamation. "Did I do anything stupid?"

"You made out with some random dude," Dylan glared at her, "then a *chick*."

"That's not stupid. That's… pretty normal."

"Then you tried to make out with me," Dylan added.

Mantis winced, face contorting wildly. "Damn. I must've been *real* hard up."

"And then… we made up a handshake." A weak smile crept onto his face.

"Oh my *God*."

"*Yup*."

"'Ey kid, do me a favor. Go get my knife… and hit me," she motioned to the center of her forehead, "*right* where you got that asshole yesterday."

***

The truck was silent except for the sound of the air conditioner blasting at full intensity. Mantis donned the dark pair of men's sunglasses she'd found in the truck's glove box. The bright sun, the whirring motor, and the wafting smell of the decomposing Texan beneath her ass were all too intense with her hangover.

"Why does this Yarost guy have to live all the way in Temple?" Betty asked, speeding up. "Who *lives* in Temple?" One hand was on the wheel, the other held the stolen accountant's papers. Her eyes danced back and forth between them and the dusty stretch of scorching asphalt. The side of the road was peppered with more deep craters, ones like the one they'd seen days before.

They soon passed a cluster of stores nestled in the middle of nowhere, each with a shattered window, each seemingly looted. Sweet Tea shook her head at the madness.

One had a spray-painted sign leaning against the wall that said, "CLOSED. Will Rebuild After Apocalypse."

"Seems like demons and earthquakes are bad for business. Everything's closed out this way." Sweet Tea said to no one in particular. Dylan nestled deeper into her shoulder. He'd fallen asleep on her miles back.

"Yeah. I'm tryin' to find a place to get a coffee and something for the *stench* in here." Betty shifted her weight on the tarp, crinkling it beneath her.

"Oh shit!" Sweet Tea jolted forward, waking Dylan. She rifled through one of the tote bags on the floor, "Mantis got air fresheners yesterday."

Awkward. She wanted to thank Mantis, but they hadn't spoken since the fight. "What kind?"

"She got," Sweet Tea read them, "black ice, new car, strawberry, vanilla, pine tree, and Hawaiian."

"All of 'em. This vehicle reeks."

Dylan watched her peel out the scented cardboard trees. He remembered those same soft hands caressing him in the dream. Kissing her…

Dylan slyly grabbed Tea's American flag cowboy hat off the seat and conspicuously placed it over the rising bulge in his lap.

Sweet Tea offered up the fresheners. Mantis wrapped their stretch bands around the mirror, leaving them bundled in an aromatic hunk. Betty took a deep whiff. The cocktail of smells was nearly as disgusting as the rotting corpse.

Suddenly, Mantis frantically slammed her palm against the air conditioning vents in front of her. The cold air stopped, and now blazing heat blew from the slots. "Son of a *bitch*," she grumbled, sinking in her seat, defeated. She twirled the knob to the *off* position.

Betty rolled down the windows and accelerated, flexing her jaw. "We need a new vehicle."

Sweet Tea warbled along to a twangy country song that came through the radio in spotty waves between bits of static, pretending she was giving Dylan a private, personal concert. *"She was amazin', ba-by! Made me high as a kite. I go back. Oh yeah, that's right. Cause..."* Sweet Tea crooned louder, *"There just ain't no rehab for a drug like her."*

Dylan laughed.

She stretched his arm and strummed it. "Time for the *gee-tar* solo!" She didn't miss a note, pressing the tendons of his wrist like strings.

Mantis turned down the radio. "How can you listen to this garbage?"

"I love it!" Sweet Tea said. "Speaks to me."

Betty squirmed wildly in the driver's seat.

"You okay, Bet?" Sweet Tea seemed concerned.

"Yeah, I really gotta go. Been holdin' it in since Post."

"Number one? Or..." Mantis looked at her.

"You're *talkin'* to me now?" Betty snarled.

Mantis exhaled a deep sigh and looked away.

"Pull over and go," Dylan said.

"Where?" Betty motioned to the barren landscape. "No cover. No privacy."

"Go anywhere. This is Texas; the whole state's a toilet," Mantis mumbled.

"Awwww! Look at that!" Sweet Tea pointed to something up ahead. "He's sooooo cute!"

Dylan scrunched his nose. "What *is* it?"

"It's an armadillo!"

The gray, armored creature scurried along the roadside as if it were trying to keep up with the truck.

"Whoa, I've never seen one of those *alive* before." Dylan squinted.

Suddenly, the animal panicked, launching itself into the road.

Betty swerved and slammed on the brakes, but she was too late.

THUD.

The truck struck it, and the animal belted out a quick, pig-like squeal of terror. Betty threw the truck into park, and everyone piled out.

Dylan, Sweet Tea, and Mantis hovered around the dying creature. After a moment, Sweet Tea screamed, "You *hit* it, Betty! Why?!"

But Betty wasn't there.

Mantis scanned the field, suddenly flashing back to Gabriel's sudden disappearance. "Betty?!"

She walked around the truck to find Betty squatting over the ground, capris and lace panties in a bundle by her ankles, covering her privates modestly with a splayed hand. "Go away! I'm," she lowered her head, *"peeing."*

Mantis erupted in an involuntary chuckle and walked back to the animal.

Dylan stared at the dying thing with reverence, "He's in pain. We need to put him out of his misery."

Sweet Tea clung to Dylan's chest, tears dragging mascara down her face like Tammy-Faye Baker.

"We need to bury him," Sweet Tea managed through the tears.

"I don't think we should touch him, baby girl." Betty rubbed her back.

"Yeah, don't those things spread leprosy and shit?" Mantis shielded her eyes from the brutal sun.

"I don't care. I'm not going anywhere until he gets a proper burial."

***

Fifteen minutes later, the gang gathered around a small hole in the arid earth. Inside, the partially flattened armadillo was curled like a roly-poly over the in-ground pool brochures they'd found on the Chevy's floorboards.

Sweet Tea looked around at the others, eyes red from mourning. "Someone should say a few words."

Dylan touched his nose, and Betty did the same. When Mantis realized they were "not it," she groaned. "Aw! C'mon!" She rolled her head to look at Sweet Tea, who was staring pitifully. "*Goddammit.*" She stepped forward lackadaisically. "Um. May the little fella rest in peace. We hope he's in Heaven... where he can't dart in front of any more pickup trucks. Ave Maria, sign'a the cross, Hare Krishna, and all that good stuff. Can we *go* now? Or do we need to sit shiva for this little fuck, too?"

"Can we stop for something to eat? I'm starving." Dylan leaned forward, placing his head between Betty and Mantis.

"Everything's closed. I'm hungry, too." Betty eyed the signs as she drove through a patch of congested traffic. They had finally reached the outskirts of Temple in all its barren glory.

"We should've eaten the armadillo." Mantis shook her head.

"No. No, we *shouldn't* have," Betty grumbled.

"Turn right... onto *Field Road*." The robotic GPS barked. Betty obeyed.

"I'd settle for a convenience store. My stomach's touchin' my spine," Dylan whined. He leaned forward and pressed his face to Mantis's headrest. Sweet Tea rubbed his back. He looked back at her and managed a smile. Her hair was down, driving him wild, wanting to run his fingers through it.

"If you see anything open, point, and we'll stop. Promise," Betty said, changing lanes.

"I could go for a hot dog right now. Tons of relish. *Lotsa* mayo. *Mmmm!*" Sweet Tea licked her full lips.

"What kind of a *monster* are you, Tea? Who the fuck puts *mayo* on a hot dog?" Mantis chewed her thumbnail. "They're disgusting enough as-*is*."

The filthy pickup slowed in the driveway of another massive estate. Betty threw it in park, killed the engine, and hopped out. The others followed.

"Do we have any sort of a *plan* with this guy?" Betty looked at Mantis.

Mantis plucked a blooming lily from the manicured patch of garden along the paver path and carried it up the porch steps, spinning it in between her fingers. "Girl, we ain't had a plan this whooooole time. I say we just wing it again."

Mantis tossed the flower in the air, clasped her hands together, and blasted the lily onto the lush lawn, using her arms as a baseball bat. She cupped her hands around her mouth and, in a half-whisper-half-scream, said, "*Ahhhhhhhh! And the crowd goes *wild*."

"Are you still *drunk*?" Betty didn't find the humor in it. She pressed the bell.

The deadbolt clicked. A security monitor beeped. The door swung wide. In the entryway, two towering men in all black hoisted their semi-automatic weapons and pointed them at their unwelcome guests. Biceps and jaws flexed as they clutched the matching matte-black AK-47s.

Mantis stepped forward casually. "Hi." She pointed to the barrel of one man's gun. "Ooh, *nice*. That an *A-K*?"

The man was not amused.

"Matches your outfit. You do that on purpose?" Mantis swallowed hard through the silence. "We're just here in the neighborhood, you know, to, uh, ask if you've accepted Jesus Christ as your Lord and *personal* savior."

The taller of the men aimed his gun right at Mantis.

"You know what?" Mantis stepped back. "It looks like you're all set. Thanks for your time."

The shorter henchman snatched up Mantis by the front of her crop top and shoved her inside. The taller one waved his gun, using the muzzle to threaten the others to follow suit. They obliged, hands lifted like hostages.

The gaggle soldiered down the hallway, and the men thrust them toward the room at the end.

"Alright," Mantis groaned. "Relax, short stuff. We all get it. You have a Napoleonic complex."

Without a word, the misfits were forced into a posh living room. The gunmen took their posts at the only way in or out. Beams of warm daylight danced off white walls, glistening across freshly waxed hardwood. Mantis eyed the white shelves, sandwiching a prominent ivory fireplace. Vibrant abstract paintings and a decorative rug added pops of saturated color through the otherwise sterile-looking room. Two white couches sat in the middle, uninviting and pristine.

An old man was seated at the table next to the bay window overlooking a well-watered farmstead. The sun's rays tickled the lapels of his exquisite Merino wool suit. His sagging eyes were transfixed on the flat screen mounted to the wall set to a low volume.

On it, the evangelist, Jeremiah Munsey, passionately shouted something at the audience in his outrageously large auditorium. Nina Hartley responded into her own mic, and the crowd cheered, raising their hands in worship.

"Ah, *zdravstvujtye!*" The old man finally looked at them, offering a greeting in Russian.

Mantis looked at Betty. "Ah, *fuck*. He doesn't speak English." Mantis looked at Dylan. "Hey, nerd? Any chance you took Russian in high school?"

Dylan stepped forward and bowed, struggling to return the greeting, "Drah…Drastv—"

"Jesus, Dylan, did you just *curtsy*?" Mantis lolled her neck in a display of irritation. She stepped toward the Russian, hearing the metallic shift of the gunmen pointing two semi-automatics at her back. She patted herself on the chest with a flattened palm. "*Hello!* My name is *Man-tis*." She spoke slow and loud as if saying it to an infant.

He spoke with a Russian accent so thick Mantis could barely understand, "I… speak… *English.*"

"Oh, thank *God,*" Mantis clutched her chest and laughed.

The shorter henchman spoke. "Were you expecting company, sir?"

"I vas not," The Russian said.

"Are you *Yarost?*"

He nodded and leaned back in his priceless-looking chair. "Have you come for the *drugs* or the *wodka*?"

"What the hell is *wodka*?" Mantis scrunched her face.

Yarost repeated the word. "No, *wodka*." As if repeating it somehow made it another word.

The taller henchman spoke, his Slavic accent thick as well. "He say… *vodka.*"

Mantis stuck her bottom jaw out. "Ohhhhhh! Hell yeah! I'd love some *wodka*."

"Mr. Yarost—" Betty started.

"Yarost, please, *only* Yarost." His wrinkled hand of paper-thin skin shook in the air.

"Yarost, we've actually come for a *different* reason." Betty placed her hands on the back of one of the white couches and squeezed until her knuckles matched.

"Yes, but we can talk about that *and* drink wodka. It's called *multitasking.*" Mantis stuck her hands in the pockets of her shorts, catching a faint whiff of dead cowboy emanating from all of them. She hoped the old man wouldn't notice.

"Didn't you get that out of your system last night? You were just throwing up a few hours ago."

"Doll, you're livin' in the *past.* That was then. This is *now.* The man's offerin' us wodka, *'kay?* Let's not be *rude.*" Mantis stared at Betty.

"Dah-lings, *hvatit.*" He struggled to rise from his chair. "Stop. *Please.*" The Russian seemed frail. He had to be in his seventies. He shuffled to a cabinet beneath the screen. A large cache of vodka bottles sat inside. He plucked one from the shelf, struggled to read the label, grabbed a few shot glasses from a rack on the cupboard door, and waddled back to the table. "*Zis* my own signature *wodka.* I make from potatoes and *'ze* corn *ve* grow right here."

Yarost motioned out the bay window. Neat rows of potato plant foliage and corn stalks disappeared into the vast acreage beyond. He filled the glasses and held two in the air. Mantis grinned and passed them out. The henchmen pointed their muzzles at her the entire way.

"I shouldn't. I'm driving." Betty politely refused hers.

"She really *shouldn't*. If you think she's a bitch sober, wait til she drinks." The jab had some venom to it.

Yarost thrust himself onto his feet and screamed, commanding their attention. "I said fucking *drink!*"

Mantis raised her brows and smiled nervously. "*Woo!* Got a bit of a *temper* there!"

The tall guard shoved the butt of his AK-47 into Betty's back. She took the shot glass and faked a smile, but inside, she was terrified. The gun in her back wasn't helping matters.

Finally, with a shot glass in every hand, Yarost hoisted his own in the air. "*Na zdorovie!*"

Mantis tried to repeat the word. "Nos-drove-me!" She sucked the shot back. Her face contorted in a look of disgust.

"*Vat*? You no like my *wodka*?" Yarost seemed offended.

"No! No, your *wodka* is *fine*. Damn *good*, even. I just," she tried not to gag, "always seem to make that face when I drink booze."

"She does," Dylan said with a nod. "She was doing it at the bar last night, too."

Yarost poured himself another shot. He held it high and looked straight through it, admiring the clarity. "If you enjoy my *wodka*, you *vill* surely love *zeh* cocaine."

"Yeah, shit," Mantis clapped her hands together giddily, "I haven't done snow in a dog's age. Are we really doin' this?"

Betty pinched the bridge of her nose. This woman was going to give her an aneurysm.

He shoved a refill at Mantis. "Ano-zer!"

Mantis stared at him, not taking it.

Silence.

"It *vasn't* a *qvestion,*" he screamed.

"Yeah, one more. Sure." A little thrown, Mantis looked at the design on the glass. A goat head in an upside-down star. It was similar to the symbol she'd seen on the baggie of cocaine in the Tax Man's warehouse. And on the bizarre statue in Hank's display case...

Mantis tossed the shot back and grimaced again as she choked it down. Yarost burst into laughter and slapped his scrawny knee.

"You *do* make *zeh* face every time!" He filled her glass again.

"Oh, no, I'm good. We're just here to—"

"*Nonsense.* I *vant* to see ze ugly *face* again."

"I'm going to *excuse* that comment and chalk it up to some sort of *language* barrier." As she held the third drink, the first hit her belly like a warm bomb, exploding in her empty stomach. She drank the shot and made the sourest face yet. "No more. I'm a projectile vomiter. So unless you want your couch to look like more like a Van Gogh—"

"Okay, *ve* stop now," he conceded, giggling like a kid. Yarost set the bottle down.

Mantis's gaze drifted to a wall adorned with a vast collection of weapons from around the world.

"May I?" She asked, pointing to the wall of weaponry.

"Sure!"

She examined a mounted soviet rifle. The barrel, the stock, the engravings...

And there it was. On the shelf below, close to the mantle of the fireplace.

The gold talisman they so desperately sought.

"Oh my God, Yarost. This! We're actually here for *this… talisman thing.*" Mantis pointed to the gold piece.

"*Zat* is *not* a talisman, my dear," Yarost chuckled. "Zat is a *reliquary*. Zer' is a difference." His words whistled. "A talisman is a piece of stone or metal, like your lucky American horseshoes or the pope's ring. A reliquary is *a container.*"

Warmth. The second and third shots hit Mantis's stomach like a woof of fire.

"A container for *what*?" The alcohol wasn't making understanding this any easier.

"*Vell,* some hold bones or fabric of a saint's clothes. *Zere* was one in *zeh* Notre Dame church in Paris *zat* held *ze* crown of Jesus."

"Mmm-hmmm," she said in disbelief. "So what would *this* reliquary hold?" Mantis lifted Yarost's golden wad of metal.

Yarost shrugged and started back toward his chair. "I do not know. It *vas* entrusted to me some time ago by strange *voman*."

"A *voman*, you say?" She mocked playfully. "How about you entrust it to *this voman*, and I give you some cash and then take my merry band of weirdos out the way we came?"

Yarost only laughed.

"How much you want for it?" Mantis stared at the gold shard, desire in her eyes. The potent liquor swept through like her insides had been rinsed in Novocaine.

Yarost grew quiet. "*Vy* would I *vant* your money? I have *everyzing* I *vant* right here."

"What about *sex*? Everyone loves sex." Mantis pointed to Sweet Tea. "Eh? Probably been a while since anyone that hot handled those dusty prunes, am I right?"

Yarost scoffed, displeased.

"What about *him*?"

Dylan's eyes grew wide and horrified.

"You more a fan of salami than salmon? I go *both* ways. I get it."

"Mantis!" Dylan protested quietly.

Mantis whispered, "Hey, it's not that bad, kid. I promise I'll buy you a donut after."

"I'm not some hooker you can bribe with snacks!" Dylan stomped his alligator-skin boot on the word *snacks* with a *clomp*.

"Not to *eat*, you dipshit. To *sit on*."

"I'm not gonna have SEX with a *man*, Mantis." Dylan turned to Yarost. His tone completely shifted. "Even though I'm sure you're a *real* catch, sir."

"Dylan, be a *team player*. Have you ever *done it* with a dude before?"

"No!"

"Then how do you know you wouldn't like it? Hmmm?" Mantis looked smug. "Don't knock it till you try it. I'm pretty sure that's one of the Ten Commandments."

Yarost yelled over the squabbling, "I *vill not* have *sex vith zeh* boy!"

"*Thank you*, sir!" Dylan exhaled, relieved.

"Well, we're at a bit of an *impasse* because we've come way *too far* to leave empty-handed." Mantis held out her hand. "Betty, give me the talisman… or *reliquary*… or whatever the *fuck* it's called."

Betty dug through her purse and handed their piece to Mantis. She took it, setting their hunk next to the shorn end of Yarost's shard. The pieces melded together as if by some miraculous force. Light danced off its molten surface as the ends entwined like lovers. Though odd and still incomplete, the act was magnificent. The scrolled detail was sealed as if it had never been separated.

Mantis tried to pick it up. It burned her palm, and she clumsily fumbled it to the wood floor with a hard *bwong*.

"Guess only one of us is getting it now. Which one's it gonna be, *gramps*?" Mantis squatted, feeling the full effect of the vodka. She blew on it with sloppy mouthfuls of air, trying to cool the metal enough to pick it up.

Yarost stepped forward, hate brewing like a turbulent storm within him. The blood in his veins coursed hard, so hard that it made him ache all over. His vision blurred from the unadulterated rage. *"Vat have you DONE?!"*

The sound of metal and fabric rustled through the silence, and once again, Mantis found herself on the wrong side of guns that were locked and loaded. Mantis could tell the shorter guard was itching to pull the trigger.

Yarost stared at the reliquary, suddenly reminded of the promise of power it came with.

Mantis gave Betty a subtle look across the room. Betty stared back blankly, sure that meant Mantis had some sort of hair-brained plan.

CRACK! The sound of wood busting echoed through the mammoth room. Yarost's withered hands held a broken piece of the table beneath him. Dylan's eyes bulged at the sudden, almost inhuman display of the Russian's brute strength.

Mantis turned to the armed men and smiled. "I'm going to ask you one more time. May I hold your gun?" She pointed to the shorter man's AK-47. "*Please.*"

After a moment of tense silence, Mantis grinned. "Well, can't say I didn't ask nicely."

Mantis kicked the scorching reliquary across the floor. It settled beneath one of the immaculate couches. Betty dropped to the floor to retrieve it.

Mantis grabbed the smaller henchman's rifle by the barrel, whipped him out into the middle of the room with all her might, and kicked the henchman squarely in the testicles with her combat boot. His chewing gum hurtled across the room, and he doubled over in crippling pain. She whipped the strap over his head and stepped back. She smashed the stock of it into the face of the other gunman, dropping him before he had a chance to fire.

"You *bitch*," he screamed from the floor, clutching his nose with a hand now slick with gushing blood.

On her knees, Betty blindly scoured beneath the couch for the reliquary, anxiety mounting, feeling nothing but floorboard with her fingertips.

The still-armed gunman aimed at Mantis. She ducked behind the other couch for cover just as he opened fire, peppering the walls with a rain of bullets that detonated the sheetrock like little plaster bombs.

Dylan's alligator-skin boot smashed into the barrel of the taller henchman's gun, blasting it out of the man's grip. Dylan picked it up and pointed it at him. The big man's hands raised in submission.

Still in the chaos, Yarost slowly aimed a remote at the fireplace. The fire suddenly roared to life in the hearth behind Mantis. He hurled the broken wooden table at her with an almost supernatural strength, and it tumbled powerfully as if it were made of cheap plastic. It slammed into the fireplace, shattering into thick hunks.

Yarost skittered to the cabinet and hurled a full bottle of vodka at Mantis. She dodged, and it exploded on the floor in front of the crackling fireplace, spattering liquid in every direction. The fire instantly expanded out into the room with a *WOOF*. Flickering orange flames lapped up the potent liquor and continued up Mantis's back.

She screamed in pain, dropped the gun, and rolled across the floor to snuff the flame. The fire on her body went out instantly, but the couch erupted into a flaming mound of stuffing and fabric.

Mantis scrambled for the AK-47, but the smaller henchman snatched it first. She rolled onto her back and kicked the weapon with both feet. It slapped against the floor in the entrance. Mantis and the henchman scrambled for their life toward the rifle, clamoring to see who would get to it first.

Mantis was so close she could almost taste it when the henchman dove onto her and latched his hands around her throat. She clasped her hands onto his wrists and slammed her boot heel into his inner thigh near his balls, dropping him to the floor in agony. Before he could blink, she was on him, powerful legs hugging him like a straight jacket.

Betty pressed her body to the plaster-speckled floor, spotted the reliquary, and scooped

187

it up. Still hot to the touch, she slapped it into her open purse with a shaky hand. She snatched up an area rug and tossed it over the blazing couch, tamping it down to prevent the inferno from spreading. Smoke filled the air.

The henchman growled and tapped a hand blindly behind him, feeling for the gun. Mantis forced him down, their bodies tangled in a mess of bent extremities. She pulled until she felt his arm lock. Then, she rolled back and pulled his arm straight with every ounce of force she could muster. She didn't stop until his arm released backward, caving in on itself, no longer held in place by rigid bone.

"Ahhhhhhhhh!" His voice bellowed in agony.

Dylan grimaced as the man's ulna and radius broke like dry tree branches.

"Go stand over there by your little Russian buddy." Dylan motioned with the AK for the larger of the henchmen to join Yarost. He wiped the trail of blood dribbling from his busted nose and hesitantly complied.

Yarost locked his wrinkled eyes on Betty.

Mantis released the smaller henchman's arm, and he tucked it like a bird wing to shelter it from further trauma.

Mantis picked up the rifle they'd been scrambling for. "See? You should have let me hold it when I *asked*."

Without another word, Mantis fired three consecutive bullets directly into the henchman's head.

BAM! BAM! BAM!

The force spattered brain matter and skull fragments onto the hardwood, and he dropped with a *clunk*, like a cord of wood. She marched with purpose, muzzle drifting toward Yarost. "Thanks for the vodka, asshole."

As she pulled the trigger, Yarost shoved the larger, looming henchman in front of himself.

Mantis had already put several bullets in the goon before she fully understood what she'd just seen.

The old bastard was *fast*; she'd give him that.

Mantis fired again.

Click-click-click-click.Out of ammo.

"*Fuck!*" Mantis roared.

Yarost heaved the slumped-and-dying henchman, knocking Dylan backward with the dying oaf's body. Yarost spryly launched himself through the bay window.

SMASH!

The old man crashed through onto the dry soil.

"Oh no, you fuckin' *don't*!" Mantis screamed. She threw down the AK and raced toward the battered window.

Yarost was already racing away, disappearing into the neat rows of corn as fast as his geriatric legs would take him.

Dylan stood again, now soaked in the henchman's warm blood. Without a word, he tossed his gun to Mantis. She tossed the strap over her head and jumped onto the ledge of the bay window. She dove through, picked herself off the glass-covered ground, and shot into the cornfield. Halfway down a row, she stopped in her tracks and aimed the rifle at him. He was nearing the edge of the cornfield and would soon be too hard to spot. She fired several shots. Orange dirt exploded into the air with every miss.

She screamed, frustrated with her aim, and raced faster, hoping to close the gap between them.

She stopped and fired again, this time taking the old man down. Yarost dropped like a brick and clutched his leg in pain.

She made her way toward him, out of breath, jogging briskly. "Why you gotta make me run? That was just *dumb*."

She poked the muzzle at the wound in his leg, and Yarost bellowed, sending a murder of crows in a nearby tree squawking as they fled.

"If there's three things I *hate* in this world, it's… morning people, fake tits, and *running*."

Yarost cackled through the pain. "I vill see you in hell."

"*Can't wait*." Mantis pointed the gun at his head and, without any hesitation, pulled the trigger.

BOOM!

His laughter died immediately.

She smacked her forehead and looked down at the Yarost's slain corpse. "Oh, and *needles*. I friggin' *hate* needles. So, I guess *four* things."

***

Mantis started back down the field toward Yarost's house, bee-lining for the shattered window. Betty snickered as Mantis kicked a random potato plant in anger, muttering a string of expletives.

Suddenly, Dylan noticed something rushing through the cornfield behind her at breakneck speed.

"Mantis!" Before he could say more, a locust-legged demon leaped from between rows of tall cornstalks, slamming her forward like a loosed bowling ball, flattening plants in their wake.

It hobbled onto its slimy black feet and jumped into the air like a grasshopper, screeching loudly. Mantis fired the AK-47 into its chest.

Bullets screamed through the air as Mantis took out her every frustration on the beast. It stuttered in the air with every bullet and flopped onto the ground, smashing foliage. Mantis grabbed the gun by the muzzle and pounded the stock into the thing's head repeatedly until it cratered in.

Mantis looked at Dylan and Betty, completely out of breath. Dripping sweat matted hunks of her short, black hair against her face. She blew a drop of perspiration off the tip of her nose. She looked back down and hit it once more, full-force, for good measure.

Inside a luxurious glass shower in the upstairs bathroom, Dylan scrubbed blood from his skin. Savoring the rich soap, the steaming water made him feel like a new man. The event was almost a spiritual experience, like the times he'd seen a new convert immersed in the *Mikveh*.

He closed his eyes hard and recalled the dream of Sweet Tea, every detail still vivid. Part of him had hoped it would fade fast. The other part hoped it *never* would, indelibly stamping his mind like a tattoo.

He remembered the feel of her soft, tan skin beneath the tips of his trembling fingers and that smile of hers that could bring a *king* to his knees.

"Lord *almighty!*" Betty u-turned like she'd just slammed headfirst into a wall.

His eyes bolted open, and his hands covered himself. But the damage was done. *She'd seen everything.* "*Betty!*"

"Dylan, I'm… I don't…" She stumbled over the words.

"Why doesn't anyone fucking *knock* anymore? Jesus, what did you *see?*" Dylan was mortified.

"Pretty much… everything." Betty shielded her eyes with her hand and stared into the nearby closet.

"*Great.*" Dylan laughed, olive cheeks stained red with embarrassment. "Now everyone in this group's   seen   my dick 'cept *literally* the *only* person I actually want to show it to."

"So…   how   come…   you   and Tea *aren't* dating again?" Betty tried to contain her laughter, picking nervously at a suit's stray string.

Dylan rinsed the lather from his black curls and shut the water off, wrapping himself in a nearby towel. "That's the million-dollar question, isn't it?"

"You should do something romantic. Like a grand gesture."

"Mantis said girls don't really dig that stuff."

"Pfft, what the heck does *Mantis* know? Do you think *she's* qualified to speak for someone like *Sweet Tea*? Trust me. Women can't resist a grand gesture. They just can't."

Dylan nodded, taking it all in as he toweled himself dry.

"And put this on." Betty slid an expensive suit roughly Dylan's size through the gap in the door.

"I'll be *way* overdressed."

"Dylan, in the words of ZZ Top, Every girl's crazy 'bout a sharp-dressed man."

***

"I'm not gonna eat a raw potato, Mantis," Sweet Tea said, disgusted.

"Don't be a pussy." Mantis took a bite of the raw potato like an apple. "It's like... fries, just... you know, rare," she said, crunching through a mouthful.

"Look at this body, Mantis. Do I look like I eat a lot of *fries*?" Sweet Tea lifted the front of her tank top, showing off her taut abdomen.

"Mmm, *damn* girl! Whaddaya say we go find ourselves a *room*?"

"Girl, you *know* I am strictly-dickly."

"Coulda fooled *me*. Dylan's been trying to give you his kosher sausage, and you've shown zero interest." Mantis popped the potato in the air a few times like a ball. "That sap's been followin' you around, fighting demons and drug lords, and still thinks the sun rises and sets over you. If you don't wanna be with him, sit his ass down and be crystal clear. Otherwise, you're wasting his time. Gonna get the damn kid killed, followin' you…"

Sweet Tea slapped her hands on the counter. "The *last* person I would ever take relationship advice from is *you*."

"Why? I have relationships all the time." Mantis grabbed two more russets and started juggling them.

"One-night stands don't count." Sweet Tea said smugly. "The last—"

SMASH!

Out of the blue, Mantis pitched a second potato at another glass cabinet like a baseball, shattering the china beyond. Shards of broken glassware tinkled onto the floor.

SMASH!

She threw her last one and turned to Sweet Tea, "Sorry, you were *saying*?"

"I was saying your last relationship, *hell*, the *only* one I've ever seen you have… didn't end well. So you shouldn't be dishing out advice, Dr. Ruth."

As soon as she saw the hurt in Mantis's eyes, Sweet Tea covered her mouth, wishing she could suck the words back inside.

"Grace didn't kill herself because I was some shitty partner, Tea, so get your facts straight. You don't know anything *about* what we had."

"I'm sorry."

"No, you wanna open this can of worms and blame me for her pulling the most selfish stunt in existence? Well, you should know it wasn't because I treated her poorly. She killed herself because I told her I got knocked up."

The silence was long and painful.

Mantis leaned forward. "Happy *now*?"

Betty burst through the entry, full of excitement. "I now present to you *Dylan 2.0.* Ta-dah!" Betty waved her hands, and Dylan walked into the kitchen. He looked stylish in Yarost's suit. "I couldn't get him to lose the gator boots, but… whaddaya think? This suit costs seven *grand*."

Sweet Tea didn't look. Her eyes were locked on the tiled island, fingers fidgeting with a potato.

"*Great*." Mantis seethed, "Can we fuckin' go now?" She grabbed a bottle of vodka from the counter and offered a pained smile. "Ya' clean up nice, kid."

As she walked out of the room, Betty knitted her brows in confusion. "What's up with y'all?"

"Don't worry about it." Sweet Tea didn't look up.

"Y'all find any food?" Dylan asked.

"Not unless you're hungry for raw potatoes." Sweet Tea mumbled.

"Ooh, I could probably whip up some *latkes*," Dylan offered with a smile. No one spoke. "On second thought, maybe we hit the road and get somethin' on the way."

***

Yarost's garage was home to a bevy of immaculate luxury cars.

"Ooooh baby, eenie, meenie, miney, *moe.*" Mantis whistled at the sexy lineup before them. "I'm all for whichever one has air-conditioning and no dead Texans smeared into the upholstery."

"This is the one." Betty beamed. One had caught her eye immediately. It was a sleek, black convertible. Freshly washed with smooth curves.

"Well, what mama wants, mama gets." Mantis pulled a set of keys off the wall under the label that read *Mustang* and tossed them to Betty.

Betty ran a finger along the chrome grill, seated herself in the driver's seat, adjusted the mirror, and said, "Let's go get my *son.*"

The convertible cruised down a long, straight stretch of highway. Despite the distance between Gabe's abduction site and their present location growing, something about the journey felt correct. It was as if the further they went, the closer she felt, in her heart, to finding him. She was skeptical at first, but there were too many things she couldn't explain away as mere coincidences.

Demons, earthquakes, looting, chaos...

These indeed were strange times they were living in.

The sign in whizzing by made her smile:

Welcome to Louisiana.

Laissez les bon temps rouler!

They were out of Texas, finally. The scenery had changed drastically in a short time. The landscape had rolled from a barren flatland into foliage-filled swamps. The setting sun in the sky felt threatening. Sooty clouds loomed over a string of overturned vehicles along a treacherous mile-long crevasse gouged in the westbound lanes.

"Jesus, the earthquakes have done a number on this place." Mantis let her unlit cigarette dangle from her lips as she lit it. She took a puff, scissoring the butt between two wispy fingers, and watched another fast food joint fly past with a CLOSED sign in its window. "I don't get it. Why is *everything* shut down? People still gotta eat."

"We'll find something soon. Louisiana doesn't play around. Cajuns love their food." Betty smiled, thinking about all the po boys she'd demolished on her last visit. "Haven't been here since before Gabriel was born."

"I've never been." Dylan watched a clump of cypress trees whirr by, wooden knees jutting out of the water at the base of their trunks. "At least there's something to *look at,* finally."

Sweet Tea mumbled, "We gotta stop at a grocery store or something. My blood sugar's *tanked.* I feel sick."

"Hey, I offered to make *latkes.*" Dylan forced a soft smile.

Sweet Tea was silent. She couldn't look at him. Mantis was right. She *had* to make her position clear to him.

Betty swerved onto an exit. Mantis grabbed the dashboard, bracing herself against the force.

"Jesus Bet, where'd you learn how to drive?"

"We could always swap," Betty sassed. "*You* could drive, and I could blow enough secondhand smoke at *you* to give you lung cancer."

"I got somethin' you can *blow.*"

The vehicle slowed at the base of the ramp.

"*Eunice.* We made it." Betty swerved hard around the remains of a car that had undoubtedly been crushed by a flaming meteor.

"Slow down! Jesus, it's bad enough we got demons and Russians and accountants and pimps trying to kill us. Now we gotta add *you* to the list," Mantis exclaimed, clutching the dash and door.

"I want my *son.* I want a *po boy.* I want to sleep in my *own* bed, in my own *home.* And I want to get this stupid piece of gold for… *whatever* reason. I don't even *know* what we're collecting this thing for! A dream you had?

We're shedding blood on a *hunch*!" Betty's eyes filled with tears.

"Chill out! Your hands are *clean*," Mantis cooed, trying to calm her.

"I just… I want Gabe back! I need to know he's *okay*. I can't take any more of the killing, the drama, or this hunger right now." Betty blinked. Inky tears streaked down her hot cheeks.

"Look." Mantis turned to her in her seat. "The sign back there said there's a hotel a half mile away. Let's get you checked in, and the rest of us'll go get the reliquary. You can take a *bubble bath* or read your *bible* or *masturbate* or whatever the fuck it is that you *do* to relax."

The light turned green. Betty looked at Mantis like a beaten pup and nodded weakly. She made the turn and barrelled down the road toward the hotel.

"We're gonna get him back, Bet. I promise. Or so help me *God*, I will *die trying*."

"616 Elmwood Road." Mantis held the handwritten paper in front of a modest home in the shadow of two willowy trees. It didn't fit the middle-class feel of the rest of the neighborhood.

Daylight was disappearing, giving the unkempt yard and all of its clutter a somewhat spooky aura.

Dylan, Mantis, and Sweet Tea hopped over a drainage ditch onto the grass. On the porch, Dylan examined some peeling paint on the siding of the neglected house. "This place looks foreclosed."

Mantis knocked. *Silence.*

She pounded harder and then flicked a crawling insect away from her torn fishnet-clad calves. "*Please* be home."

Sweet Tea spotted a pile of packages mounded by the door. She read one aloud. "*Maxcollect75?*"

"Probably his e-commerce handle. Looks like he might have a bit of a spending problem from the looks of it." Dylan tore his eyes from the pile and turned to Mantis. "Hey, if he answers, can I take the reins on this one?"

Mantis looks pleasantly surprised. "Yeah? All yours, kid."

Dylan pounded on the door, rattling the glass of the tiny built-in windows at the top. "Max! Max, bud, you in there?"

After a few more silent seconds, the door cracked open. A sickly-looking man peered through the chain-locked gap between the door and its frame with sunken, beet-red eyes.

"Max! Buddy! It's been years!" Dylan exclaimed like he'd grown up with the man. "What's it been? Ten, *twelve years*? How ya been?"

"Do I... know you?" The voice was meek.

"Dude! We went to high school together! It's me, *Dylan*!"

"Oh." The man nervously chuckled. "Yeah, I think I *do* remember you, Dylan."

"You gonna let us in or not?"

Mantis had never seen Dylan so confident before. She stood in silent awe of what she was witnessing.

"Who are *they*?" The man's eyes darted to the women.

"They're my friends. Open up, man. I'll explain everything. We drove a long way to see you." Dylan's tone was genuine and friendly.

The door rammed shut. The chain slid, and the door creaked all the way open. The man inside was a bag of bones in desperate need of a haircut. His long, scraggly locks were as neglected as his yard. His pasty skin was so white it was almost transparent. He waved a bony arm, motioning for them to follow him in. "Come in, come in."

The spindly man led them down a cluttered hallway stacked with mountains of dusty newspapers and old magazines.

Mantis flashed Dylan an ultra-impressed look. They silently performed their secret handshake. Sweet Tea rolled her eyes.

Max's living room, if one could call it that, was anything but livable. He'd taken hoarding to a new extreme. The space was littered with floor-to-ceiling boxes, stacked records, heaped textiles, precariously balanced knick-knacks, and a boat-load of collectibles in their original packaging.

"Sorry 'bout the mess." He pushed over a stack of junk and laughed. "There's a couch around here somewhere, I promise."

"Got a lotta cool stuff here, Max," Dylan lied, eyeing the disgusting amount of hoarded clutter.

The man beamed at the compliment. His head popped up behind a tall stack of accumulated items like a sallow gopher. "Thanks!" Max heaved an armful of hardcovers onto another pile, "it's my little treasure trove."

"That it certainly *is*." Dylan fought the urge to wince at the man's golem-like features.

"Sit." Max patted the dingy couch cushion he'd excavated from the heap.

The red flag with a goat's head and upside-down star on a wall caught Mantis's eye. "That symbol. What is that? I've been seeing it *everywhere*."

Max smiled at it like an old friend. "That's *Baphomet*."

Mantis made a strange face, unwilling to try to pronounce it.

"It's the sabbatic goat. It's the heathen idol for occultism and mysticism. That thing symbolizes the sum of the universe. Men and women, good and evil, yada yada." Max waved his hand as if he didn't care to go on.

"So it's like a fugly *yin-yang*?"

He laughed a little. "Sort of. It's used in Satanism and all that." Max sifted through a similarly disorganized heap, searching for another seat to offer his standing guests.

"So judging from the big ass *flag*, I take it you're a Satanist, then?" Mantis tried to sound casual so as not to spook him.

"I was pretty hardcore into it for a while. It's crazy what a man'll do to impress a woman."

Betty and Mantis's eyes shifted to Dylan. He wiped a small cockroach off the strap of Max's stained wife-beater. "Chin up. Some girls just don't know how to appreciate a good thing when it's right in front of them." Dylan looked at Sweet Tea, making sure to drive the point home.

"You said it…"

"Dylan."

"Dylan. Yeah, you said it, Dylan. I mean, I joined the Church of Satan for a while, *the whole nine.* I mean," Max laughed nervously, "I was gonna sacrifice *animals* for this broad. Speakin' of, there's a dog runnin' 'round here somewhere. He's little, so just watch where you step. He likes to get underfoot." He raised onto his toes and scanned the room. "Ain't seen him in a while, though."

"So this girl—" Dylan changed the subject.

"Ah, yeah. Turns out she was fuckin' 'round with some Anton LaVey-lookin' dick she met off *Devil Date.* Lyin' whore…"

"*Devil Date?*" Mantis wondered just how much deeper the insanity would get.

"Yeah, Devildate.com. It's for followers of the Dark Lord that wanna place to mingle without judgment." He suddenly found himself entranced by Dylan's suit. "Man, looks like you've really done well for yourself since I last saw ya." Max tugged at the lapel, pulling Dylan off-balance.

"That's not a cheap suit. I mean that style, that brand, we're talkin' $5700, at *least*."

"$7000. But who's counting?" Dylan smiled, thinking about the receipt he'd found in the bag with it that morning. New boots, new duds... maybe after the chaos settled down, he'd reinvent himself style-wise.

"Mmmm, maybe *retail*, but who's *dumb enough* to buy off the rack these days? Willin' to part with it? I could sell that online like *that*." He snapped his slim fingers. "Give you $500 for it. *Cash.* Right now." Peering up at Dylan, his eyes so brown they looked black in the dim room. "I don't need the shirt. Shirt's worthless. Could pick up one of those online for a few bucks. But the *jacket*... and the *pants*..."

Mantis flashed Dylan a smug look that said: *What now, leader?*

"Know what, Max?" Dylan sighed. "Actually, I *would* be willing to give you the suit. Absolutely." Dylan put his hands on his hips. "But... I don't want your money."

"Damn, boy!" Mantis howled out the dropped top of the black convertible as it barreled down the darkened, humid roads of Eunice. "You could talk the panties off a *nun*!"

Dylan sat in a pair of black boxer shorts, alligator boots, and nothing else. He fidgeted with the newly acquired portion of the golden reliquary.

"I admire you, kid. If it were me, I woulda threatened to burn that goddamn tinderbox to the ground. But you went in like a skilled surgeon and cut through all the bullshit with *precision*. No *murder*. No *arson*. No *guns in my face*. I love it, kid. It's fuckin' refreshing!"

Mantis dragged an Iron Pillar out of the pack with her lips and lobbed the smokes onto the center console. She yanked her Zippo out of her shorts pocket.

"You were," she said through the filter, "like the son I never h—" She stopped and cleared her throat, unwilling to finish the sentence. Instead, she said, "First round's on me tonight."

***

Mantis blew into the hotel room like a hurricane. Betty was on the bed, Bible in hand, watching television with a distraught expression. On TV, Jeremiah Munsey shouted with ferocity about the *mark of the true Christian*. Betty lowered the volume. "How'd it go?"

Mantis set down stuffed canvas totes on the second, still-made bed. "Seems ol' Dylan here has a talent for bullshit."

"Aww, shucks!" He waved her away.

"That didn't sound like a compliment." Betty watched Mantis intently.

"No, it *was*." Mantis grinned, rifling through the items. "It absolutely *was*."

"You get the…" Betty clicked her fingers, unable to remember what Yarost had called it. "The thing! The *gold* thing."

"The reliquary? No."

Silence. Stillness.

Then Mantis beamed pridefully. "But *he* did."

Dylan presented the hunk of scrolled gold to Betty, and she took it, overjoyed.

"That was *fast!*" Betty took it to the ornate box they'd acquired. She opened it and placed it beside the large, already-melded piece. The hot metal fused together in seconds.

They were close to completing it.

They only needed one more piece.

…But then what, Betty thought. She managed a weak smile and shut the box. "What's all that?"

"Food! Dylan literally traded the shirt off his back for it. Got that little fucker to throw in some canned shit to sweeten the deal."

Sweet Tea tossed Betty a can of beets. Betty looked at them and smiled. "Ooh, my favorite!"

"I know." Sweet Tea smiled and lowered herself into the chair by the door.

"Little weirdo gave us this, too." Mantis tossed her a can-opener. "He had *five* of them. Total hoarder." She tore into a can of mandarin oranges. "Poor Dylan needs some clothes. Left there with nothin' but skivvies and those stupid boots." Mantis waltzed out the open door and poured the sugary juice from the can over the railing onto the pool platform below. She walked back in and tossed the lid at the trash. She missed but made no attempt to pick it up. Betty stared at it, unable to focus on anything else.

Mantis twisted her fingers into a makeshift spoon and shoveled orange slices into her mouth like a ravenous animal.

"Shit," Mantis shoveled more, speaking through sloppy chews, "if Sweet Tea don't want ya, Dylan, I'll take ya." Mantis emitted an orgasmic moan into the can and downed the rest like a giant shot.

"Good Lord, Mantis." Betty twisted her face, "You look *feral*."

Sweet Tea cracked into a container of canned meat. She took a sniff and yanked it away from her face, appalled. She sniffed again and then groaned. "We got any forks?"

Betty searched the bags.

"Just eat it like me," Mantis said innocently.

"No, thanks. I'm not a *barbarian*. I'll find something." Sweet Tea set the can down on the nightstand, rifled through the bags, and clung to a box of plain crackers. "Yes!"

"Dylan, why aren't you eatin'?" Mantis asked, choking down another gob of food.

"I will. Ladies first. It's fine."

"Is this the same kid who was at the diner deep-throating fries like *Linda Lovelace?*"

"Well, right now, I'm not high as a kite off pot brownies either, *am I?*" Dylan chuckled.

"*Touché.*" Mantis smiled.

Betty cranked the volume on the television. Munsey pointed emphatically to the swarm of people seated in his colossal venue. Thousands of faces peered up from the crowd, hanging on his every word. "Nehemiah chapter nine, verse eighteen says: you did not desert them, even when they cast for themselves an image of a calf and said, 'This is your God, who brought you up out of Egypt,' or when they committed awful blasphemies." He scanned the crowd.

"This is because God, our God, the Almighty, he is a *forgiving* God. A *compassionate* God. A *gracious* God. He *knows* he made us all with imperfections. He *knows* we all have doubts. He *knows* that we don't always know the *right* way to go. They didn't either!" Munsey patted his forehead with a handkerchief from the front pocket of his pure-white suit jacket.

Nina Hartley flashed on the screen and raised her hands high, "*Amen!*"

"This is why verse nineteen goes on to say, 'Because of your great compassion, *oh Lord*, you did not abandon them in the wilderness!" Munsey's tone grew hushed. "He didn't abandon them. *No.*" He stuffed his handkerchief in his pocket and spoke louder. "*Then* it says, 'by day, the pillar of cloud did not fail to guide them on their path, nor the pillar of fire by night, to shine on the way they were to take.' It did not *fail* to guide them on their path. And you know what that means?" Munsey panted from his theatrical display. "God *is* the path!" He paused. "When you are lost, yes, he will lead you on the path of *righteousness*!"

The audience cheered.

"He will lead you! In these dark, troubling times, it may seem hopeless. But that storm cloud lingering overhead, it's not there to rain down on you, no." Munsey's voice boomed for the big finale. "It's no storm at all. It's a *beacon*! It's *God* showin' you *the way!*"

Mantis opened a can of carrots and drank the juice, eyes fixated on the screen.

Nina held up both hands. On her right palm, in bold, permanent marker, the numbers 9:19 were prominent. "God is showing you the way! Praise *Jesus*!" She pressed her palms together and chanted silently to herself.

Munsey shouted, "If you believe God is *the way*, hold up your right hands!" The camera flashed to the audience. Thousands of men and women waved their right hands.

"I know *I* believe that *God* is the way. He is the *path*. I want you to reach under your seats. You'll see a marker placed there. If you believe *God will lead you*, if you believe that *he is the way,* I want you to write chapter 9, verse 19 proudly. So that he can *see it from the Heavens!*"

Munsey held up his hand. He, too, had a bold 9:19 written in black on his palm.

The camera panned over the crowd, who obediently followed orders, scribbling numbers on their palms.

"Every time you look at that, I want you to remember you have *God on your side.* I want you to remember that he will *navigate you to glory*! Go forth into the world now, share this message of hope, this pledge and decree of your faithfulness to him, with others! Show them that *the great Almighty God* can be a beacon for them, *too*!"

Munsey held his inked hand high. Mantis tilted her head to see the image on the television upside down and giggled. Through a mouth full of vegetables, Mantis said, "Wow, Betty, that looks just like the symbol on that demon's palm."

As much as she wanted to deny it, Mantis had a point. Anxiety swelled in her chest.

"Little ironic, don't you think? That he's bearin' the *Mark of the Beast.*" Dylan scoffed.

"*What-oo-oo-mean?*" Mantis said, struggling to keep the soft hunks of carrot in her mouth.

"Well, in Revelations, John of Patmos said that during the end of days, a sorta seductive Antichrist will emerge during the apocalypse and will mark on people's foreheads or right hands with the mark of the beast."

"I thought that was like 666 or some shit." Mantis popped a carrot slice in the air, leaned back, and caught it in her mouth.

"There's some speculation because printed versions of the Bible say the number is 666. But they actually found a fragment of the piece of papyrus that Revelations was originally written on and found that it actually said *616.*"

"That's a big whoopsie," Sweet Tea added, scooping meat out of the can with her crackers.

A swell of tears rushed to Betty's eyes, and she sobbed. She raced into the bathroom and slammed the door.

"Way to go, *Dylan.*" Mantis snickered. "Just kiddin', man. Her hormones are all outta whack. It's probably *Shark Week.*"

The Yeehaw Country Bar bustled with life. Unlike anywhere else they'd been, the arrival of vicious demons, meteors, and global quakes seemed to be surprisingly good for business. The Cajuns seemed to want to drink like nothing was wrong. Mantis found it quite refreshing. She knocked back her second shot of tequila and sucked hard on a fat slice of lime. She slammed the glass on the counter and motioned to the bartender. "*Another.*"

"What? No porchcrawlers tonight?" Betty had more than a hint of judgment in her voice.

"Fuck no, not after last night."

Betty sipped daintily on her Shirley Temple, annoyed the bar was savagely up-charging for garnishes because of the recent food scarcity.

The upbeat country music blared. Dylan's gator skin boots, for once, didn't seem so out of place. He stomped them to the beat on the sawdust-covered floor, following the moves of the ginger line dancer beside him, grinning wild.

Sweet Tea slammed her palms on the bar by Betty, irritated. "Whiskey sour, please. Make it strong."

Mantis grinned, grabbing the full shot glass from the bartender.

"What?" Sweet Tea lowered her head.

"You're jealous." Mantis downed it and made a sour face.

"You're ridiculous." But Tea was transparent, envy obvious.

"You're jealous of that lil' tramp fawning all over Outlaw *Jew-sy Wales* over there."

Sweet Tea adjusted her obnoxiously colorful cowboy hat and shook her head as if the notion were preposterous.

Mantis leaned against the bar. "Poor bastard followed you through three fuckin' states full'a dangerous dipshits just so you could give him the silent treatment all afternoon."

The bartender slid the stiff drink in front of Sweet Tea, and she started drinking it quickly.

She leaned towards Sweet Tea's ear. "If you don't wanna be with the kid, plenty of other chicks will jump at the chance." Mantis stepped away and pointed with two fingers, unlit cigarette clenched tight between them. "Mark my words."

Mantis coolly approached a group of gorgeous girls in Western wear at a nearby table. "How we doin' tonight, ladies?"

Sweet Tea watched Dylan. The redhead next to him laughed at something he said and put a hand playfully on his shoulder. Sweet Tea picked up her drink and walked up to a random middle-aged man at the end of the bar.

Dylan excused himself and stepped up next to Sweet Tea with a smile. He smiled at the bartender through neon-tinted smoke. "Shot of tequila, please. Bottom shelf. Cheapest stuff you got." He looked over his shoulder and saw that Mantis was across the room. He lowered his voice, "Scratch that, sir. Can I get a *sex on the beach*, instead?"

The bartender stared for a long moment. Disappointed, he said, "Yeah, comin' right up."

Dylan leaned toward Sweet Tea. "Everything okay here?"

"Sure! Me and Stan here are getting to know each other." She giggled.

The patron offered his hand to Dylan. "It's Dan, actually. Hi."

Dylan shook it. "Dylan. Cool. Well, I just wanted to make sure you were good here."

"We're *great*." Sweet Tea's tone was cold.

"Good." Dylan faked a big, happy smile.

Dylan drifted over to Betty. The bartender slid a two-tone drink to him, and Dylan handed over some cash.

"Kinda makes you think," Betty looked out over the dancing crowd, "what would Hollywood Hank do?"

Dylan took his drink and walked away.

Beside Betty, a gaggle of women giggled. She turned to see Mantis squeezing the hottest one's biceps and saying something about her "impressive guns." Betty laughed as she watched it. Mantis was fearless. She always had a way with women way out of her league.

Suddenly, the music died. Everyone's attention shifted to the DJ booth in the corner near the out-of-order mechanical bull. The DJ patted Dylan on the back and handed him a cordless mic. The DJ pointed to the stage. Dylan sucked down the last of his drink, made a face at the brain freeze, and then walked out onto the middle of it.

"Oh, this oughta be good," Mantis said, leaning back against the table to give him her full attention.

Everyone was watching now, waiting with bated breath.

Dylan tapped the mic. "Testing, testing."

"*Oh, Jesus.*" Sweet Tea partially covered her face in embarrassment and horror.

The DJ pushed a button, and a white spotlight blasted on him from the par-cans mounted to the truss above. Mantis whistled loudly through the silence.

"Hello, everyone. I'm Dylan." He cleared his throat nervously. "I want to start by apologizing. I'm sorry that I'm not some big, handsome Hollywood actor with some award-winning Jerry Maguire-type speech prepared. I don't know how to write poetry. I've never seen a hot air balloon. I've never *been* to *Philadelphia*. But I *have* been in love." He looked at the floor and then up at Sweet Tea. "Loved so hard that it hurts to be *around* that person—"

"*Get off 'da stage!*" A drunken coonass hollered.

Mantis assumed a threatening stance. "Hey, asshole! Say something else, and I'll slit your fuckin' throat."

Dylan looked at the man, gravely serious. "She'll *do* it."

The man growled and shook his head, opting not to start a war with a woman.

"I've longed for this person I've loved to the point that... I can't even *sleep* some nights. I just toss and turn, wishing I was with her. It tears me apart inside to pretend, *day after day*, that nothing *exists* between us. Some days, I'm *tortured* by what I feel for you."

Sweet Tea chugged her whiskey sour.

"I want to *know* you. I want to know your hopes and *dreams*. I want to know your real *name*, for God's sake!" Dylan's trembling hands shook

214

the mic. "It's come to my attention that, until now, I may not have been clear enough with you, Tea. So let me say it. Now. In front of all of these people." His voice quivered, "I don't *want* to be your *friend*. I... just want to be *yours*. I'm addicted to you, Tea, and, to quote a country song, there is simply no *rehab* for a drug like you."

A few people in the audience clapped at the reference.

"I *love* you." Dylan said, looking only at her. "I am shouting it from the rooftops, Tea. I love you."

It felt so freeing to *finally* say the words aloud. *To confess it all.*

"I know you watch these movies with these big, romantic gestures." His green eyes glittered in the light. "Well, this was *mine*."

Mantis cheered and motioned for others to do the same. They erupted in a cacophony of whistles and claps.

Sweet Tea dug into the pocket of her shorts and thrust a wad of singles onto the bar. She wiped a tear from her eye and rushed out of the building.

The others stared at each other, dumbfounded.

Dylan's heart sank as the bar's door thunked closed.

Betty slid the card key. A green light flashed, and she burst through the door. Sweet Tea was lying on her belly watching the news in one of the hotel beds, wearing nothing but a bra and stretch pajama shorts, propped on her elbows.

Betty was livid.

"Look, Betty, I love you, but *stay out of this*. I wasn't making myself clear enough with him. I'm not trying to *hurt* him—"

"That was *heartbreaking*." Betty put her fists on her hips. "What is *wrong* with you? Dylan's a great guy!"

"I strip for old, married men for cash. I've sold my soul a piece at a time on a pole. I've got nothin' of value left to give."

"Oh, *bull*!" Betty glowered.

"Tell me, Betty. What've I got to show for my life beyond a purse full of singles? I've got feet full of scars from grinding my cooch on strangers in acrylic heels. I've got more baggage than an international airline. I'm a dented can, *Bet*. It is what it is. I'm not *mother* material. I'm not *wife* material. Hell, I'm not even *girlfriend* material. People like *me*, who do what I do, we don't end up with the Dylan's of the world."

"You're an *idiot*, Tea. He *loves* you. Do you know how many of us in the world would *kill* for that kind of adoration?"

Outside, muffled singing arose, and something scratched at the door. When Betty opened it, Mantis and Dylan staggered in, arm-over-shoulder, laughing.

"I… couldn't get the… thingy in the thingy." Dylan pointed at the lock with his card.

Mantis slurred the song, "*And the girls said yeeeeeee-haw. And the* boys *said?*" She pointed to Dylan.

"*Yeeeeeeehaw!*" He belted loudly.

"Shhhhhh! Keep it down. Other people are tryin' to sleep," Betty whispered, pulling them in.

Dylan tried several times to put the room card in his pants, missing his jeans pocket every time. He whirled it onto the nightstand.

"So! What'd *you* do tonight, Dylan?" Mantis raised her thick brows high.

Dylan sang the words like a twangy country song, "*Got muh heart ripped out of muh chest. 'N stomped on the grouuuuund.*" He danced toward the door, joining the rooms. "You know, I think I finally *get* country music. It's not *just* a bunch of whiny—" He pointed at the adjoining room. "Is this *our* room?"

"Yup!" Mantis giggled.

Dylan struggled with the door. When he finally got it open, he yelled, "Yahtzee!"

"Did you see those *girls*? Oh, those *girls*, Dylan," Mantis swooned like a cartoon skunk in love. "That brunette was *sooooo* feelin' me. Did you see that? Did you see the brunette?"

"She was diggin' you!" Dylan agreed enthusiastically.

"Ugh, tequila always makes me so *horny*." Mantis ran her hands down her thighs seductively, then locked eyes with him and flirted. "How *you* doin'?"

Dylan snickered at the serious look on her face. Her intense blue eyes sized him up like a piece of meat. She flashed him a sexy sideways grin. "No, really. How about it? *You're* single. *I'm* single. We're adults." She slid a hand down the crotch of his jeans and pressed her forehead to his. "I already know you're workin' with a stellar rig..."

"I—" Dylan tried to protest. She pressed a finger to his lips and then replaced them with her mouth.

Betty cleared her throat, embarrassed to be witnessing such a thing.

"Sweet Tea doesn't care. *Do* ya, Tea?" Mantis kissed his neck, and his knees nearly buckled.

"Nope. Knock yourselves out." Tea stared at the TV.

"Great." Mantis kissed him deeply, running her fingers through his curly hair and drawing him to her. A switch flipped, and Dylan kissed her back, bowing her backward. Betty's jaw dropped.

"We should probably get some priv—" Dylan kissed her hard and pressed her backward into their adjoined room, and slammed the door behind him.

Sweet Tea lifted the remote and cranked the volume up a few notches.

***

Inside the room, Dylan sat on one bed, and Mantis sprawled across the other. Dylan covered his mouth to stop himself from laughing aloud. Dylan whispered, "Holy shit, did you see her face? That totally worked!"

"Told you," Mantis whispered back. "You don't know what you got 'til it's gone."

"That was a solid performance. The singing," he gave her a thumbs up, "was a nice touch. They really think we're *hammered*." Dylan looked down at his crotch and covered it with a pillow. "Damn, I'm all worked up."

"Oh, we're not done *yet*. Take off your clothes." Mantis flashed a wicked grin.

***

The sounds of a bed squeaking rhythmically in the neighboring room drove Sweet Tea mad. She tried to concentrate on a reporter who discussed the intercontinental impact of the demon attacks, but it was no use. She tossed the remote to Betty, rolled over, and punched her pillow. "I'm goin' to sleep."

The sound of pounding springs cut through the quiet. Muffled moans wafted through the door.

A tear rolled down Sweet Tea's reddened face as she stared at the hideous hotel curtains.

"You okay?" Betty whispered over the loud, breathy moans.

Sweet Tea sobbed.

***

Dylan jumped enthusiastically on one of the beds in his boxers. Mantis lay on the other bed, still clothed, moaning pornographically with the rhythm of his jumps. She motioned for him to do the same. He shut his eyes and grunted.

She motioned for Dylan to get up and press both of his hands on the adjoining door. He nodded in understanding and slammed his weight against it, over and over, rattling the door against the jamb. Mantis stood against the wall nearby and moaned. "Ooooooh, Dylan. Yes! Yes! Ugh, yes, baby. Jesus, you're so... *big*."

He whispered, still banging on the door. "Don't *oversell* it."

Mantis broke character and whispered back, "I've *seen* that monster. I ain't oversellin' *anything*."

Dylan grinned and shook his head, pounding his weight harder against the door.

"Oooooh, baby. Right there. Oh yeah, right there. Harder. *Harder*, Dylan."

She whispered to him again. "I'm gonna cum. You ready?"

Dylan nodded.

Mantis grew louder yet. "Oh, oh, ohhhhhhhh, Dylannnnn. Oh my God. Yes, right there."

"There?" He moaned, playing along.

Mantis moaned harder. "Ohhhhhhhhhh yeah. Don't stop, baby." Mantis screamed out with pleasure, pretending to climax. *Hard.*

It was everything Dylan could do to not laugh.

Silence.

He removed his weight from the door and stood back.

"And now... we wait," she whispered.

***

Minutes later, Mantis burst through the adjoining door, fishnets draped across her arm, hair even messier than usual. She scoured through the canvas totes on the dresser. "Do we have any more," Mantis plucked a can out of one of the bags and searched for the can opener, "ravioli. Yeah, here we go!" She opened the can. "Man, I really worked up an appetite."

In their room, Dylan sat on the edge of the unmade bed and adjusted the crotch of his boxers.

After a moment of silence, Sweet Tea whipped back her covers, strode to Mantis, and slapped her across the face with a loud *smack*.

"I thought you were my friend!"

"Yeah, well," the slap didn't seem to phase her, "You claim Dylan's your friend, too. Look at where that got *him*."

Sweet Tea stormed into the adjoining room and screamed, "What is *wrong with you*? I turn you down... so you go and fuck my *friend*?"

Dylan stood without a word and met Sweet Tea in the middle of the room with a deep, passionate kiss that came from seemingly out of nowhere.

Mantis walked over and closed the dividing door between the rooms, shutting Tea and Dylan in together. She plopped down on Sweet Tea's bed and snatched up the remote.

"You think it *worked*?" Betty tried hard to fight her smile.

Mantis smiled at her, cheek pink from the slap. "Man, I fuckin' hope so."

Hungry

Dylan pressed Sweet Tea against the wall. She shoved him sharply backward. "What the hell are you doing? Mantis wasn't *enough*? You gotta fuck your way through the whole *group*?"

Dylan's response wasn't verbal. He stared her down. Hungry for her *touch*. Hungry for her *body*. He tilted her face up toward his.

Rage and jealousy burned deep within her.

He traced his finger down her throat, down the curves of her ample breasts, down her tight abdomen.

She slapped him. *Hard.* A chaotic mix of emotions swirled through her. Jealousy had her spinning out of control.

They stared in silence, his face burning from the impact of her palm. But through it all, something was different now. He could *see* the desire burning in her hazel eyes.

It was all-or-nothing tonight.

Dylan pulled her close and kissed her. She clutched the nape of his neck and drew him closer, kissing him back, intoxicated by their tongues entwining. He walked her until her bare back was touching the door dividing the rooms and unclasped her bra as he kissed her neck. The only sound she could muster was dizzied pants.

He tossed her bra to the side and reveled in the sight of the curves and angles of her perfect body. Though he'd seen them on stage a thousand times, it paled in comparison to touching them.

The scent of wildflowers filled his senses, and he couldn't help but kiss her deeper, as though to meld her and the door as one single organism.

His lips moved down to her nipples, enveloping them with warm lips as her breasts heaved from her deep breaths and soft moans. He was anxious to taste every square inch of her.

PART FIVE: DEATH

The sun peered over the tree-lined horizon, spraying the morning sky with rays of golden light. The wheat whispered gently in the breeze, and a blanket of fog dissipated. Clarity fell over the land.

In the middle of it all, the grotesque lamb with seven horns blinked all seven eyes and nudged open more pages of the tome with its hoof.

The patchwork creature hissed, this time with a dire gravity to his voice. "You are almossssssssst out of time. The sssssssseal will be broken sssssssssoon."

All three of his eyes *begged* her to succeed.

He truly was a monstrosity.

"Come and ssssssee," he hissed.

From the lifting fog appeared a man on a sage-green stallion. The horse was frail and sickly. Its bony hips jutted, every rib visible through matted fur. Its eyes oozed mucus, dripping in long strings like pale, green drool. It moved slowly, as if on the very *brink* of death.

The rider was as malnourished as the horse. He donned no armor, carrying only a sharpened sickle in his frail hands. He wore a green mask with small, sunken eye holes. Atop his head, he, too, bore a gory demon-finger crown.

A pack of hungry coyotes stalked the pale horse from the treeline behind him. Eyes locked, fur mangy and matted with blood. They bared their teeth, shoulders hunched. Ready to *pounce*.

A strange sound started behind them and grew to an almost deafening decibel.

Bugs. *Thousands of them. Locusts.*

There was a swarm flying through the field toward her.

And men. A group of them, emaciated, dressed in black tattered clothes, emerged from the trees.

"What's happening?" Mantis looked at the amalgamated patchwork creature.

The pale green rider turned his head toward her. He held up one fist. Then, he raised it. At the exact same moment, every man, locust, and coyote raced toward her. Mantis ran in the opposite direction. The patchwork creature trailed swiftly behind. Sticks and rocks sliced her bare feet. The harsh wheat whipped past her, whooshing like rattlesnake tails.

Small pillars of light burst forth from the ground everywhere her bleeding feet touched down. The beings avoided the light at all costs, dodging the gleaming pillars.

The coyotes caught up to Mantis and her three-eyed companion. The patchwork creature was tackled. Coyotes savagely shredded his limbs. He screamed in agony.

"*Deathhhhhhhhhhhhhh!*" The final word came from his dying breath. Another coyote gnashed at its face and dragged it by the mane into the wheat.

Mantis spun to regain her sense of direction. The locusts swarmed near the beams of blinding light, careful not to touch them. Their faces had strangely humanistic qualities. Tiny gold barbs formed crowns atop their minuscule heads. One gnawed at her, taking little hunks of flesh out of her forearm with its tiny teeth.

"Mantis, wake up!" Betty yelled, pinching her forearm. "We gotta go."

Mantis looked around, trying to sort out where she was, her heart still thumping from the realism of the horrific dream.

"The last address is in some town called Reserve, three hours away."

Mantis rose slowly. "I've been havin' the most fucked up dreams—"

"Can we talk about it from the *road*?" Betty asked, swiping the curtains back to the daylight flood in. But only darkness oozed in.

Betty looked at her watch, confused.

What the… it's 9:03 a.m. Sun should've been up hours ago." Betty was concerned. "Did… my watch die?"

Mantis looked at the alarm on the nightstand. 9:03. "Nope."

"This week gets more bizarre by the minute." Betty stomped toward the door. "Let's hit the road. Will you wake the love birds and meet me in the 'stang when you're ready?"

Mantis nodded, still groggy.

***

Sweet Tea gasped sharply near Dylan's ear, nibbling on his lobe. She writhed on her back and ran her teal fingernails through his thick, black head of hair. "*Oh… yeah,*" she moaned again, low, sexy.

"*You like that?*" Dylan nuzzled her ear as he thrust his hips slowly, entwined between her tan, well-toned legs. Sweat formed on their writhing bodies as they squirmed and tangled.

"*Yes,*" Sweet Tea breathed and kissed him gently, savoring the taste of his bottom lip.

He brushed some blonde hair from her face lovingly and allowed his hand to linger on her soft skin. He never wanted this moment to end. Being inside of her felt like a stealing piece of Heaven.

"*I love you,*" he whispered tenderly before thrusting deeply into her.

She arched her back, and her breathing quickened. "*Dylan...*"

Hearing his breathy name roll off her honeyed tongue drove him wild. He kissed her breasts.

"*Tia.*" Sweet Tea's voice barely formed words.

"*Green.*" Her eyes closed.

Dylan thrust into her deeply again and smiled, taking her breath away. "Is this some kind of a riddle? Hmmm?" Dylan trailed kisses up to her ear.

"No," she hid her smile in the pillow. "My real name."

He thrust into her again, and she moaned louder. "Your name is *Tia Green*?"

She nodded bashfully.

"Can I call you *Green Tea* from now on?" Dylan joked.

Sweet Tea giggled. "Not if you value your *life.*"

Dylan pinned her wrists against the bed, and his kisses drifted down to her abdomen. He disappeared under the sheets and probed her most intimate places with his tongue. She gasped.

He spoke, muffled slightly by her athletic thighs. "*Tell me more.*"

He leaned in again to dive in, to taste her.

Mantis burst through the door, not expecting to interrupt such an intimate display. "*Whoa!*"

Sweet Tea scrambled to cover herself with the sheet, pulling it off Dylan's feet. Dylan surfaced.

"Well! Glad to see you finally found your appetite." Mantis grinned and slapped his cheek playfully. "Aww, a man after my own heart. I take it last night went well?"

Dylan shrugged casually. "*Yeah.*"

The lovers burst into a fit of laughter, embarrassed by the intrusion.

"As soon as you're done with your, um, *breakfast*, we're hitting the road. Betty's antsy."

Mantis shut the dividing door, and there was a moment of silence before Dylan dove beneath the covers like an animal. Sweet Tea shrieked and dropped back onto her pillow.

Nina Hartley was a stone-cold bitch when she wanted to be. She had an expression of anger in her repertoire that made people forget what favor they were begging the church for in the first place. She was making it *now*. Nina looked up from the game on Munsey's television with a furrowed brow and set down the sermon she'd been proofreading.

"You see *this*?" Nina pointed to the set, still intently watching.

"Yep." Munsey looked up at her over a mess of index cards, agitated by her scathing tone. He could never get a moment of peace when Nina was around. And Nina was *always* around.

"These men are out here in front 'a God and everybody dressed like *the Pope*." Nina scowled.

Munsey looked up at the screen. His irritation morphed into a look of satisfaction. A group of fans cheered in a football stadium dressed in black-and-gold papal dresses with gold miter hats. They waved at the crowd sporting bold black-markered numbers on their palms. One of the men held a large black banner with the words "Nehemiah 9:19" on it in gold marker. The arena was a sea of gold and black.

"These sacrilegious rabbit-turds are dressed like the *Pope*, and you're telling me you got no problem with this?"

"You kiddin', right? This's gonna have the same impact as those bible scriptures on Tebow's eye-black. These guys are pretending to be *saints*. As long as it spreads *our message*, who cares? We're reachin' the masses."

"We *already* reach the masses," Nina argued. Growing up in the ninth ward had made Nina street-savvy. She could smell bullshit a mile away. And Munsey had *that* in spades. But despite the weakness in his convictions, she knew they were doing the Lord's work.

"It's *immoral*! We cannot start condoning impiety, Jeremiah. These people need to show some *reverence* for the Lord! *'Specially* if they're advertising *our* message." Nina leaned in. "I can't stand the thought of people out there making a mockery of religion in *our names*. I will not stand by idly and let some disgusting display like *this* be the message we send. The Bible says—"

Munsey interrupted, "Nina, for *fuck's sake*, I *know* what the Bible says. I *sent* them, alright?"

"You *what*?!" Nina clutched the neckline of her prim, pastel dress.

"I sent them! Do you *have any idea* how many people are at that game right now? Seein' our banner? Seein' our message on their hands?! We should be thankin' our lucky *stars* that we got in front of a crowd *this size*!"

Nina was hurt. *They were supposed to be partners.* "I don't even know who you *are* anymore. When we started this ministry together, you were…"

Munsey glared. "These are delicate times. People are looking for God more than ever, what with all the natural disasters and those demons runnin' amok. We have to maximize the spread of our message."

"It's that *woman*, isn't it? The one out *there*." Nina pointed to the office door. "Ever since she and that kid showed up, you've been actin' so strange. I don't even *know you* when she's around." Nina furrowed her brow and walked out of the room, slamming the door behind her.

In the dim transept, Nina stomped across the marble floor to the center pew and looked around the church. "You need to leave," Nina hollered into the air. "Both of you. Your free ride is over. Whatever deal Munsey made with you is over."

Silence.

"Where are you?" Nina looked around the shadowy church for any sign of life.

A boy giggled, and Nina looked up.

"*Timber!*" Lucy laughed as she dropped a gold candelabra over the edge of the balcony. It smashed on the white marble below, warping it forever. Three candlesticks clattered in different directions.

Gabriel giggled and shielded his face from Nina's cruel scowl.

"Stop that *immediately*!" Nina shouted.

Lucy raised the matching candelabra a few feet away and hurled it at Nina below. The metal bounced, landing on a pew. Candles shattered into wax hunks around her.

"I'm sorry, I couldn't hear you. What were you saying?" Lucy's tone was smug.

Nina stormed toward the basement door, offended. Once she disappeared through the door, Lucy sat on the floor beside Gabriel.

"That was cool," Gabriel giggled, "but also kinda mean."

"You think *that* was mean?" Lucy chuckled. "One time, your dad let me kill a guy's entire *family*. He let me give him pus-filled skin sores and butcher *all* of his livestock, daughters, *everything*."

Gabriel flashed a look of fear with his sapphire eyes.

"He watched me take *everything* the guy had just to prove a point to me."

"Do you feel *bad* about it?"

"Of *course* I do. The guy didn't do anything *wrong*." The memories of it still weighed heavily on Lucy's mind. *The torture… the anguish…*

Gabriel put his hand in hers. "God knows what's in your heart. If you're sorry, he knows."

Lucy laid her head back against the rail and stared at the painted ceiling of the church.

"Lucy?"

She looked at his pure face. "Yes?"

"When can I see the bomb?" Gabriel's question sounded so innocent, so matter-of-fact.

Lucy smoothed the child's black hair with her hand. "Just as soon as your mom gets here. That way, you can go to Heaven together."

"Meet up by the register when you're ready to go," Betty said as they all exited the Mustang. Betty looked at the black sky, still in disbelief that it was morning.

A massive hole was smashed through the front window of the store, presumably from a car driving through the building.

Mantis motioned for Betty to enter. "*Apres vous.*"

The store had been ravaged by looters. Items were strewn about. Displays had been overturned. Most of the necessities had been stolen in the days prior. The grocery section had been raided thoroughly.

Mantis crunched through a welcome mat of shattered glass and looked around at the ravaged ruins of a once-bustling place of commerce. "Well, let's go shopping!"

Betty headed through the main aisles with her rattling cart. She soon found herself in sporting goods, shuffling through the shattered glass display case. In the pillaged mess, she located a partial box of .38 bullets and put them in her basket. She turned the corner and headed into the toy section in search of a hopeful gift to welcome her son home. Once there, terrible thoughts of never seeing Gabriel again crowded her thoughts.

Before a large row of adorable stuffed animals, Betty released her grip on her cart, dropped to her knees, pressed her hands together, and prayed for her son.

Mantis breezed past the isle and backtracked when she realized what she'd seen. "The faith is *strong* in this one."

Betty finished her prayer, stood, and dusted herself off. She smiled weakly and grabbed a stuffed bear for Gabriel.

"Does God ever answer you back?" Mantis asked genuinely. "Or is it always a one-way convo?"

"If he were to talk back, that wouldn't require much faith from me, would it?"

Mantis changed the subject. "What do you think of this?" She twirled, showing off her new black leather jacket. "It's got a preacher's collar instead of lapels. I can never find these."

***

"I know you're not going to like this, but just hear me out..." Sweet Tea kissed Dylan lightly on the lips.

"I already don't like where this is going."

"Try this on for me?" She produced a pink V-neck shirt from behind her back.

"There's no *friggin way* I'm puttin' that on." Dylan looked at the shirt like it was diseased.

"Why?" Sweet Tea pouted.

"Because it's *pink*!"

"It's *salmon*, actually."

"Salmon's *pink*. There's no way in HELL you're getting me to wear that." He stated confidently.

***

Dylan scratched the tag in the neck of his new salmon-colored V-neck as he approached Mantis. The group hovered around the manager's office door in the back of the store.

"Do we really need to do this?" Mantis whined, opening the door.

"Yes, we really need to do this. Otherwise, this is *stealing,* and I'm not going to start breaking commandments just because it may or may not be the end of the world."

"The jacket was $120, got a couple new shirts, a pair a' black pants, and four cartons of Pillars." Mantis flashed an embarrassed smile.

"Do you really need *four cartons*?"

"Let's be *real*, Bet. This shit's gonna last me, like, four days at the rate I smoke. Plus, if things get bad, we can use 'em as currency."

"This isn't *prison*," Sweet Tea said.

"What about *you* guys?" Mantis peered into the cart. Betty pointed at various items, estimating the total mentally.

"With my clothes, shoes, hair spray, the teddy bear, fresh panties, and bullets—" Betty tallied the numbers in her head.

"Did anyone find any food?" Mantis interrupted.

"I found a box of smashed Lil Debbies under a display rack." Dylan tossed them into Betty's basket. "But I won't be eating 'em. Last time I had a brownie, it didn't go so well."

"Together all this, plus the brownies… we are around $460." Betty looked up at Mantis. "They were out of the size of bullets for the AK."

Mantis shrugged. "It's okay. I might have a few left."

Sweet Tea shuffled through her tote. "I got lipstick aaaaand condoms—"

Mantis winked at Dylan. He blushed.

"Ooh, I also got—"

"How about you give a rough total. We don't need an itemized list." Betty was growing antsy.

"$200, maybe less," Sweet Tea said.

"Let's leave $700 to be safe with tax and everything." Betty peeled $700 off of the pile.

Mantis sighed deeply. This was idiotic. "Where should we leave it? I don't want some other *asswad* to loot this place and take it."

"Put it inside the desk." Betty handed the money to Mantis.

Mantis pulled out the bottom drawer of the manager's desk and gasped. "Holy mother of mercy, would you look at that!"

It was chock-full of beef sticks, desserts, and snacks. "*Jackpot.*"

"St. John's Parish, huh?" Betty smiled at the reflective sign slicing brightly through the black sky. "Seems pretty fitting."

"I have no clue what you're talking about." Mantis propped her dirty, bare feet on the dash.

"St. John the Baptist. You know, the prophet who wrote about Revelations and the *apocalypse*."

"I got no clue what you're talkin' about, Bet." Mantis pointed to the black halter Betty had on. "Speaking of fitting, that shirt looks good on you. Old Betty is back! I knew you could do it."

Suddenly, her seat bowed forward from the force of an elbow shoving into it.

"Take it *easy* back there." Mantis warned. "Am I gonna have to turn a hose on you two?"

"You're like two dogs in *hea*t." Betty laughed. She glanced at the amenities on the sign and drifted onto the off-ramp. "We're close, guys."

Dylan sat up quickly and wiped a bit of Sweet Tea's pink lipstick from his lips. She sat up and adjusted her tank top.

"We need gas. We're on fumes." Betty stopped at the base of the ramp. "Hopefully, this place'll *have* some."

"I gotta take a piss, too." Mantis took her feet off the dash and shoved them in her untied boots.

"*Classy.*" Betty rolled into a gas station parking lot. She turned the car off.

Mantis got out. "Grab me some coffin nails, would ya? Iron Pillars." Without waiting for an answer, she was off in search of a bathroom.

Betty peered into the back seat at Dylan and Sweet Tea, both trying to look casual.

"Coming?" Betty asked.

"We're trying." Sweet Tea muttered. "It's hard, though, in a car full of *people*."

"*Sickos*." Betty shook her head.

Mantis walked into the women's bathroom. The putrid smell was overpowering. Green-tinted halogens buzzed overhead. Someone rustled in the only stall. While she waited, Mantis leaned into the toward a spattered mirror and scrunched her wild waves of black hair.

The stall creaked open. The occupant stepped out. Mantis forced a smile, a polite nicety, but it washed from her face like a tide.

The woman's features were pale and elegant. And all-too-familiar. Years of history flashed before her in an instant, and her heart felt wrung out like a dish sponge.

It was Grace.

***

Betty crossed the darkened lot and opened the door of the convertible, tossing two packs of condoms in the back. "Pumps are out of order. They were all out of Iron Pillars. --The attendant, well… his *head* is missing, so I guess we'll just have to—"

Betty shrieked.

Dylan and Sweet Tea sat up from the back seat, frantically tugging at their clothes, trying to make themselves decent. Dylan zipped his fly, pinching the hem of his pink shirt with his chin. "*Sorry!* We thought we had a couple minutes…"

"You have *five* minutes." Disgusted, Betty slammed the door and strode across the parking lot.

Sweet Tea grinned. Dylan kissed her deeply, pressing her back down onto the back seat.

***

Mantis didn't know what to say. She wasn't often speechless either. Quite the contrary.

"Don't go to the church," Grace urgently warned.

"I… haven't been to a church in years." She wanted to touch Grace but couldn't bring herself to do it. The sudden appearance of tears pricked her eyes. "You *died*. How—"

Grace touched Mantis's face, skin molten-hot. *"Promise me you won't go to the church."*

Grace kissed her softly, but her lips were scorching. Mantis pulled away, a look of confused horror plastered on her face.

"Promise me," Grace said again, stepping toward the door. Her delicate mouth frowned, eyes full of dread. She bolted out the door into the parking lot, and Mantis shot out the door behind her.

But Grace was gone. An ethereal whisper in the darkness... vanished without a trace.

Mantis stared at the black bayou trailing beside the blurred shoulder of the highway whizzing past. The convertible's high beams made the dewy leaves shimmer white through the velvet mass of black.

"I *know* what I saw," Mantis grumbled, voice slightly shaking.

"Hun, it isn't *possible.* Sweet Tea and I were there when they lowered her into the ground." Betty said calmly, flying down Highway 61 well above the speed limit.

"Slow down."

"We're almost on empty. I'm trying to get us as far as I can before we run completely out."

Mantis chewed her fingernail in silence for a moment and then said, "She told me not to go to the church."

"Who?"

"*Grace,* goddammit!"

"Okay, jeez! What *church*?" It scared Betty to see Mantis this rattled.

"I don't *know*," Mantis barked, catching a glimpse of reflective alligator eyes in the murky water. *Lots* of them.

"How long were you and Grace together?" Dylan asked, curious.

"*Mind your business,*" Mantis rasped.

Betty answered for her. "They were together a long time, Dylan."

"Okay, I'm just gonna ask it, then. What happened between y'all?"

"She killed herself because I got *pregnant*." Mantis punched the dash three times, bloodying her knuckles. She roared with fury and shouted, "She thought I was fuckin' around on her!"

"Mantis was protecting me," Betty said somberly. "In addition to pimping me out, Johnny was beating the crap out of me. Put me in the hospital with a broken rib and a coupla' broken fingers. I called Mantis. Asked for her help."

"Don't. This isn't any 'a their *business*, Bet." Mantis seethed.

Betty continued, "I called her after I got out of the hospital. Told her I was in El Paso and that I needed to get out. She came to pick me up, but Johnny wasn't about to just let me walk. I was his top earner. His, quote, '*bottom bitch.*'"

"*Humble brag,*" Mantis scoffed, staring out the window.

"What? How come I'm *just* hearin' all this?" Sweet Tea asked.

"Johnny told Mantis I was available for *rent*, but if she wanted to '*purchase*' me, it was going to cost her. Next thing I know, she's drained her bank accounts, comes back with a *stack* of cash. Everything she had." Betty swerved to avoid an abandoned car in the middle of the road. Its door was shorn off. The driver inside was torn to gory ribbons of glistening meat. Busted glass laid across the asphalt like sparkling glitter.

"Johnny said the money wasn't enough. He wouldn't let me go until she agreed to—"

"Dude said if I wanted Betty, I had to let him *nail* me, *alright?*" Mantis grew more hostile. "Fucker knocked me up."

"There was a *bit* of an altercation." Betty switched lanes again to avoid a broken hunk of earthquake-ravaged asphalt. "And I *may or may not have* cut his finger off before we left."

Mantis chuckled through the anger and grasped at the floorboard for her pack of Iron Pillars. "That part was badass, actually. Not gonna lie."

"I always thought you and Mantis had a... *thing*?" Sweet Tea spoke up. "I always just assumed—"

"Yeah, *you* and *Grace* and *every-fuckin'-body-else* on the goddamned planet," Mantis snarled, finally locating the pack. *Empty*. She let out a frustrated sigh and tossed the crumpled remains to the floor.

"I didn't know Grace thought *we*—" Betty looked at Mantis but didn't finish.

"We fought *constantly* about you," Mantis swiped a messy chunk of hair behind her ear. "She thought I was cheating with *everyone*. Then, when the pregnancy test came back positive," Mantis laughed sarcastically, "that was all the proof she needed. She waited until she knew I'd be at work, took a razor, and sliced herself up the highway."

The GPS chirped, "In *.2 miles*, turn right onto *Hickory Drive*. Destination is on the right."

"Oh, thank *God*! We're gonna make it." Betty rejoiced, preparing for the turn. The convertible puttered, slowing in speed.

"No, no, no!" Betty moaned, carefully pulling onto the shoulder of the two-lane bridge. She smacked the steering wheel, and the car died.

Mantis held her hand out. "Gimme another pack of Pillars, Tea."

Sweet Tea handed up a carton. "We only have *one* ozone layer, you know."

"Would you look at that," Mantis pointed to the cardboard, "this box comes with a free *lecture*."

"What are we supposed to do now?" Betty felt a tidal wave of panic overwhelm her.

"Let's walk. It ain't far. We'll go deal with *this dipshit*. Then, after, we'll siphon gas once from one of these broken-down cars or somethin'." Mantis shoved a cigarette in her mouth. "Or maybe this guy'll have a can for his lawn mower we can buy off of him."

Betty was boiling over. "This freakin' week just keeps gettin' *better and better*."

"*Chill*. It'll be fine. Pop the trunk so I can get the AK."

"You can't just walk around with a semi-automatic rifle," Betty warned.

"Uh, the Second Amendment says I *can*. Louisiana's open carry. This is *'Murica*, baby."

Betty rolled her eyes as they all filed out. "That's for handguns, not *AK-47s*. You need a permit."

"Permit, shmer-mit. When was the last time you saw a *cop*, Betty? It's been *days*. They have kinda a lot goin' on right now, what with the fucking meteors, and earthquakes, and homicidal creatures roamin' about. So just... pop the goddamn *trunk*."

Betty pushed the button on the fob, and the hatch clicked open. Mantis dug the rifle out from under their morning Supercenter spoils. "What's this fucker's name again?"

"The Tax Man's sheet said *Adam*."

Mantis strung the rifle strap over her head and slammed the trunk. The road groaned the moment the hatch closed, and the highway's shoulder crumbled beneath their feet.

"S*hit!*"

They jumped back just in time to see a massive portion of the bridge crumble into the bayou below, taking their vehicle with it. The black convertible careened gracefully into the waters below.

SPLASH!

The group gathered silently at the railing, watching in shock as the Mustang was dragged beneath the glistening surface.

Betty walked in a circle, looked out calmly over the water, and then screamed. "FUUUUUUUUUCK!"

Despite the serious situation, Mantis couldn't help but snicker with immaturity. Never in decades of knowing her had she ever heard Betty swear.

Mantis nudged a savagely eviscerated body with the barrel of her rifle. Day-old entrails were strewn behind what remained of the man's lower half, reminding her of the cowboy who so generously offered up his vehicle to them just days before.

Near the end of the bridge, a gnarled motorcycle lay on its side, front wheel off the edge, dangling precariously over the dark bayou some forty feet below. Mantis squatted and fished around in the corpse's pockets.

Betty shouted, eyes bulging, "Get out of his pockets right this instant!"

"I'm just gonna see if he has anyt—"

Betty stomped. "I said *now!*"

Mantis wiped her hand on her new black jeans. "Okay! Jesus. You don't have to go all *mom mode* on me."

Mantis leaped onto the grass and stared up at a street sign that read: HICKORY DRIVE. "*Four cartons.* Four fucking cartons of Iron Pillars, just, *bam*, down the drain." She shook her head in disgust.

"I still have all the beef sticks." Sweet Tea patted her teal children's backpack. The tag dangled from it like a fluttering leaf.

"The bear I just bought for Gabe is at the bottom of the swamp now," Betty muttered.

"*Rest in peace, condoms.*" Dylan sounded genuinely mournful.

As the group took the turn into the residential neighborhood, Mantis heard nearby foliage rustle.

She pointed her rifle at the dense thicket. "Who's there?"

A raccoon scurried from the treeline and stood on its hind legs when it saw them.

"Aw!" Sweet Tea cooed. "How cute! You hungry, lil' fella?"

Suddenly, the raccoon dropped to all fours and raced toward them, chittering with ferocity.

"Oh shit!" Mantis took aim at the creature.

The chubby ball of fur leaped at Sweet Tea. She screamed, and Betty punched the furry beast, knocking it into the air. Mantis fired several shots, and it rolled limply down the slope, stopping at the water's edge.

"No! Why'd you do that?! Mantis, he was just hungry!" Sweet Tea shouted, staring at the still creature face-down in the grass.

"Yeah, for your fuckin' *jugular*!" Mantis laughed a little in disbelief. "That thing wanted blood!"

"Uh… Mantis?" Dylan sounded panicked.

She turned to look, following his index finger to the thicket.

Eight reflective eyes stared, unblinking. Four more coons had appeared, each with the same hungry look. All at once, the group of hungry creatures scampered toward them, tiny mouths bared.

Mantis opened fire, dropping each with a loud *POP*!

Tea screamed again. Mantis turned to mutter something sarcastic but soon realized Tea was focused on a massive alligator on the bayou's edge, hungrily chomping the first murdered coon.

"Holy *fuck*!" Mantis was frozen by the sight of the leathery beast. The alligator gulped and raced up the bank toward them.

"Kill it!" Dylan shouted.

Mantis skidded backward, putting more space between her and the prehistoric beast. She stepped on the ever-untied shoelace of her boot and toppled backward to the ground.

The gator charged, and she scrambled to re-aim, scooting through the grass and mud, digging her heels in to propel her.

Betty pulled the .38 from her purse and shakily loaded it.

Mantis screamed as the gator's open maw lurched toward her, swiping its thick tail for propulsion. She unloaded the AK in its mouth until the rifle only clicked.

Out of ammo. Again.

The gator flattened against the ground, slowing to its final place of rest, surrounded by bullet-addled 'coon carcasses.

"Holy shit!" Dylan ran a sweaty hand through his curly hair.

Betty clicked the revolver closed moments too late. Mantis stood, unstrapped the rifle, and hurled the spent AK onto the ground. "There ya go, Dyl-do. Another pair of gator-skin *boots* for your collection."

"I *told* ya. You got-ta-tie-your-shoes," Dylan nagged, karate-chopping the side of his hand into his other palm.

"Hey, you had better thank your lucky stars I'm outta bullets, kid."

The neighborhood was silent. Thick groupings of trees between spaced-out properties offered this middle-class suburb a slice of tranquil seclusion.

As they approached the address, Mantis noticed a beat-up, windowless panel van by the road. Its pastel-green shade made it stand out in the darkness like a night light. "Dude's got a friggin' chi-mo van."

"What's a *chi-mo* van?" Dylan asked, grabbing up Sweet Tea's hand with his own.

"You know… *child molester. Pederast.* This thing just needs 'FREE CANDY' spray-painted on the side."

"Who's taking the lead here?" Dylan looked around.

"I vote you, Captain Big Dick. You handled Max like a champ." Mantis performed her secret handshake with him. Sweet Tea rolled her eyes.

"No. Let *me* handle this one." Betty knocked on the front door. The others waited patiently behind her.

Mantis looked at her watch, marveling that it was still only afternoon and yet looked dark as night.

A voice called out, "It's open."

Adam was a good-looking man. Fit, with pecs that pressed against the fabric of his tight T-shirt. As they followed him into his home, Adam slid a tightly wound power cord up his tan arm.

Black-and-white concert stills and music memorabilia lined the walls like a fanatic's shrine, all action shots of a chiseled man in makeup and glitter performing shirtless on stage.

"Hi. Sorry to bother you, but are you, Adam?" Betty asked politely.

"Yep," he fidgeted with the battery pack in his hand. "I'm in a hurry. So, let's cut to the chase. What do you want me to autograph?"

"We don't want an autograph. Frankly, I don't know you from Adam." She burst into a fit of giggles from the unintentional joke. "I just meant, we don't know, really, who you are. We are searching for something." Betty pulled the nearly-completed reliquary from her purse. "We are looking for the last piece of this thing. A *friend* told us *you* had it."

"Was it that coked-out accountant?" Adam searched through some cabinets. "If so, you need better friends. Guy's a creep." He grabbed a set of keys off the kitchen counter. "I don't have it anymore. As if my prick *twin* hasn't taken enough from me already, he ended up with that, too."

"*Fuck*," Mantis whispered.

Betty stepped forward. "Okay, where can we find him? It's important."

"He's at a gig right now down in the Quarter. The 'End of the World' thing they got goin' on down there. Fish is headlining tonight."

"*Fish?*" Mantis smirked.

Adam looked at her strangely. "Yeah. What? Do you live under a *rock*? He's *Fish*. Of *Fish and the Fantasy Girls.*"

Dylan gasped. "You're kidding! Your brother is *that* Fish?"

Sweet Tea squealed. "*What?!* I dance to *Fistful of Feathers* all the *time* on stage!"

"Fish and the Fantasy Girls are, like, *the* glam rock band of our generation." Dylan was fangirling now. "That's your *brother*?"

Adam oozed disdain. "Yeah, we're fraternal, not identical, you yutz. You know that little twerp just signed a six-figure contract to be the new 'face of Progressive Shadows' makeup? They said he's gonna be their poster boy for trans culture."

"Fish, huh? That's a… *dumb* name." Mantis laughed.

"Our last name is *Fisher*." Adam's stare cut through her. "Originally, Stephen did vocals, and I wrote the songs and played lead guitar. That was until that fuckin' Judas cut me outta everything."

"I thought it was *Adam and Eve*, not Adam and *Steve*," Dylan joked.

Adam sighed. "Yeah, never heard *that one* before." He grabbed a pedal and a cable from the floor and kept walking. "Maybe I looked a little more like him, *I'd* have been the one with the Benz and the bitches. Instead, I *schlep* cable and struggle to make my mortgage. I wrote every song on *Glitter Gypsy* AND *Troubador*. Where'd it get me? I shoulda eaten that asshole in the uterus when I had the chance."

"Could you get us into that *show*?" Mantis batted her lashes at him.

"He's not gonna just let you have that gold thing, whatever it is. If he knows you want it, he'll keep it from you. It's what he does."

"*Please.*" Betty begged.

***

Adam hauled ass through the narrow, pot-hole-filled streets of New Orleans in the pale, green van. "I don't even know what it is. Some chick gave us each a hunk of gold after a show *years* ago." He swerved to pass a group of horn-playing musicians who were fending off two bat-like demons on the corner of Canal and Bourbon.

Adam continued, seemingly unphased by the brutal violence, "Anyway, the chick told us if we kept 'em safe, I'd get *one hell of a reward* later. I was hoping she meant, you know, like a *hummer* or somethin', but she never came back. Steve kept both of 'em together in a hollowed-out book that he takes on tour to stash his passport and crap in." He scoffed. "Like anyone would believe that self-absorbed dick *reads*."

Adam stopped at a red light and tapped his fingers anxiously. His eyes darted around, on high alert for the deadly creatures running amok in the streets.

"You're handling this apocalypse well," Betty noted.

"Shit, you shoulda seen how crazy this town was before. It ain't that much different now. I feel like we were groomed for this." A smile crept onto his face. "Anyway, Steve comes back from the tour, opens the book, and there's only one piece. Said he had no clue what happened to my half. Real shame, too. I thought if it was *real*, I'da had

had it melted down to buy a new hot water heater." The light turned green. Adam mashed the accelerator. "I wanna go tank-less."

Moments later, he whipped into a cramped, public parking lot and rolled over a woman's severed leg to nestle into a tight space. "I can get y'all backstage so you can look for it if you want."

"Seriously?" Mantis said, fearful it was all too easy.

"You'd be willing to do that?" Betty chirped.

"Sure. I don't give a rat's ass. Rob him blind for all I fuckin' care." Adam grabbed his gear and squeezed out of the van.

Sweet Tea got out and looked around. "So, this is 'Nawlins, huh?"

"Yup. My advice is to stay away from wharf rats. They get as big as fuckin' toddlers down by the riverboat launch, and this lack 'a sun seems to be driving everyone and every*thing* a little madder'n usual." He hoisted twenty bucks up. "$20 for whoever wants to take a shit in Steve's shoes for me."

"*Sucker.*" Mantis snatched the bill and stuffed it in her boot. "I'da done it for free."

Adam led the group down Decatur Street. Its disheveled appearance added a strange charm to the historical area.

"Always wanted to go to New Orleans." Sweet Tea looked up at a gutted building. Only the haunting, pink front of the structure remained.

"Smells like vomit and shame," Mantis joked. "My kind of place."

A woman in a leather catsuit passed the group, and Mantis turned around so quick she nearly gave herself whiplash. She looked at Adam, jaw agape in awe as the woman walked away.

"Tip of the iceberg," Adam said. "Never know what you're gonna see in 'Nawlins. Everyone lets their freak flag fly here."

"I'm never leaving," Mantis said firmly, still looking at the woman's ass.

They turned into a small brick alley between two multi-story buildings, bee-lining for the chiseled black man at the end. The pounding bass seeped through the walls.

Sweet Tea gasped when she recognized the tune. "Ahhh! *Jezebel Lipstick*!" She grooved to the tune on the sidewalk, dipping low. Dylan stared, and she grinned. "What's the matter, you don't like my dancing anymore?"

"Oh, baby, on the contrary." His eyes scanned her form, and she pulled him close, kissing him deeply.

Mantis looked at Betty. "We're gonna have to get her spayed."

"Jonah, I want you to meet a few friends of mine. They've volunteered as free hands for trash pick-up after the show. They need wristbands."

Jonah scoffed and waved in a way that told Adam he didn't need to bother with such formalities. Then, he said, "They packed *wayyyy* beyond capacity tonight."

"Pfft, like the *fire department's gonna come*."

"I think Steve's only got two songs left before the encore," Jonah said, staring at Mantis.

"Wait, *what*?!" Adam looked at his watch. "He wasn't supposed to even go *on* for another, like, 15 minutes. He asked me to run home and get some stuff. What the fuck happened?"

"He didn't wanna wait. Threw a fit backstage. Started yelling at the stagehands, '*Do you know who I am?*'"

"Great, so," Adam looked at the items in his hand, "yet another waste of my time. *Typical.*"

They brushed past Jonah and piled through the alley door.

Jonah leaned in and smiled at Mantis, "Hey sha, whatchu doin' after the show?"

"Maybe *you*, if you play your cards right." Mantis tried to stifle a smile.

Adam waved them forward, "Dressing room's up that way."

The song ended. The crowd went berserk.

Mantis hollered over the cheering fans, "Betty and I'll go. Y'all stay. Text Betty when he's done playing. Having all of us back in one place might draw too much attention. We'll text and meet outside once we got it, okay?"

Dylan saluted like a soldier. Mantis and Betty followed Adam down a maze of claustrophobic corridors through the back.

As the next song came on, vibrant stage lights lit the place up like an electric-blue wonderland.

It was an intimate venue packed to the gills with adoring fans, some in states of undress. Frenzied screams echoed off the exposed brick.

"I can't believe we're seeing *Fish and the Fantasy Girls*! I'm freaking out right now." Sweet Tea squealed, fascinated by the pageantry.

But Dylan could only see her and the way the lights glimmered in her hazel eyes.

A cobalt-blue banner hung in the rear of the stage sporting the cover of Fish's newest album, *Graven Image*. On it, Fish's twenty-foot airbrushed face sat in the center of a glitter pentagram, shining like a ringed star made of diamonds. The banner was sandwiched by angled walls covered in a collage of mirrors.

A gleaming-white spotlight illuminated Steven. The crowd roared. His back was turned to them, spotlight lighting his sequin pants like a disco ball. Radiant orbs of refracted light danced across his ecstatic fans as he shook his ass.

A topless girl in the front row screamed, "*I love you!*"

Dylan pulled Sweet Tea down the side aisle toward the bar in the back. Once there, he waved two fingers. "Yo! Shot of tequila, please."

The bartender nodded and yelled, "Thirty-three."

Dylan's eyes bulged. "Whoa, sounded like you said *thirty-three*."

The man nodded.

"Like, dollars?"

"Well, I'm not talkin' British *pounds*."

"I only want one shot. Not *four*."

"That *is* for one."

"Holy FUCK!" Dylan shook his head in disbelief. "That's… fucking *robbery*!"

"In case you haven't noticed, it's anarchy out there. Liquor's getting harder to come by with all the looting and shit. *Supply and demand*, buddy."

"Wait, how much for a *sex on the beach*?" Dylan asked out of curiosity.

"Mixed drinks are fifty-eight."

"*How do you sleep at night?!*" Dylan hollered.

"Hey, no one's twisting your arm, princess. Buy it. Don't buy it. I don't care either way."

Fish turned around, fluttering fractals of light across the venue. His muscular chest was home to a massive tattoo up his side. Dylan and Sweet Tea recognized it immediately as the goat-headed Baphomet. Fish's features were masculine, but his heavy makeup added a seductive touch of androgyny. He peered at the audience, eyes rimmed in thick liner.

They screamed.

He spoke, voice low and manly, "As a boy, I grew up in church, worshiping at the altar every Sunday. But one day, I woke up. I *opened my eyes*. I became a *man*. I see the world clearly now, without the fear of Hell. Romans always made me laugh. In 6:16, it says, *we have a choice*."

Sweet Tea and Dylan looked at each other with cocked eyebrows, confused by the turn the concert had taken.

"We are a slave to whom we obey. We can choose a path of lightness… or the *darkness*." A wicked smile crept onto his freshly shaven face. "We can be a slave to *sin*, or we can be a slave to obedience. *Which one sounds like more fun?!*"

The audience erupted into chaotic cheers.

"What would *you* rather be a slave to?" Fish hollered, riling the crowd.

"*Sin! Sin! Sin!*" They chanted.

Fish raised his palms skyward in worship. *6:16* was written in his right hand in marker. "Then let's embrace some *fucking sin* already!"

The crowd exploded in a jovial celebration. A woman on a man's shoulders ripped off her top, baring her breasts for all.

Fish leaned into the mic again and spoke with glossy lips. "This song's from my new album. I call it *Slave of the Flesh.* Everyone put your fucking hands together, for *you* are home at last among your *fellow* sinners!"

The drummer's foot pounded the pedal, slamming the mallet rhythmically into the bass drum. She nodded to the beat, but her short, gelled hair stayed neatly in place.

Fish sauntered to a full-length pivoting mirror propped in the center of the stage and pressed his body against it.

The bass guitarist strummed. She was slender and wore a thin tank with no bra. Men's sunglasses adorned her face, seated below the bangs of her pixie cut.

Sex oozed from every word from Fish's lips as he sang:

Serve me in this palace of flesh
Show me your obedience
Worship me, allegiant servant
You sanctimonious convenience

The audience cheered emphatically. Fish sang louder, grinding sensually to the beat.

I'm the tortured son of pleasure
You're my wretched puppet of pain
Slave to the one that you obey
Over you, I reign
Sexy marionette, down on your knees
Vexing siren, this God will pull your strings

Feel my eternal, bitter sting
Bow before the Dragon King
***

Music thumped the walls backstage as Mantis and Betty rifled through the rockstar's belongings. Posters lined the walls. In each, Fish modeled for the camera in front of colorful backdrops in various states of undress. The last of which was a nude of Fish standing, legs splayed, clutching a microphone crotch-height as if it were his phallus.

The music rattled the large vanity mirror. A slew of colorful makeup products cluttered its surface. Mantis picked up a tube of glitter lip gloss.

"Jesus, this guy's got more makeup than you and Tea *combined*." She stuffed the gloss in the pocket of her jeans and continued searching. She whipped open a suitcase and sifted through its contents. She dumped the case on the floor.

"Mantis!" Betty whispered, panicked.

"Do you want this fuckin' gold thing or *not*?" Mantis bit back.

Suddenly, the music died. The screams of the fans swelled. Mantis looked at Betty.

Betty gasped and felt around in her purse. "I think I might have left my phone in the car!"

"Why would you even have it out in his car?!"

"Not his car. The mustang! The one in the freaking bottom of the swamp! It was in the window mount for the GPS!" She pressed her wrist to her forehead, about to cry.

"Fuck." Mantis tossed Fish's belongings back in the suitcase, and Betty dug beneath a black futon, utilizing the last few seconds before they'd be caught.

A man outside the door screamed. Mantis recognized the voice. *It was Adam.*

"No, Steve, you have to do an encore!"

"No!" Fish burst through the door, pouting petulantly.

"It's a hometown show, Fish. *Do the fucking encore.*"

"You don't *own* me." Fish stepped forward to intimidate Adam with his posture.

When he did, Adam spotted Betty and Mantis over his shoulder, frozen like deer in headlights. Behind his brother's back, Adam subtly pointed for them to look higher at the top of the closet.

Mantis and Betty followed the silent instruction and silently continued their search just a few short feet away from the musician.

"Hear that, asshole? Those are *my* fans. They're cheering for *my* band. Screaming about *my* music. They don't even know who *you* are." Fish barked arrogantly in Adam's face.

Mantis discovered the faux book amid a spaghetti'd pile of feather boas on the top shelf. The front read HOLY BIBLE. The edges of the page glistened with metallic silver foil. Inside, a compartment had been cut into the center. They silently rejoiced.

"You are so conceited," Adam said in disgust as the audience chanted, demanding an encore.

Mantis plucked the final piece of the reliquary from the book's hollow and handed it to Betty. Betty pressed its jagged end against the rest of the reliquary. The two pieces miraculously melded, in an instant, finally completing the golden cross. The metal scorched her skin, and she let it fall into her purse. She bit her lip to keep from howling out in pain.

The floor rumbled.

Everyone looked down in confusion.

"You wanna go, you narcissistic prick? Take your best shot." Adam touched his chin.

"You're pathetic." Fish swung around, suddenly finding himself face-to-face with Mantis and Betty."What the *fuck* are *you* doing in here?"

Betty stuttered. "Uh-um, we-we're groupies."

"Nah," Mantis shook her head and decked Fish in the face with a closed fist. He fell to the floor, caught completely off-guard. Adam doubled over in uncontrollable laughter.

Betty gasped. "Mantis, I was handling it."

Mantis waved her fist loosely in the air in agony. "Holy mother of *fucks*, that hurt! What is your skull made of? Concrete?"

Adam peered down at his brother with tears of joy in his eyes.

Mantis stared down at Fish. "Your music fuckin' *sucks*."

"Sorry." Betty apologized politely as she stepped over him.

Fish latched furiously onto Betty's leg. Without thinking, she ground her high heel into Fish's tattooed ribs. He yowled out in pain.

Mantis yanked Betty free from Fish's grasp, and they raced down the corridor.

"Get back here!" Fish growled through bloodied lips. He hobbled toward them, clutching his side.

Betty dug into her purse and retrieved a wad of rubber-banded cash. When Mantis and Betty exited the corridor to the main theater, Fish was only inches behind, grabbing at hair and skin, not quite finding purchase.

As soon as they were in the aisle next to the chaotic crowd, Betty ripped off the rubber band and threw the currency into the air. Cash rained down from the sky like twirling confetti, and the audience went crazy trying to catch it.

The mob of fans soon turned their frenzied attention from the bills to Fish and mobbed him.

"That was fucking *awesome*!" Mantis exclaimed, laughing as the gang raced through the alley and out onto the cobbled sidewalk.

"Did you get it?" Sweet Tea giggled.

"Yeah! You should have seen it! Betty just made it *rain* in there."

Sweet Tea squealed. "Oh my God! That's awesome!"

Silence.

"So… now what?" Dylan asked.

It was at that moment that they realized there had not been a plan beyond attaining the reliquary.

"Can I see it?" Sweet Tea held her hand out. Betty handed it over. It was cooler now and could be handled without issue. After a moment of examining it, Dylan spoke.

"What are these words on the tips? They're hard to read. Looks like the top says *JOXX*, and the bottom… I dunno. *LUKE*?"

The flickering gaslights above them illuminated a small compartment in the very center of it.

Betty looked closely. "It's *John*, not Joxx. The letters are pushed together so tightly it's hard to make it out. But it says: John and Luke on the top and bottom and Matt and Mark on the crossbar."

"Why is it only those four and not the rest of the disciples?" Dylan furrowed his brow.

"Luke and Mark aren't disciples. These names are the *Evangelists*. All four of their gospels in the Bible include a lot of the same stories. This is an *Evangelist Cross*."

"Looks like all that dumb-ass *Good News Network* you watch finally just paid off." Mantis seemed impressed.

Dylan walked away, pulled out his phone, and started typing in the browser.

"I actually watched a documentary on the Evangelists once." Betty smiled.

"That… sounds like the most boring fuckin' documentary I've literally *ever* heard of," Mantis said brashly.

"I don't know what to do with it." Betty twisted the hefty hunk of decorated metal in her hand, feeling defeated.

"*This* guy might." Dylan held up his cell. It was a photo of Jeremiah Munsey. "He's that televangelist you watch, right?"

Betty nodded.

"Says his church is here." Dylan showed Betty the GPS map. "Like, literally, here. Like two blocks or so."

Mantis scoffed and then said nervously, "Well, ain't that convenient."

***

The gang headed through a set of tall wrought-iron gates adorned with fleur-de-lis post-toppers that screamed *New Orleans*. Beyond it, a swirling path surrounded several bronze statues bathed in sodium vapor streetlights.

An ice-cold breeze wafted through the air, sending a sudden chill right through them all. Mantis zipped her leather jacket and looked up at the church, with its steeple looming high overhead.

Decorative stained glass windows adorned the front. An engraved stone banner read *Church of St. John the Evangelist* above its entrance. A wide, stone staircase spanned the length of the building like a tiered welcome mat.

In front of the massive wooden double doors, a black demon feasted on the remains of a street musician, tearing into the man's shredded throat with its gnashing teeth. Near the body, the man's blue saxophone lay dented on its side.

Two more creatures slunk out from behind one side of the church together, sniffing the air until they, too, found the corpse.

Don't go to the church.

Grace's words swam in Mantis's head. Unease washed over her. "*Fuck*," she whispered, watching them through the bushes at the fenced edge of the grounds. "*Think we can take all three?*"

No one dared to answer.

A fourth demon rounded the corner, prowling the walkway in search of gory sustenance. A glowing, orange, magma-like substance seethed from the wide crags in its skin. This one was more insect-like, with long, locust legs jutting from its chest.

As soon as it reached the corpse, it unhinged its jaw unnaturally, roaring at the others. The others cowered, skittering away from the locust-like creature.

It crunched into the man's skull like it was chewing a mouthful of stone. It shook with vigor, splashing dark blood across the side of the church, separating the head. Tendrils of slick veins and tissue dangled. The demon spat it into the air, and it returned to the ground with a dampened crunch as it smashed against the slate walkway.

One of the smaller demons chased after it, thrilled for the scraps.

"*Bet, how many bullets you got in your .38?*" Mantis pulled her switchblade from her pocket and triggered it. It was tiny in comparison to the beasts before them.

"It's *not the bullets I'm worried about; it's the reload time. It only holds six shots. What if those things take a few shots to go down?*" Betty whispered back.

"*Shit.*"

Two more demons made their way to the front of the building.

"*Jesus! How many of these are there?*"

"*Look!*" Betty pointed to two more demons making their way toward them from two blocks away. One leaped onto a covered metal trash can and screeched. The terrifying sound echoed through the darkened French Quarter.

"*Mother-fuck,*" Mantis growled.

"*I got this,*" Sweet Tea hissed. "*As soon as they're gone, you hightail it inside.*"

"*What are you doing?*" Dylan asked, panic in his voice.

"I'm *gonna distract them.*" Sweet Tea took off her teal jacket and backpack and handed them to Betty.

"*With what? Your tits? This ain't The Classy Lassie,*" Mantis said.

"I'll *get them to chase me, then I'll give them the slip and meet you back inside.*"

"*Just like that, huh?*"

"*I used to run track. I still run almost every day. Tips are shit for a chubby stripper.*" Sweet felt adrenaline surge through her body.

"*You can't be ser—*" Dylan was interrupted as Sweet Tea kissed him. Before he could protest, she was gone. She bolted out of the gate into the middle of Decatur, drawing the attention of the nearby demons away from the dead musician. They leaped, nearly in unison, toward her, racing past the statues and out the gate in an ashen flurry.

Sweet Tea hollered joyfully, her voice bouncing off the French-style balconies and brick buildings. They bared their fangs, scuttling after her, leaving the bloody church steps completely vacated in seconds.

The others followed Mantis across the park path, through the other gate, and up the gore-splattered steps. Mantis yanked the bloodied handle of the front door. It didn't budge.

"Are you *kidding* me?!"

Mantis kicked the door in anger, smearing the sax player's life fluids on it with her boot.

"*Over here!*" Dylan hissed loudly, hand on the knob of an open side door.

***

Nina Hartley watched the church's new visitors from the altar in the apse of the church. A gold cross stood ten feet high behind her. It was an exact, large-scale version of the reliquary, sans compartment. Betty's heart leaped with joy when she spotted it. They were on the right track. They *had* to be. That couldn't possibly be a coincidence.

"May I help you?" Nina bellowed, dark skin and hair bathed dandelion-yellow from the chandeliers overhead. She set a polished chalice on the altar and folded her rag neatly.

"You can't hide out from the *Locusta Acrididae* in here. I'm sorry, but you need to leave."

Mantis laughed. "Turning us away in a time of crisis. How very *Christian* of you."

She peered up at a large plaque above the looming cross. It said:

And this is the condemnation, that light is come into the world, and men loved darkness rather than light, because their deeds were evil.
John 3:19

Betty looked down at the bloody footprints she'd tracked onto the marble aisle and then back at Nina apologetically. "None of them followed us in."

"I know. They can't come in here." Nina was clearly irritated. "They never seem to make it past the steps."

"What's a *Locussa Crididee*?" Mantis couldn't quite remember what Nina had called it.

Nina rattled off the memorized scripture, "*And he opened the pit of the abyss; and there went up a smoke out of the pit, as the smoke of a great furnace; and the sun and the air were darkened. And from the smoke... came locusts upon the earth.*" Nina stepped forward onto the sanctuary. "*Revelations.*"

"*Shocker*," Mantis retorted with sarcasm. "Those don't look like any locust *I've* ever seen. But then again, bugs in the south *do* get pretty damn big—"

"We're searching for Jeremiah Munsey." Betty interrupted. "We just need a *moment* of his time. I'm trying to find my son. And… we have to ask him about this." Betty wasn't sure how to make those two concepts cohesive. She stepped toward Nina, pulling the reliquary from her purse.

When Nina caught sight of it, her eyes widened as if she were standing before God himself. "Where did you get that?!"

"*Finally*." Lucy's voice echoed from the balcony. "*Took you long enough.*"

Lucy smiled down at them, chestnut-brown hair draped over her shoulder, breasts heaving from the pressure of her skin corset.

A lustful grin grew on Mantis's face.

Lucy looked down at Nina. "Be a doll and fetch Munsey. Tell him I said it's *time.*"

"Time for *what?*" Nina grabbed the railing to the raised transept with both hands.

Lucy didn't answer.

Nina imagined that the banister was Lucy's throat for a moment, subtly choking the life out of it. "Sure thing. Anything *else* you'd like while I'm at it? Shine your *shoes*, perhaps?"

Lucy waved her away and started down the staircase on the side of the church. Nina disappeared into a door in the back.

Mantis turned to Betty and whispered. "Oh my *God*. I think I'm in *love*."

Munsey rushed out of his office, Nina trailing with a sullen expression.

Dylan stared at the side door, hoping Sweet Tea would burst through at any moment.

Mantis gawked at Lucy's long, sexy legs as she made her way down the last of the steps.

At the bottom, Lucy traipsed lackadaisically. "Your boy is a *trip*, Betty."

"My *boy*?" Betty gasped and covered her mouth with both hands for a moment. Tears filled her eyes, and her knees felt like they would collapse. "You've seen my *Gabriel*?" A barrage of tears poured down her face. "Where is he? Is he *okay*?"

"Oh, he's fine." Lucy crossed her arms in front of her voluptuous breasts. It was only then that Betty and Mantis started to comprehend what her gruesome outfit was made of. "We've been having an amazing time together. He's *very* bright. Figured out who I was like *that*." Lucy snapped her fingers.

"And who's that?" Mantis asked, grabbing Lucy's hand and kissing the back of it. "*Enchente*."

"Oh, you all have *so many* names for me." Lucy pulled her hand away and smiled. "Beelzebub, Belial, Tempter, *Abbadon*... ugh, I *never* liked that one. Makes me sound like the fat little boy on the playground that no one likes. *Morning Star* was always my favorite, but you can call me Lucy." She grinned, cheeks dimpling. "Short for *Lucifer*."

"So... you're, uh, allegedly *Satan*, huh?" Mantis flashed Betty a look that said *This chick is crazy*.

"Oh, *Satan*. Yes, that *is* another one."

"I've been hearing stories about the devil my whole life, and I never pictured him to be some fine-ass honey with a sweet rack."

"*Right*? Well," Lucy looked down at her tits, "she's only a *rental*. I was lucky. She was sort of a dent-and-bent floor model. Possessed the bitch *right* as she was dying, which, believe *me*, is *weirdly* hard to do." She was tickled by her own admission. "Check *this* out."

Lucy turned and lifted her hair to reveal a huge chunk of the back of her head was gone. It was a concave mess of skull, meat, and shattered vertebrae. They could see the back of Lucy's teeth and tongue through the gaping hole.

"*Oh fuck!*" Mantis covered her mouth.

Nina flashed a furious glance for the blasphemous outburst.

Lucy twirled back around. "This thing's barely got any miles on it, and the interior's *all stock,* if you know what I mean."

Mantis stared at the curtain of hair through the hole in the back of Lucy's mouth when she spoke.

"Not an ounce of silicone. I couldn't believe it. Finally, God did *somethin'* right."

Nina's eyes shot to Lucy now, her Creole face twisted in disgust.

"*What the fuck?!*" Mantis yelled, wiping her dark hair back in shock.

"Watch your language! You are in the holy house of the *Lord,*" Nina scolded.

"On the *contrary,* Nina. This is *my* church."

"*Excuse* me?"

"Yes, you *are* excused." Lucy said with a grin, waving Nina away. "They're here now. You can go."

Mantis and Betty flashed each other puzzled looks.

"Munsey! You gonna let her talk to me like this?" Nina slammed her hands onto her hips.

Munsey shrugged without a care. "She's right. You can go."

"Wh-what are you *talking* about?" Nina bellowed. "I've been by your side since the *beginning*. Back when you were just… *Jerry Beck*! I have *slaved* for St. John's Min—"

Munsey cut her off with a scream. "We said *get out!*" He pointed to the front door.

"You can't just toss me to the side like I'm *nothing*. You've been acting so strange since *she* came around."

Lucy laughed and covered her mouth. "I'm *sorry,* you are just *so pathetic.*"

The church's front doors rattled vigorously. Dylan rushed over to the side door and waved Sweet Tea in through the side entrance.

Once inside, Dylan kissed her. "Don't you *ever* fucking do that to me again!"

"What'd I miss?" Sweet Tea asked, panting heavily. She wiped the sweat from her brow, and he handed her jacket and backpack back to her.

Dylan pointed at Lucy. "Chick thinks she's *Lucifer.*"

Sweet Tea stared at him, confused, trying to catch her breath. "Come again?"

Mantis stepped forward. "Even if I *did* believe in Hell, which I *don't*, I don't believe you're *Old Scratch.*"

"You fucking mortals and your need for *proof.* Then again, I suppose if more of you were capable of faith, I wouldn't be *overrun* by you little bastards down there. You'll believe a book with talking *snakes* and spontaneously combusting bushes, but when a woman says she's the *Great Deceiver*, you suddenly require forensic proof." Lucy sighed. "How's this?" Lucy untied the braided hair laces of her flesh corset, exposing her breasts as it fell to the floor.

Mantis grinned, "Alright, now we're talkin'."

Betty noticed that Lucy's hand bore the 616 symbol. But instead of being in marker, it glowed like molten metal in the carved-open meat of her palm.

Betty thought about Gabriel's bear and how the same sooty numbers appeared in its fur. And the severed hand Mantis brought into her home. And Fish...

Nina covered her eyes, completely appalled at the nudity before her. "This is a *Church, for God's sake*!"

Lucy wriggled out of her brimstone-yellow skirt, revealing her entire naked form in all of its perfection. "Why is it always for *God's* sake and never *mine*? I gave you rock-n-roll!"

She ran one fingernail across her throat. It sliced through the skin, separating her flesh cleanly.

Dylan screamed, shocked by the sight.

Lucy's wound didn't bleed. She pried back, peeling her skin away from the meat beneath like a sheet of cling wrap.

"And *birth control*, so you could bang your brains out and not have a dozen little *rugrats* running around." Lucy looked Sweet Tea up and down, face completely degloved, and added, "You're *welcome!*"

Lucy slit the skin from her throat to her navel.

"And *porn* and *David Lee Roth*."

She grabbed the edges of her skin like the lapels of a coat and flapped them back. The newly uncovered muscles of her abdomen shifted bizarrely. A being burst forth from it, the color of a garnet gemstone, glistening. Two black horns shoved through its forehead, curling up toward the light.

Its muscles expanded, making the creature appear bulkier. Sharp, piranha-like teeth burst through its gums. Long, black fingernails forced their way through her hands.

Lucy transformed before them into a nightmarish being, easily over four hundred pounds.

None of the gawking observers had ever seen anything like it. It was no longer male or female and was, instead, completely *monstrous*, with a faint resemblance to the Baphomet they'd seen all along.

Nina screamed and raced toward the door, stopping short and using Betty and Mantis as a shield.

Munsey, however, seemed unaffected by Lucy's transformation.

The beast growled in a low, demonic tone, "Is this more like what you pictured?"

Mantis nodded, heart thumping wild. "Yeah. I k-kinda liked you better the other way."

The beast let out a sinister chuckle and compressed back down to the size and mass of a mortal. The claws and teeth retracted into the meat. The horns sucked inside. It picked up the woman's flesh and wriggled back in like a tight bathing suit.

Nina nearly fainted and held Betty's arm to steady herself.

Mantis squirmed as she watched the beast finish its jaw-dropping retreat into the beautiful female it was before. "I am *weirdly* turned on right now."

Lucy redressed and cocked one now-normal eyebrow at Mantis. "So, Esther Levy, now that you *know* I'm the *Destroyer of Worlds*, can we get down to business?"

Mantis was completely shocked as her real name fell from Lucy's lips. She nodded slowly, in complete awe.

"*Really?*" Betty whipped her head. "*Esther Levy? That's* your real *name?*"

Mantis rolled her eyes. "I'm named after my *grandma.*"

Sweet Tea snorted. "No wonder you go by Mantis! Shoot, I would, too."

"It was my *grandmother's* name," Mantis uttered quietly, eyes locked on Lucy.

"Wait, *Levy?*" Dylan chuckled. "You're *Jewish?*"

Mantis held up her thumb and index finger, spread an inch apart. "Little bit, yeah."

Dylan doubled over, roaring with laughter. "You gave me all that shit about me being—"

"616." Betty pointed to Lucy's hands, interrupting Dylan. "You *were* the one that took my son!"

"I *did.*" Lucy nodded. "Although we both know he's not *your* son."

"I may not have given birth to him, but he's still *my son.*" Betty trembled from the rage at the insinuation.

"Wait," Sweet Tea turned to Betty, "Gabe's not—"

"He's *mine,*" Mantis volunteered. "*Technically.*"

"*What*?!" Sweet Tea's grew loud.

"After that piece-a-shit pimp knocked me up, Betty rode in on her pro-life high horse and begged me not to have an abortion."

"After everything he put me through, physically, I couldn't have any of my *own*," Betty added.

"Betty watched me like a hawk. Agreed to take the baby when I calved out. I told her if I did, she'd have to leave." She pointed to herself. "Because this girl was *not* built for motherhood."

Lucy waltzed up to the altar and picked up a decanter of wine.

"What do you think you're doing?!" Nina bellowed. "That's the blood of *Christ*!" Nina spat.

"This? The blood of Christ? *Please*, it's *fermented grapes.* You sanctimonious Evangelicals aren't even supposed to *believe* in transubstantiation. The very fact that you worship a *meal* is, *itself*, idolatry. That's what you all do. You pick and choose and pick and choose and pick—" Lucy poured the burgundy liquid into the holy chalice and gulped some before offering it to the others. Wine dribbled out the back of Lucy's skull down her pale, yellow skirt.

"Why not. We should celebrate." Munsey took a sip from the chalice and stood obediently beside Lucy.

Nina felt as if she had been eviscerated.

"Esther, no one's gonna give you sympathy for being the *Madonna*." Lucy rolled her stunning eyes.

"First, it's *Mantis.* Second, what the *hell* does *the Material Girl* have to do with any of this?"

"Not *Madonna*, you idiot. *The* Madonna. The bearer of the *second coming*." Lucy finished off the chalice of wine and crammed some communion wafers in her mouth. She looked at Munsey, spitting crumbs everywhere. "Why do you even *have* this stuff? I specifically told you to pretend to be an *Evangelist*. Didn't we *talk* about this? Like, at *length?*"

Munsey cleared his throat. "We *did.* This stuff was for the monthly mass we added a few months ago. I was trying to hook a group of on-the-fence Catholics. Worked, actually. Every time someone came up for a wafer and wine, you could just see this absolutely *vacant* look in their eyes. Like they'd checked out. Just going through the motions. Oh, you'd *love it*, Lucy. None of 'em had any clue why they were doing it."

"Good work." She patted Munsey on the top of his head like a puppy.

"God's *flock* is the perfect way to describe them. These *sheep* believe anything a guy with a suit and a mic says. They don't think for themselves. Religion has become mechanical. It's almost," Munsey wolfed down more crackers, "*too* easy to lead them astray."

"Is that why you pulled the little *mark of the beast stunt?*" Lucy asked in a disapproving tone. "Because it was too tempting not to?"

"They were gonna die anyway. I just wanted to see if I could pull it off."

"You moron, if you lead them *astray* and they die without the *cleansing,* they go *where?*" Lucy cupped her ear and waited for an answer to her quiz.

Munsey cleared his throat and mumbled. "To *Hell*. They go to Hell."

Lucy smacked Munsey hard in the back of the head. "That was the *opposite* of what we wanted. *Right*?"

Munsey nodded like an abused spouse.

"Woah, hold up. What *exactly* do you mean, a *second coming*?"

"Oh, wow, you're still on *that*?" Lucy sighed. "How do I put this in the words of a *Springer* guest? *I was a huge fan of that show, by the way.* It was like getting a brief preview of who's comin' to see me soon." She leaned forward, wagging her finger. "*Johnny Fo'-Fingas wasn't yo' baby-daddy.*"

Mantis couldn't focus. She'd never been more confused in her life.

"You were preggo *two weeks* before you even *went* to El Paso to play *Captain-Save-a-Ho* with Black-Eyed Betty here."

"Not possible," Mantis asserted confidently. "I'd *only* ever been with Grace for, like, *years* before that."

"It's called an *immaculate conception,* dummy." Lucy smacked her hand on the altar. "Seven years ago, Esther here, she gave birth to the *Son of Man*. I tried to make a push to end this all way back *then,* but for a broad who just squeezed a seven-pound wrecking ball from her clown-hole, you bounced back quick."

Betty looked at Mantis, eyes huge. "That's why those creatures stopped! That never made any sense to me."

She looked at Dylan and Sweet Tea to explain further. "Right after Gabe was born, we killed, like, ten of those *things* when he was in the NICU on the ventilator the night he was born." She looked up at Lucy. "And then they just... *stopped.*"

"Yeah, that was almost *really* bad. I called 'em off. It wasn't the right time to make my move. See, I needed Gabe to be older because I found out this whole thing actually doesn't work without his *consent.* I *totally* almost blew it. In retrospect, I waged war prematurely. *Not the first time*, I'm afraid."

"Why *me?* Out of all the people on the *planet.* That makes no sense." Mantis was flustered by the logic.

Lucy shrugged. "Who knows. Mary Magdeline was a prostitute. Noah hung around in his vineyard, getting drunk. Jacob lied and cheated Esau out of his birthright. Paul was a Christian-hating *chief* of sinners at one point. And, hell, Lazarus... Lazarus was fuckin' *dead.*" Lucy looked up into the air. "He's always 'got his grand *plans.*"

Betty spoke. "God always seems to choose imperfect people for the important tasks."

"Also, it probably helps that you also have Christ's lineage on your father's side." Lucy pressed another communion wafer between her lips.

"Oh, *bullshit.*" Mantis waved away the ridiculous notion.

"Every generation dilutes it a bit more, but I assure you, it's true."

"Then why not one of my *relatives?*" Mantis asked.

"Like *who*? You're an only child." Lucy waited for another smart-ass reply. None came.

"Why not my cousin, um…" Mantis snapped her fingers. "*Claire*?"

"Claire's not really your uncle's kid. Her daddy's some postal worker who used to bang her mom." Lucy pointed up into the air. "If you wanna know *more*, you could always ask *Him*."

Mantis scoffed. "God and I don't exactly have an open line of communication currently."

Lucy laughed hard. "I feel you on that one. Been a while since we've had a *heart-to-heart* as well." She turned to Jeremiah. "Munsey is all my doing. *My protege*." She wagged his chin as she would a baby. "*My widdle Antichrist*." She shoved Munsey's face. "Pairing with you, Nina, was all *his* idea. He said every Jim needs a Tammy Faye to sell the image. Looks like he was right."

"Why would I believe anything you say? You're *Beelzebub*. Your temple is built on *lies* and *deception*," Nina growled through gritted teeth.

"Well, thank you. That's very kind. It's less of a *temple* and really more of a rancid pit where the self-indulgent scourge of the earth is allowed to commit all of their hedonistic crimes at will. It's basically *Florida* but *marginally* hotter. You should be *thanking me*, Nina. I'm the *best friend* the church has *ever* had. Without such a terrifying force, no one would fear the consequences of their actions. There'd be *anarchy*. I've been doing Him a *favor*. No one would adhere to the Bible or its mish-mash of rules and commandments without *terror*. The blacker the darkness, the brighter *His light* can shine, *right*?"

"Don't you have your *own* flock of ritualistic heathens to damn with your Church of Satan?" Nina spouted.

Lucy was tickled by the comment. "Oh, they don't believe I exist any more than *you all* did a few minutes ago." Lucy pointed to Mantis. "They think I'm some sort of *fabled creature* that symbolizes their opposition to figures like Christ. They don't worship *me*. They only put faith in the tangible, *earthly* things, and they believe I'm just a symbol of that. They worship *themselves*. It's part of their doctrine. And, while I can respect their pride, they're misguided. LeVey made it sound like you have to be an *elitist genius* to worship me, and *I assure you* that is *not* the case. Any ol' self-serving lecherous asshole will do."

Lucy continued. "Oh! And to top it all off, I have to deal with idiots like *Fish* trying to steer people in my direction with pentagrams made of *glitter*. But... the biggest help I get expanding my *'flock'* is, like, Baptist pastors who picket gay funerals and spout hate speech." Lucy purred. The thought of it made her feel all fuzzy inside.

"Or men who dress in white robes and pointy hoods swearing to uphold *Christian morality* by burning crosses on people's lawns in *His* name. Or *televangelists* who steal millions from the church to build a fucking *theme park* or who lock newly-homeless parishioners outside their megachurch during a *flood*. Those," she smiled, "turn more people from God than I ever could."

Lucy looked around. "You guys don't have any *real* food on you, do you?"

Everyone stood in stunned silence. Sweet Tea clutched her backpack strap tighter.

"Eh, worth a shot. Been living off bread and crackers for *days,* waitin' for the lot of you to arrive. I'm trying not to ruin this body with too many carbs. That'd be the *real* sin here." Lucy joked. "I don't know how you mortals do it. Some of you eat, like, three times a *day*. It's *exhausting*."

Sweet Tea glowered. "Yeah, well, it doesn't help that the water's now been filled with toxic meteors, and the crops are gonna die from a lack of sun."

"First, your water was *already* toxic, as many chemicals as *you humans* dump into it. I mean, ask the people of Flint, okay? Second, *bitch, it's not easy* to black out the *sun*! I had to pull a lot of strings to do that! I assure you, the book of Revelations has *not* been easy for me to recreate. That John of Patmos had a real flair for the *dramatics*."

Lucy sighed, bored with having to explain it all. "Here's the deal. I *so* don't have time for this, so I'm just gonna cut to the chase. Bottom line: Hell is *full*. And I'm not talking just a *little* full as in, like, nearing *maximum capacity*; I mean, it is butts-to-nuts *packed* down there. Sometimes, I come to earth just to get away because I can't even hear myself *think* with all the screams. I used to *love* the sound of tortured souls!"

"I would think it being full would please *you* to no end," Betty sassed.

"Right? *Except...* that you guys keep breeding and breeding. And I never *chose* to lord over billions of degenerates."

"Sure you did," Betty retorted. "When you tried to *usurp* God's throne."

"Look, I did some things in Heaven without fully grasping the consequences." Lucy sighed. "Admittedly, I got a little too big for my britches. But c'mon, an *eternity* of this? You guys fuck up, break every commandment and then you go get baptized and suddenly you're saved. How's that fair?"

"But you've had centuries to make some big power play. What the hell's so special about right now?" Mantis asked.

"Well, funny you should ask. The problem down there... it's getting *exponentially* worse. I mean, I thought the Holy Wars were *bad,* but this age breeds sin *everywhere.* Church attendance is down. New sites crop up every day for casual sex encounters, apps specifically for adultery, or random hookups. *Just swipe right to get laid by a total stranger.*"

"What apps are those? Like, specifically." Mantis looked like she was about to take notes.

Betty elbowed her hard. "Stop!"

"People aren't even *hiding* their depravity anymore. Instead, they're casting wider nets. Prisons are overflowing with thieves and murderers while pedophiles and rapists are getting off scot-free. People pitch a tent overnight to worship new versions of a smartphone that's almost identical to the one in their pocket, but where are they on the *Sabbath,* huh? People have grown covetous in their vapid attempts to *keep up with the Joneses.* So I ask you, where the *fuck* are they all supposed to *go*?"

"So you *faked* the end of the world?" Betty was appalled. "What could you *possibly* get out of *forcing* an apocalypse? Wouldn't you be stuck with even *more* people down there?"

Lucy sighed. "Normally yes, but *not* if the second coming of Christ is *martyred* first, cleansing people of all their sins with yet another sacrificial lamb of God."

Lucy raised an eyebrow and smiled. "Now, if worldwide demolition occurs after *that*, all of the sin-free souls ascend to Heaven. With nobody left on earth, Hell's doors close for good. He can deal with His fuckin' angels and me, my demons. Plus, seeing the events of Revelations come to light has already made *billions* drop to their *knees* to beg for God's forgiveness. In the last four *days*, there have been more baptisms, prayers, Hail Marys, and talk-in-tongues than *ever* before." She looked at Nina and pointed to herself. "*See*? Church's best friend."

"So, let me make sure I understand you. You're trying to send everyone… to *Heaven*?" Betty was trying to wrap her mind around the concept.

"Yes!" Lucy slammed her hand on the altar again.

"You're not gonna sacrifice my *son* for *your* agenda," Betty yelled.

"Correct. *Her* son is gonna sacrifice *himself*." She pointed to Mantis.

"No." Mantis assumed a courageous stance. "Absolutely not."

Lucy spoke condescendingly, "Aw, *you're cute*."

Mantis flirted back, "You're pretty hot yourself. What do you say after this—"

"Mantis!" Betty screamed. "*Focus*!"

Mantis cleared her throat and grew serious. "Why do you need this… stupid…*reliquary* then? We just went on a wild goose chase—"

Lucy waved for them to follow her.

"Enough chit-chat. *Come*. It's time for the show. You get the best seats in the house." Lucy walked down the aisle toward the stairs.

"We're not going anywhere until you answer me. We *killed* for this thing!" Mantis exclaimed, pointing to Betty's purse.

"Yeah," Dylan said meekly, "actually, like, a *lot* of people."

Lucy snapped her fingers. "Walk and talk, walk and talk." She started up the steps, and the others hesitantly followed. Nina brought up the rear, arms crossed.

"Seven years ago, Grace helped me hide the pieces so the reliquary couldn't be destroyed while we regrouped from the botched attempt."

Lucy barely got the words out before Mantis raced up the steps quickly behind her. "Grace? *My* Grace?"

"I chose someone who could get close to you. She hand-selected the seven men, all known for their unique transgressions and exceptional spiritual shortcomings."

She ran her fingers along the glossy railing as they neared the top and spoke eloquently in Latin, "*Luxuria, Avaritia, Acedia, Ira, Gula, Invidia, et Superbia.* The men were charged with protecting each piece in exchange for an elevated position in Hell, which, of course, was a *lie*." Lucy chuckled, "*I do that sometimes*."

"So, you're telling me that my *dead* ex-girlfriend just sent us on a four-day *scavenger hunt*?" Mantis locked her jaws together in anger.

Lucy turned, looming slightly over the others from the top step. "She could've hidden the pieces anywhere in the world. How about a little *gratitude*?"

They followed Lucy to the second-level balcony, unprepared for what they'd see. Beyond several rows of pews, a black orb, with smoky tendrils flitting from its edges, swirled against the wall like a gaping portal. The hole in the center of it looked like a sooty, twisted tunnel that went through the wall.

Below the portal sat a small wooden chair with Gabriel in its seat. Several small blood bags sat on a folding table beside the boy. A smile crept onto his drained face as Betty came into sight. "Mommy!"

Beside him, Grace was there, labeling another bag of blood. She set it down and locked eyes with Mantis but made no attempt to greet her.

Betty raced toward Gabriel, but Munsey snatched her mid-stride by the arm.

"Let me go!" Betty screamed. "You can't keep me from my *son*!"

Munsey didn't budge. Instead, he gripped her arm so tight it would surely bruise.

"Ow!" Betty attempted to wriggle free from Munsey's powerful grasp. "Gabe, are you okay? Did they hurt you?"

Gabriel managed to speak, though weak. "I'm okay. Miss Lucy said I'm going to save everyone, just like Jesus did." There was such innocence in his glacier-blue eyes. "I'm *helping*, mommy."

Betty couldn't control the tears. "What are they doing to you?"

Even from twenty feet, Betty could see the needle marks and burst veins that marred his arms.

"It's okayy." Gabriel looked down at the marks. "Miss Lucy just needs some more of my blood."

Betty's head swung around, and she glared at Lucy. "Why would you do this? He's just a child!"

Munsey wrenched her arm again with his freakish grip.

"Give Jeremiah the reliquary, and you can go to your son," Lucy stated.

She looked to Mantis for approval, but Mantis had her eyes locked on Grace. Betty pulled the gold cross from her purse and handed it to Munsey. He released his grip, and blood rushed through her arm like a burst dam.

Betty raced to her son, crashing to her knees before the boy.

Lucy grinned as she took the ornate golden cross from Munsey.

Mantis stalked toward Grace like a tiger, ready to shred the throat of a zebra. Finding out that Grace had a role in Lucy's plan was beyond a betrayal. Hatred burned for the woman she once loved.

Lucy crossed her arms, pressing her breasts out front and center. "She lured you here, not to see you again but to gain a better foothold in *my* kingdom. Suicide was the only way to ensure such a loyal follower would come straight down to me." She neared Mantis. "It hurts to be cast aside by the one you love the most. Trust me, I know."

Still staring at Grace, Mantis could only mutter, "*I loved you.*"

Lucy laughed.

"You think this is *funny*?" Sweet Tea was offended. "You like watching people *suffer*?"

"Yeah. It's kinda *my thing*."

"You used to be an *angel*! How did you even become… *this*?"

"Tea, don't," Dylan reached out, trying to pull her back, but Sweet Tea jerked away.

"*God* made me like this! I didn't want to be in charge of the world's degenerates like some eternal *prison warden.* I made a *mistake.* One stupid, lousy mistake. Where was his never-ending forgiveness *then*?!"

"Tell me this isn't real. Tell me Lucy's lying." Mantis stepped toward Grace.

Silence.

"Tell me she's full of shit, Grace! *Seven years*, I've been *destroyed* over losing you. Thinking your death was *my* fault."

"I *told you* not to come," Grace said smugly.

Lucy laughed again, and Sweet Tea lunged at her. The force knocked Lucy to the ground by the balcony rail, and she wailed on her face with closed fists. Munsey grabbed Sweet Tea by the waist, ripping her off Lucy.

"Put her down!" Dylan screamed, furiously grabbing Jeremiah by the jacket. But the evangelist was overpowering.

Thrashing in his arm, Sweet Tea elbowed Munsey in the face. It didn't phase him. Dylan savagely punched him in the base of his skull and yanked back on Munsey's white jacket with all of his weight.

But it wasn't enough. Munsey moved forward like a rolling boulder and hurled Sweet Tea over the edge of the balcony.

Dylan's scream echoed throughout the church, even louder than the sound of the crash below. They could hear the sound of Sweet Tea's spine as it snapped atop an oak pew. Her body lay still, draped in an awkward position across the wood.

Mantis and Betty rushed to the railing and looked down in absolute horror. Betty shrieked. The veins in Dylan's neck throbbed as he screamed, doubled over the rails, tears raining down, spanning the vast distance to the first floor.

Stillness. Quiet. Nobody moved.

Sweet Tea's eyes stared blankly affixed to the painting of John of Patmos on the ceiling.

Dylan's heart pounded as he flung himself down the massive stairway, barely making it down upright. He skidded to the marbled floor at her feet. Panic swelled in his chest, attacking him, making it impossible to breathe. He wheezed through the tears.

"Tea! *Tia!*" Dylan shoved an oak pew away to make room, crying so hard he could barely see. "Tea, baby. *No!*"

Sweet Tea blinked and swallowed hard, choking on a mouthful of blood. She tried to lift her head but couldn't. Her eyes strained to look at him. Dylan crawled onto the pew beside her and held her hand to his tear-streaked cheek, rocking in place with it.

"I love you." He whispered through the tears and kissed her palm. "Hear me? I love you, Tia Green."

Dylan watched, devastated. The light behind Sweet Tea's hazel eyes extinguished. As her hand went limp, he felt a piece of his soul die.

Eyes flooded with tears, Betty pulled the revolver from her purse and pointed it at Munsey. "You bastard!"

Grace lurched forward and snatched Betty up by the hair. She yanked Betty's head to the side and wrenched the gun away, firing it in the process. The shot missed Gabriel by an inch and blew a hole in Lucy's abdomen.

Lucy groaned. Her rumbling muscles squeezed the metal casing back out of the hole.

"Grace! What the fuck?!" Lucy pointed to Gabriel. "*You could have killed him!*"

Grace looked down, filled with shame. "I beg forgiveness, Morning Star."

"Grace, if you weren't already dead, I'd fucking kill you," Lucy screamed.

"Ditto, bitch," Mantis yelled at her ex.

Nina backed away from Munsey, appalled by the monster standing before her. She'd spent nearly a decade preaching the word of God by his side but somehow knew so *little* of his *true* intentions. Nina's eyes were open now. "Seven years I've been helping you lead innocent people astray." She turned to face the stairs, unable to look at Jeremiah. "*What have I done?*"

Munsey placed his hands on the sides of her face lovingly. "Nina. None of them were *truly* innocent."

He twisted, snapping her neck effortlessly. Nina slumped in his grasp. He gave her a shove, and her lifeless body toppled down the staircase, bashing limply against the steps until she was splayed across the marble floor. Munsey smiled at the broken corpse.

Betty snatched up Gabriel, but he struggled. "Noooooo!" He wriggled out of her grasp and raced to the edge of the balcony. Before Betty could catch up to him, Gabriel had scrambled up the divider. He balanced precariously on the railing of the balcony, wavering.

"Gabriel, no!" Mantis hollered.

"I *want* to do this!" Gabriel yelled, pleading, staring with innocent blue eyes. "Miss Lucy told me *everything*. I'm the second son of God. My sacrifice can save everyone. Just like Jesus, Mom!"

"Not yet, Gabriel," Lucy pointed to the floor. "Come down."

Gabriel complied, carefully climbing back down. Betty scooped him into her arms and held him tight. He hugged her back and whispered, "I just want to help."

"I know you do, baby." Betty pressed her lips to the crown of Gabriel's head.

"Take the boy down to the office, Grace," Lucy ordered. "The adults need to talk.

Grace nodded obediently and stepped toward the boy.

Betty growled, "Don't you even *think* about touching my *son*."

Betty felt the barrel of the .38 press against the side of her head. Grace whispered, "Unless you want to face your judgment in front of the boy before the cleansing, you'll come with me."

Betty complied with Grace's order, still clutching Gabriel. Grace shoved them toward the stairs forcefully.

"Take Dylan with you," Mantis said calmly. The echos of his heartbreaking sobs made her want to bawl, too.

Once on the ground floor, Betty held her hand out for Dylan. Betty's breath hitched as she saw Sweet Tea's lifeless gaze.

"No!" He yelled, still cradling her hand.

Grace nudged Betty with the gun, and they continued toward the office door in the transept, leaving Dylan to mourn.

"Let's move on. Shall we?" Lucy retrieved a scalpel from a small stack of supplies by the blood donation station, lifted a full plastic sack, and drove the blade in. The portal hungrily slurped the vital fluid sideways, defying gravity.

The ground shuddered beneath their feet, and a deafening rumble rose from the earth below. Jagged hunks of painted ceiling loosened, crashing down onto pews.

Chunks of drywall and wood rained down, dusting everything with a fine coat of powder. Chandeliers danced as the building rumbled from the brutal earthquake.

"Dylan!" Mantis screamed over the rail as one of the massive chandeliers came careening down through the air. Dylan rolled beneath a pew just in time. The fixture smashed down onto Sweet Tea, exploding shattered glass and warped metal in every direction.

Dylan crawled out. The sight of Sweet Tea's hand beneath the rubble infuriated him. He darted for the stairs, momentarily stunned by the sight of Nina's body in a tangle at the bottom. He steadied himself through the vicious rumbling and scrambled up the steps.

Lucy spoke, buttery voice rising optimistically above the chaos. "Another global earthquake. The final plague." She held up the last bag of blood and smiled at Jeremiah. "*It's time.*"

Munsey stepped forward with the reliquary, unbuckling the tiny chamber in the center. Lucy took several steps away from the portal and stabbed the bag with the scalpel, and poured the blood into the golden cross.

The rattling halted immediately.

"Now, there's only one thing left." Lucy motioned to Mantis. "I just need a little bit of your blood for—"

"*Fuck you,*" Mantis spat defiantly. "If Gabe's the second coming, you don't need *shit* from me."

"His blood alone can bring down mountains and fill rivers with blood. It can make the earth quake. But the blood of *both* of you in the portal together…" She moved her fingers like a firework. "*Boom.*"

Mantis stood stunned, taking all of the craziness and chaos in for a moment.

"I call it an *Adam* Bomb," she joked. "According to that almighty book, civilization started with an Adam. Now, it can end with one, too."

Munsey snatched Mantis's arms from behind, taking her by surprise. She struggled to free herself from his inhuman grasp.

Dylan glared at Munsey from the top of the staircase, hatred burning in his reddened eyes.

"When Gabriel is martyred, the sins of man are washed away again. And once this goes in with your blood, God's cruel science experiment here on earth finally comes to an end."

Arms cranked behind her, Mantis pulled the switchblade from her jean pocket. Munsey noticed, throwing her to the ground with brute force. She slammed hard. The force knocked the blade several feet away until the blade hung over the edge of the balcony, ready to fall at any moment.

Mantis groaned in pain, wondering if her ribs had shattered, but fought the evangelist with every shred of strength left in her.

Dylan dashed forward and picked up the knife. He leaped onto Munsey's back and buried the blade into the front of the reverend's throat, all the way to the hilt.

"You piece of shit!" Dylan yanked the knife out and forced the entire blade in again. *And again.*

Munsey choked on his own blood but did not go down. He locked eyes with Mantis, and he clutched his neck. Dylan stabbed again. The blade sliced through Munsey's hand, and he pulled it away, staring in horror at the stuck blade all the way through his palm.

Munsey leaned down, swinging at Mantis, catching her in the face with a slap that drove the knife through her cheek.

She howled in pain as Munsey's blood rained down on her. He reared his hand back and swiped at her again, this time slicing her jaw. Dylan still held on, dangling from him like a thrashing howler monkey.

"Good work, Munsey. Just… make sure to get some in here." Lucy calmly handed the reliquary down to the dying man. Through wet, dying wheezes, he lowered the reliquary to Mantis's face.

"Rot in hell." Mantis hocked a wad of spit into his face, and the bloody loogie landed near his eye. She smiled, molars visible through the gash in her face.

Where it landed, the sanguine liquid ulcerated a hole into his face like acid. The skin melted away. A sliver of white light shot out of the burned hole, just as the ground had done in her dreams.

"*Holy shit…*"

Munsey bucked like a wild bronco in pain. Dylan let go of the reverend. Mantis spat again. Another gaping hole opened in the evangelist's head, shining pure-white light onto her.

Munsey flopped backward and clutched himself in an infantile pose. Mantis tugged the knife from Jeremiah's hand and sliced her own palm with the blade. Mantis wiped her blood down his skin, and Munsey erupted in a nightmarish scream. Bold light poured through the now-gaping wound.

Mantis hobbled to her feet, certain of broken ribs with every labored breath. She smeared blood down the quivering man's back in the shape of a cross. Light shined through. Munsey struggled to stand, blinded by pain. Dylan grabbed him again by the lapels of his once-white suit and hurled him over the balcony. Munsey crashed loudly onto the rubble below. His guttural screams faded, and the beams of light dancing throughout the ruined church dimmed with them.

Mantis waltzed bravely up to Lucy, brandishing her bleeding palm as if it were a weapon to be feared. *But Lucy didn't flinch.*

"Your turn."

"Yes! Please!" Lucy's laugh was chilling. "Me next!"

Mantis pulled back, confused by Lucy's willingness to die.

"Go check on Betty and Gabe. I don't like them being in there with Grace," Mantis whispered to Dylan.

"You got it." He sniffled and wiped his eyes. He raced down the stairs, skittered through the rubble, and disappeared into the office.

"You've been scorned, beaten, raped, pissed on, pissed off, tossed aside, and put through the *wringer* by those who never even loved you back. So why not sit back and enjoy a front-row seat as we watch this world *burn*?"

***

"Don't *shoot!*" Dylan entered with his hands up in a display of submission.

Grace aimed the gun at his face. "Sit down." She motioned to the empty chair by Betty.

Gabriel watched the news on Munsey's television. "She... she couldn't have done this." His face twisted into a panicked frown. "I was with Miss Lucy the whole time."

Dylan walked toward the chair. With his back to Grace, his eyes locked with Betty's and bulged, alerting her that something was about to happen. He nodded toward the window. Betty gave him a subtle nod.

As soon as Dylan reached the chair, he picked it up and swung it, smashing it into Grace. The .38 in her hand went off, shattering the light fixture above them. Broken halogen snowed down on them. Betty scrambled through the darkness for her son.

As the muffled shot rang out, Mantis felt a wave of dread wash over her.

Lucy peered over the railing at the office, waiting for someone to emerge. While Lucy was distracted, Mantis's eyes settled on a sound station in front of several yellow drapes set up for church musicians and for mixing the onstage mic levels during Munsey's sermons.

"Grace?! Everyone okay down there? Is Gabriel safe?" Lucy hollered.

No answer.

Mantis crawled beneath the soundboard and pressed her injured hands together in prayer. "You *there*, God?" She panted, frantic to get the thoughts out before Lucy discovered her piss-poor hiding spot. "Look, I know I maybe haven't been your ideal baby mama up 'til this point. I'm new to this whole *repenting* thing. I guess... I'm sorry. For the killing. *And* for the lying. And the whoring around. Also, I shouldn't have convinced that guy in high school that I was a *Jehovah*. That's wasn't cool. I see that *now*."

She unclasped her hands, reached into her jean pockets, and pulled out the lighter and photo of Grace and her in Paris.

"I'm sure there's a laundry list of stuff I need to apologize for, God, but if you let us live, I will get right on that. Right now, I don't have enough time to itemize my sins. All I can say is... I am so *sorry*."

She rubbed her thumb over the faded inscription on the lighter. A present from Grace.

From another lifetime.

For the one who sets my heart ablaze, it said.

She flipped the top and spun the flint wheel a few times until the wick stayed lit.

Beneath the soundboard, she could see Lucy's feet waltz through blood, searching.

"Lord, I don't know why you entrusted me with something so important. Most people wouldn't trust me to watch their *dog* for a few hours." Mantis held the flame to Grace's face. The photo ignited. She leaned out from underneath the soundboard and tossed the lit picture beneath one of the yellow drapes.

"I'm sorry I wasn't everything you wanted me to be."

Lucy heard the whispering and rushed to the soundboard.

The flame crawled gracefully up the curtain, growing in size and scorching the white paint beneath it.

"I'm sorry, God, for what I'm about to do."

"Suddenly praying to God when you're in trouble? *How original.*" Lucy tapped the reliquary on the soundboard. "How 'bout we make this fast so that you can tell him in person."

Mantis continued her prayer, louder now that she'd been discovered. "Please let Betty know that I never meant for any of this to happen. And please let Dyl-do know that he really grew on me." Fire woofed through the balcony, filling the air with smoke. "Dyl-do is Dylan, by the way, just so we're clear." Mantis coughed. "Take care of Gabe, Lord. He's a good kid. You did good with him. Sure as hell didn't get that from *me*."

Grace limped her way up to the steps.

"Who's watching the kid?" Lucy asked, alarmed.

"There's been a…" Grace struggled to get the word out, "problem."

Below the soundboard, Mantis ran her tongue along the gash in her cheek and nodded, "*Amen.*"

Mantis lifted her legs and shoved, smashing the soundboard table sideways into the women. The force blasted Grace through the gap in the broken railing. She careened through the air, crashed down, and impaled on the chandelier's remains.

Mantis latched onto Lucy with both arms and whipped her into the wall of flames.

"*Forgive me, Father,*" Mantis grunted. She placed her sliced-open hand on the edge of one of the engulfed curtains and screamed as the burn of melting nylon consumed her, sticking to her wounded flesh like molten glue. She twisted into the curtain, wrapping the burning fabric around Lucy and herself like a flaming cocoon.

The women screamed in agonizing unison as Mantis hurled them off the edge of the destroyed balcony. They plummeted through the billowing cloud onto the jagged rubble below.

The black swirling portal shrunk to nothingness as life extinguished from Lucy's mortal form.

Mantis heard more bones break on impact. She wasn't sure who produced the noise. All she knew was that every square inch of her body hurt.

Mantis coughed weakly through the dense smoke and struggled to free herself from the charred curtain.

The devastated church grew blurry. Mantis rolled onto her back next to Lucy. She opened her eyes to see Grace's impaled body transform into weightless ash before the whole world faded from view.

As death mounted, the unfathomable pain melted away. Darkness enveloped her as she took her final breath.

The sun had returned, slicing through the ominous obsidian sky like a shiny steel beam. Betty and Dylan coughed as they dragged Mantis from the church through a maze of demon carcasses littering the steps. A trail of plaster trickled out from beneath her limp, sizzling legs.

They rested her on the walkway in front of the church. Betty checked frantically for a pulse and performed CPR, though she knew it was pointless.

Gabriel peered through the side door of the church at Lucy's corpse. Tears welled in his innocent eyes at the sight of her lifeless body. Nina, Sweet Tea, and Munsey lay in their own twisted displays of fragile mortality.

"Come on, Mantis!" Betty cried between chest-compressions.

Dylan joined Gabriel at the door and wiped the tears from his soot-covered face.

Gabriel clung to Dylan, shielding himself from the carnage. "Miss Lucy said I could save everyone."

"I know." Dylan rubbed the child's hair.

Betty screamed, drained of the energy needed to continue the useless act. *It was too late.*

No heartbeat.No sign of life.

Only silence.

Mantis was gone.

The beam in the sky widened until the city had become bathed in its singular, radiant beam.

Gabriel looked up at the parted clouds. "And God said let there be light," his tiny voice offered some optimism, "and there was light."

Betty's shoulders slumped as she prayed over Mantis. Gabriel ran to her, embracing Betty with all the strength he could muster.

Dylan stood near the church doors, lost. She motioned with her outstretched hand for him to come closer. Dylan dropped to his knees and hugged Betty and Gabriel tightly.

"You guys... aren't going to start singin' K*umbaya*, are you?" The weak voice beneath them managed.

"Mantis?!" Betty gasped.

Mantis coughed and then growled at the painful broken bones in her chest.

"You were *dead*!" Betty shouted.

"Yeah, I don't quite understand it, either." Mantis stared up at the beam of light from the sky, equally in shock that she'd survived.

As the growing light bathed her, she thought about Sweet Tea, Grace, the demons, her broken ribs, the devil... The last few day's events swirled in her mind like a flushed toilet. But as the light warmed her skin, she thought about how grateful she was to see the blue sky again. She thought about her lineage, their journey, and all they had survived.

"I need a cigarette," she said and let her head rest back down on the bloodied cobblestone walkway of the French Quarter.

EPILOGUE

Mantis awoke to the sound of keys jingling against the doorknob, and she buried her face into the couch pillow. Dylan opened the door and motioned to Gabriel. "After you, good sir."

"Why, thank *you*." Gabriel raced into the living room, hopping onto Mantis.

"There's the birthday boy." Mantis rolled onto her back and looked at Gabriel. His chin was covered in soot. He stared out from underneath a tiny hard hat. "How old are you today? Thirty-three?" She narrowed her eyes at him.

"I'm eight!" Gabriel rolled his.

"You sure? That amount of facial hair just ain't right on a kid your age. You know, you get that from my side of the family for sure." Mantis wiped the smudges. "Shoulda gotten you a shaving kit for your birthday."

"That's not hair, it's ash." Gabriel lounged, still sitting on Mantis's side.

"Oh yeah? What are you doin' playing around in ash, huh?" Mantis poked him in the sides playfully, coaxing a delighted giggle.

"Uncle Dylan gave me a job!"

"He gave you a *job*? Holy smokes, the only job Dylan knows how to give is a hand—"

"Mantis!" Dylan threw a couch pillow at her and set his helmet on the dinner table. He sifted through a pile of mail. "Hired him on my post-apocalyptic cleaning crew. *Tea's Double-D's* has taken off."

Mantis snickered. "That name never gets old. Perfect name for a demon-disposal company."

"Did you see the logo Betty drew up for us? It's on Gabe's shirt," Dylan said, pointing to the kid. Mantis glanced at a cartoon logo of Sweet Tea holding a trash bag with a demon claw sticking out of the top.

"Nice!" Mantis laughed. "Pretty smart idea, too. I heard they're melting them down and making all sorts of things out of 'em these days. They said on the news they're making 'em into asphalt and bricks, hell, even built housing material out of 'em in Oklahoma."

"It just felt right. She was always big on making the earth a cleaner place." Dylan's smile was melancholic. "I was scrapin' one of those locust ones off the street today, and I caught just a slight whiff of someone's wildflowers. Made me think of her."

Mantis didn't know what to say.

Gabriel picked at a piece of plastic wrap taped onto Mantis's arm. "Can I pleeeeeease see it now?"

"Sure, why not." Mantis peeled the plastic off of her arm to reveal that her *Grace* tattoo had been revised. More words had been added between the healed burn scars. The tattoo now read: *There, but for the Grace of God, go I.*

"Wow, they matched the font and everything."

"Yeah, but I don't think it's gonna get me a lot of," Mantis looked into Gabe's hopeful face and decided to spell it, "V-A-G. But at least now—"

Gabriel's face contorted in confusion. "*Vag*? Is that like a bag?"

307

Dylan's eyes grew large. He struggled to choke back his laughter and looked to Mantis, hoping she would skillfully evade Gabe's awkward question.

"Whoa, look who knows how to spell and forgot to tell Auntie Mantis."

"Yeah, Mantis?" Dylan joked. "Is it like a *bag*? Can you put stuff in it?"

"Yes, you can. And you should! As often as possible. And always with consent." Mantis poked Gabriel in the chest. "Gabe, *honey*, why don't you go whip auntie up a lil' mid-afternoon porchcrawler?"

"*No!*" Dylan said firmly. "No teaching him how to make porchcrawlers. He's eight."

"I wasn't *gonna* teach him." She sat up. "He already *knows* how. Taught him last week. He's still a *little* heavy-handed with the *vodka*, but, hey, Rome wasn't built in a day."

SCRITCH-SCRITCH-SCRIIIIIITCH.

The noise came from inside the coat closet.

Gabriel gasped. "What's that?"

Dylan looked around for a weapon, face tense. Mantis casually walked to the door and scratched her ass through her loose-fitting sweatpants. She caught a glimpse of herself in the mirror by the door and tried to smooth down a thick chunk of disheveled hair.

Silence.

The scratches stopped abruptly.

She sighed deeply and grabbed the baseball bat propped by the front door. She spoke in a low announcer's voice. "And now, Mantis is up to bat."

She readied it and grinned back at Gabriel and Dylan.

"The pitcher fires it to the plate," Mantis continued as she threw open the door.

A snarling, emaciated demon swayed uneasily and lurched forward, dead eyes locked on her. Magma-orange drool dripped from its ashen maw.

"The batter swings!" Mantis swung the bat with all of her might, battering the creature's tar-slick head with a deep *smack*. The force knocked the creature off balance. It hit the floor with a moist thud. Mantis straddled the beast and yanked the bat from its caved-in head. She smashed the weapon down again on its three-clawed hand. "She heads to first!"

Mantis bashed its teeth in. "She made it to *second*! Oh, she rounds to third..." She drove the handle of the bat into its chest cavity.

REEEEEEEEEAAAAAAAWWWW!

The demon screeched and collapsed to the ground.

"She... could... go... all... the.... way!" She spun and bashed in its groin.

"Oh!" She yelled, tossing the bat down the hall. "It's a *homer*!"

"You got 'em!" Gabe raced gleefully to the couch and jumped on the cushions with excitement.

"*Gabe*." Dylan warned, trying to control his laughter. "No jumping on the couch." Gabriel hopped back onto the floor. "Now go get your shovel. Auntie Mantis got a fresh one for ya."

On his way out, Gabriel tripped over the demon's corpse and got up rapidly, unfazed.

"Oh, and Gabe, sweetheart," Mantis hollered, "don't tell your mother about this when she gets home with your cake. She'll have my ass."

Erica Summers is an independent filmmaker, artist, film industry grip, and writer with an unwavering passion for horror. Several of her award-winning feature films have screened worldwide including Obsidian, Mister White, & Loverboy (available on most streaming services.)

Though born and raised in Wyoming, Erica spent most of her life in the swampy American South. She now resides in Connecticut where she works in film and writes and illustrates genre fiction. In her downtime, the bizarre bisexual is typically slathered in garden dirt, kayak fishing, or devouring horror movies with her boyfriend and their two jack russell terrors.

Erica also writes romance fiction under the pen name Odessa Alba and cozy mysteries under the name Trixie Fairdale.

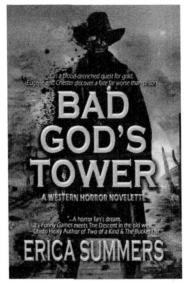

BAD GOD'S TOWER
A Western Horror Novelette
By Erica Summers

Available in paperback, hardcover, e-book, & audiobook

Vicious criminals, Eugene Dempsey and Chester Craven, escape Wyoming Territorial Prison armed with nothing but striped prisoner pajamas and a Lakota's hand-drawn map that, according to legend, will lead them to unfathomable riches below Devil's Tower. With two determined buffalo soldiers nipping their heels, the sadistic escapees will soon realize all the gold in the land isn't worth what lies in wait for them in the claustrophobic underground beneath.

WRITHE
By Erica Summers and H. M. Wohl

Releases February 27, 2024 on paperback, ebook, and audiobook

Garrett was a normal New Yorker, appeasing annoying neighbors and paying over-inflated rent for a dumpy little 4th-story apartment in Hell's Kitchen. *Until the larvae hatched.*

As Garrett unleashes his violent wrath upon the unsuspecting city of Manhattan, NYPD'S-own Luca Han and Mel Tredo are on a tense mission to find the lunatic before he can murder again.

The Choice is Yours: Yakshar's Lost Treasure
By Rowen Sikora and Erica Summers
Available worldwide in paperback

Third graders, Rowen and Ella, take you on an adventure on their homemade boat to find Yakshar's legendary lost treasure. Danger lurks around nearly every corner and only YOU can guide these third graders to the gold and riches they seek! *Yahskar's Lost Treasure* is a fun, full-color adventure where you choose your path! It features multiple endings so it can be enjoyed again and again. For fans of the *Geronimo Stilton* books or the classic *Choose Your Own Adventure* series.

The Billionaire's Assistant
By Odessa Alba
Releases March 19, 2024 in paperback, discrete hardcover, ebook, and audiobook

Welcome to Greenwich, Connecticut. Unable to don his outrageously-expensive, bespoke suits and perform everyday tasks now that he's injured, attractive billionaire, Eric, is desperate for an assistant. He hires temporary help, Kira, to run errands and help with his daughter, Bella, but the moment the wild blonde arrives, Eric's tense, cold life is completely upended. But with every caress, every stolen kiss... *they're playing with fire.*

This is book one of the New England Billionaires Series. It can be read as a standalone or as a sequential part of the series. *Guaranteed HEA & no cheating.*

From Ashes: Book One of the Illuminator Saga
By Heather Wohl

Available now in paperback, hardcover, & ebook!

Elf blacksmith, Quistix, suffers a tragic loss the night a bandit invades her humble Bellaneau home in search of "The Illuminator." After months of crushing loneliness, the disheveled half-elf is out for blood, seeking revenge on the man who shattered her once-contented life and answers about why this alleged Illuminator is so highly sought-after. A wounded wyl, a brilliant esteg, and child-like dragonling soon join her on her cross-country adventure, banding together in a riotous, misfit crew. But Destoria is a dangerous place. The isle is bursting with clever hybrid creatures, floating magical cities, bandits, and a sadistic, dikeeka-peddling new queen: Exos Tempest.